Zoe Cook

I grew up by the sea in Cornwall, spending my summers on the beach. I left to study History at Oxford University, before starting a career in television during which I was lucky enough to travel the world interviewing incredible authors for the Richard & Judy Book Club. Fast forward ten years I'm now married to a lovely man called James and have a daughter who keeps us on our toes. Oh, and a very furry cat called Bobby.

You can follow me on Twitter @mezoecook.

One Last Summer at Hideaway Bay

ZOE COOK

A division of HarperCollins*Publishers*
www.harpercollins.co.uk

HarperImpulse an imprint of
HarperCollins*Publishers*
1 London Bridge Street
London SE1 9GF

www.harpercollins.co.uk

A Paperback Original 2016

First published in Great Britain in ebook format by Harper*Impulse* 2016

A catalogue record for this book
is available from the British Library

ISBN: 9780008194468

This novel is entirely a work of fiction.
The names, characters and incidents portrayed in it are
the work of the author's imagination. Any resemblance to
actual persons, living or dead, events or localities is
entirely coincidental.

Set in Minion by Palimpsest Book Production Limited, Falkirk, Stirlingshire

Printed and bound in Great Britain

MIX
Paper from
responsible sources
FSC www.fsc.org **FSC™ C007454**

FSC™ is a non-profit international organisation established to promote
the responsible management of the world's forests. Products carrying the
FSC label are independently certified to assure consumers that they come
from forests that are managed to meet the social, economic and
ecological needs of present and future generations,
and other controlled sources.

Find out more about HarperCollins and the environment at
www.harpercollins.co.uk/green

For James and Lara, the loves of my life.

Prologue

September, 2005

Can you believe that after all these years I have to write this in a letter because I can't say it to you, can't get the words out right?

I know you think I'm running away. You're probably right. But what do you think I have if I stay here? There are too many ghosts here, Tom, too many memories. It's like walking around in my own nightmare sometimes, and it will drive me mad.

I wish we weren't fighting about this. I don't know what I expected you to think or to say about it all, but I didn't expect you to be so angry with me. I feel like you're taking it the wrong way. It's not you I want to leave; it's this place.

If you knew how many hours I've spent thinking about what the hell to do — honestly, the thought of being without you is unbearable. But I didn't want to put you in this position, to do what I'm about to do now. I didn't want to ask you to come with me, to leave everything you have here. This place means so much to you, and you have so many reasons to stay.

But I guess I am selfish, like you say I am. Because I want you to come with me, Tom. I can't do the London thing on my own, I don't want to. I don't want a life that doesn't have you in it. I can't

1

really see the point in that. Is that pathetic? You are everything that's good in my life.

I know you'll need time, but can you think about it? About coming with me? Starting a life away from here? It would be the adventure we've always talked about, wouldn't it? I mean I know it's not exactly South America or Thailand, but you know...

I'm doing that jokey thing you get cross with me for, aren't I? Trivialising things because I'm nervous and awkward.

I'm rambling now. And I don't even know if I'll ever give this to you. Part of me thinks I should just go and leave you here to live your life without me. I think you might be better off that way. I want you to be happy, Tom. I love you more than words. If nothing else, I hope you always know that.

Lucy

1

London, July, 2010

Lucy tipped the white powder from a carefully folded lottery ticket onto the mirror of her compact. She scraped it into a neat line with her credit card and took the rolled bank note from the back of her wallet. She sniffed quickly and quietly, pausing for a second to feel the immediate hit of energy. She placed the folded paper and card in the zipped section of her purse, straightened herself up and walked out of the toilet cubicle back to her desk.

It was 5:55pm before Lucy had time to check her personal emails on Tuesday. Work was manic, as it always was in the lead-up to an awards ceremony. For Spectrum, the Screenies were the event of the year, a real prestige project and a massive money-spinner. The grand-scale, live-broadcast awards show at the Metropolis on Park Lane, which celebrated all things TV, dominated spring at Spectrum, with a huge production team recruited, doubling the number of people in the office for the months leading up to the show. Emma had too many meetings to fit into each day and, as her PA, it was Lucy's job to make them all happen – somehow. Emma's mood alternated between manic happiness at the prospect of an evening of guaranteed attention, and sudden bursts of furious disappointment at the team she employed to run Spectrum TV's events. Lucy had mostly escaped her wrath, instead taking the role of confidante, which she actually felt even less comfortable with. Every time she was called into Emma's office she dreaded the instruction to 'close the door', which signaled an imminent verbal assassination. Lucy hated how Emma dragged her into her bitter inner world of hatred towards the production team, most of whom had absolutely no idea they had done anything to upset her. Already this week she'd heard how angry Emma was with Frankie, the lovely associate producer working on the awards, because she'd cut her long hair short so close to the event.

'I would never have employed her looking so butch,' Emma had spat.

'We'll have to reassign her role for the evening, she can't be talent-facing now,' she'd sighed, as if Frankie's new hairstyle might prove too much for any delicate celebrity-type unfortunate enough to set eyes on her at the ceremony. Lucy hated herself for not standing up for anyone, for just sitting there listening to it all, making herself complicit by her inaction. She wanted an easy life with Emma, she'd seen what happened to people who dared to disagree and she valued her career too much to be the next person bullied out of their job. She needed it, needed the money. It had taken so long to earn a wage that meant she could afford her own flat, or near enough afford it, at least; she couldn't entertain the prospect of having to start on a lower salary else-where. So she sat there, like the baddy's little lap dog, being stroked and kicked alternately, depending on the day, Emma's mood, the weather – taking whatever shit Emma threw her way and never standing up for anything or anyone.

Emma was having one of her good days today. Lucy had found it relatively easy to juggle her schedule, field her calls and keep her happy. She hadn't sat down at her desk for more than five minutes at a time and her feet hurt like hell in her new heels, but that didn't matter too much. The day was nearly done, Emma was due at an event at 7pm, so a car would be picking her up at 6:30pm and Lucy could get out at a reasonable hour for the first time in weeks. She scanned through her inbox, deleting junky emails and opening a couple of 'funny' round robins – was she the only person in the world who hated those cat videos? Her eyes were drawn to the email sent at 11:47pm the night before. Subject line: 'Hello', from: Thomas Barton.

Her first thought was that it couldn't be him, that it was a coincidence. Tom never called himself 'Thomas', he thought it sounded stuffy and old. Clicking the bold 'Hello', her heart began to race at the possibility that it *was* him, and she ran her eyes over the long email that opened on her screen to the bottom of the page. 'I still think about you and I hope you're okay,' she read. It was signed off 'Tom'.

Emma called for Lucy to help her into her dress before she could read his words. She guiltily shut her MacBook at the call of her name, afraid of being caught reading something from Tom, something personal. Not that Emma would have had a clue who he was, no one in the office would, but Lucy felt exposed, made vulnerable, even, by his electronic presence. In Emma's office, sounds and voices appeared as if she was under water and she remembered the sensation of noise bursting into technicolour each time she came up for breath in swimming galas as a young girl. She desperately wanted to get outside for some fresh air, or to the toilets for another line to sharpen her thoughts.

'Anyway it just won't do,' she finally tuned in to Emma's snapping voice, 'You'll have to tell her tomorrow that it's not her job to do that.' Emma had finished and Lucy had no idea what, or who, she had been talking about. 'Absolutely,' Lucy smiled at her boss in what she hoped was a normal manner.

'How do I look?' Emma spun around, her dress lifting far too high with the hideously girlish action, revealing her black underwear and cellulite at the tops of her thighs. 'Fantastic,' Lucy lied, 'Really great.'

Lucy walked to the station too fast, she was breathless and clammy by the time she reached her platform. Her heart raced and she felt a familiar pang of fear about just how much damage she might be doing to herself with her habit. She forced the thoughts aside and focused instead on the rare victory of securing a seat, which she slipped into self-consciously. The drugs always made her feel a little paranoid. As they pulled out of the platform towards Scott's flat, Lucy hovered over Tom's email, debating half-heartedly whether to read it now or later. She opened it, unable to resist, and read his words, hearing his voice rather than her own.

From: Thomas Barton
To: Lucy Robertson
Subject: Hello

Lucy, hi, it's Tom. How are you? It's been a while. I hope you're really good. I've been meaning to get in touch for a while. It's hard to know how to after so much time has passed. I'm sure you understand that more than most. Nina tells me you're doing really well up there. I knew you would be, good on you. You did it!

Everything's good down here, same as ever, really, but good. Mum and Dad send their love. The café's doing well, just starting to get busy now with the good old tourists. God bless them.

You should come here, come and see everyone, see how little it's all changed. That's why I'm writing to you, actually. I know you're busy, Nina tells me you're some kind of TV high-flyer, which sounds fun, but definitely busy, so I know it's probably difficult. But you should come, Luce. Nina and Kristian are up for it, we've been speaking loads recently and we all want to get the gang back together again one more time. They're coming for August, staying here in the house, and you should come too. The four of us, a summer on the beach, like old times. We all want you here for it. I want you here for it. It's been so long since I saw you.

Just think about it, anyway. Promise me that much. Promise me you won't just stubbornly decide 'no' and refuse to consider it. Maybe it's a stupid idea – we both know I have plenty of those, but it would be fun, wouldn't it? Humour an old friend?

I know we haven't spoken in a really long time, but I still think about you and I hope you're okay.

Tom

When she reached the bottom of the email Lucy took a deep breath and counted to ten; she'd done that ever since she was little when she felt like she might cry. It had been five years since she'd spoken to Tom, five years since she'd seen him. She knew he was still in Hideaway Bay; Nina had kept her vaguely informed with updates. But Nina had left too, with Kristian – travelled the world with him after university, and although those two were still in touch with Tom, they knew better than to talk much about him to Lucy.

The idea of going to Cornwall was preposterous, of course. She had a job, responsibilities, a flat, for Christ's sake. The idea that she could take August off work for some nostalgic road trip to her home town and a reunion with her ex-boyfriend would almost be laughable if it wasn't so bloody annoying that he'd even thought he could ask. Who the hell did he think he was, suggesting she just ditch all of her own plans to fit in with his pipe dream of a summer reunion? Asking her to *promise* him things. What did he actually want? To relive their happy summers before she'd left and he'd refused to come with her, the summers before he'd given up on them and let her leave without ever looking back?

How had Nina not told her about this? They'd only spoken a few days ago and seemingly she knew all about this stupid plan.

Had Nina thought it was a good idea for Tom to get in touch, go for the weak spot and perhaps Lucy would just melt into a pathetic little puddle at the sound of his name all over again? She wouldn't go. She'd ignore the email; maybe send a polite response in a couple of days to show that she wasn't petty, that she was over it. She looked out of the window as the train doors bleeped shut and swore out loud, too loudly, judging by the shocked faces glaring at her from around the busy carriage. She'd just missed her stop.

2

Hideaway Bay, 2003

Tom took Lucy's hand in his as they walked up the hill to her parents' house. She could feel his eyes on her, but pretended she didn't know he was watching her; he had a habit of observing her doing the most mundane things. 'You look beautiful today,' he said, kissing her on the cheek.

'I'm sweaty,' she replied, laughing. 'You're mad.'

'You're sweaty and beautiful,' he said, lifting her arm and spinning her into him. She groaned and then smiled as she nuzzled into his chest, stopping now to kiss him properly.

'That view,' he said, turning towards the sea. 'It still gets me every time.'

'I know,' Lucy said. She couldn't imagine anyone failing to be stunned by the sight, the vast expanse of blue, soaring from a pale crystal at the sand's edge to deep navy where it met the sky. You could still hear the buzz of the beach, the squeals of delighted children over the gentle roar of the pulling tide. It was the most calming sound in the world, somehow blending the magnificence of nature perfectly with the human pursuit of pleasure.

'Are your parents in?' Tom asked, as they began walking again.

'I don't think so,' Lucy said, 'Dad wanted to take the boat out to "make the most of the weather".' She did her best impersonation of her father.

'Richie?' Tom asked.

'Don't know,' Lucy said, 'Why, are you hoping we'll have the place to ourselves?' She nudged him gently and skipped ahead of him slightly. Tom reached out for her hand again and smiled at her. 'Well, I could deal with that,' he said. Lucy kissed him again, before opening the gate with a code on the keypad.

'No cars,' she said, 'looks like you're in luck.'

3

London, 2010

In the lobby of the glass and stainless-steel building, home to Scott's very expensive waterfront flat, Lucy took the lift to the fourteenth floor and knocked on the heavy, dark door. Scott's face was a more welcome sight than Lucy had imagined, and he held his arms out for her suddenly weary body as she leaned into his arms and let him kiss her hair.

'Hello, darling girl,' he said, 'Come in, I've cooked for you.'

In his lounge Scott had set the table and put flowers in a silver-rimmed glass vase. She smiled at the gesture and leant down to smell the purple and pink hyacinths – her favourite.

'Sit down, Luce,' Scott called from the kitchen, 'Dinner's just coming. I hope you're hungry.'

He'd cooked what looked like a very good lasagna, which Lucy's heart dropped at the sight of. She couldn't eat it. She knew immediately, her body filling with panic at the sight of all that pasta and cheese. She took a slice and filled her plate with salad.

'This looks absolutely delicious,' she said, looking at Scott and his lovely face, his chiseled jawline and cute, perfect nose. He was so bloody handsome. Lucy acknowledged this often, but he was just a bit too keen to be truly sexy. She knew this thought made her a bitch and she wished she was less of a cliché. The sad truth was that she knew she'd like him more if he didn't like her.

She spent dinner cutting up pieces of lasagna and pushing them around her plate and under her salad, listening to Scott talk about his clients, the office politics at his city law firm and about the football match he was looking forward to at the weekend. When he went to get a second bottle of wine, Lucy reached for her handbag, took a tissue from a packet and wrapped as much of her lasagna as she could fit in it, and put it in her bag, praying it wouldn't seep through. She was drunk, she realised now, her movements were clumsy and it felt like her hands were too big for her arms. It was a feeling she loved, that warm fuzz of wine running through her body, numbing all the sparking connections in her brain, dulling everything down enough to make life feel easy.

Scott poured her another glass of red before taking her nearly empty plate away.

'You really liked that, huh?' He kissed her on the mouth, hard, and Lucy realised he was drunk too. He put her plate back down on the table and kissed her again, stroking his hand through her hair, pulling her head back slightly and running his tongue down her neck. Lucy unbuttoned his shirt. He looked good in his work clothes; his body was beautiful. She put her hands on his smooth chest and reached for his jeans. Scott lifted her up from her chair and sat her on the dining table.

In bed, Lucy wore Scott's t-shirt, her hair tied up, her neck still hot. She took her phone from her handbag and set an alarm for 6am. She had a missed call, from Nina, and the wine fuzz began to turn to more of an ache as she recalled the email on the train. She leant over to kiss Scott goodnight. 'I love you, Lucy,' he said, rolling towards her and putting his arm across her empty stomach.

'Goodnight sweetheart,' she replied, hurting at her inability to tell him she loved him too. Scott fell asleep with an immediacy that always made Lucy envious. Sleep was not her friend. She lay completely still, staring at the ceiling, trying to make out shapes in the plaster, trying not to think about Tom. This was the curse of her habit. Well, one of them. She needed to stop doing it so late into the evening. No amount of wine could totally take the edge off, and once things were quiet and it was dark, the fear could creep in. Her heart raced and she began to feel hot, as though someone was pressing down onto her chest. She reached for the glass of water on the bedside table and watched it shake as she pulled it to her lips. Lying back down, she tried to calm herself by breathing slowly and steadily. Eventually her heart seemed to settle, she felt her eyelids begin to become heavy, her thoughts start to spiral into sleep.

They came to her again in her dream. All of them, this time. There was always Richie, and this time he ran towards her, beaming. This time her parents stood quietly behind him, waving. She was so happy to see them, reaching out for Richie's warm little body, his spindly arms and crazy hair. She kept looking up to check that her parents were still there too, so pleased that they looked happy. She began to realise that it was taking too long for Richie to reach her. She looked again and could see now that he was running almost as if in slow motion. His arms and legs were moving strangely, as if he was being pulled down, wading through something thick. She tried to call out to him, to move towards him, but she was suddenly sinking into the ground too, it had turned to marsh beneath her feet. She felt panic rising as she looked around for her parents now. They were further away than before and their faces were wretched with despair. They weren't waving any more, they were desperately pleading for her help. But she couldn't move. Richie was crying now and drifting further away from her. Lucy tried to scream for help but her voice wouldn't come; instead the screams seemed to stab sharp pains through her chest. Her eyesight began to fail her, as if a thick fog had fallen on them all. She couldn't breathe now, and she couldn't see her parents.

She woke, sweating, out of breath. She reached to her side to feel Scott, still fast asleep, as if touching another human being would confirm that she was real and this was real and the dream was over. She felt sick and her heart ached. She pressed her fingers into her eyes to stop the tears that began to form. She'd been having this dream, or versions of it, for years. It never got any easier to cope with. It always knocked her more heavily than she felt was reasonable after all this time. Looking at her phone she saw it was 5am and decided that wasn't too early to get up for the day. She'd only had around four hours' sleep, but that was better than the prospect of closing her eyes and returning to her nightmares.

She stepped out of Scott's bed quietly, still shaking slightly and cold now. It was the day of the awards and she felt like utter shit. It was going to be a long, long day.

4

Park Lane was as busy as ever, six lanes of traffic coughing out hot fumes into the hazy blue sky. Hyde Park was filled with the usual mixture of tourists meandering and office workers rushing on their way to work. As Lucy stepped out of her Addison Lee car in front of the Metropolis Hotel she had an unwelcome flashback of last year's awards ceremony and the A-list – well, lower A-list, maybe B-list, really – celebrity getting papped, up-skirt, by the scummy photographer who lay on the floor as she got out of the car. The fallout from those pictures breaking in the red tops the next day had led to some seriously awkward calls from the agent about Spectrum's 'failure to safeguard'. Lucy entered the hotel, smiling at the doorman, and was greeted by the familiar smell of marble, dark old wood, and something she couldn't pinpoint but which, judging by the surroundings, might well have been the smell of money. The atmosphere of the Metropolis still excited her, even after all these years of working on Spectrum's televised events at the hotel. The bar was littered with small groups of ladies drinking tea, with fine china plates of pastel-coloured cakes decorating the tables, their feet obscured by an assortment of sturdy, ribbon-handled shopping bags from New Bond Street's boutiques. It felt like a place full of possibilities, of secret meetings, and of a life she'd probably never be able to afford.

In the production suite people had dumped piles of coats and bags in the corner, and a rail of evening dresses was already nearly full. Lucy hung her black-lace dress, grabbed a copy of the running order, a polystyrene cup of grainy coffee from the machine and headed to the script meeting in the ballroom. It was Lucy's third awards ceremony as Emma's PA, and it became more and more difficult to concentrate during the longwinded script read-through. It was a point of pride for Emma that she ran this meeting in such a unique way. She insisted on a full run-through in which she took the role of both the main presenters, all of the individual awards' presenters and every winner, often delivering Oscar-worthy acceptance speeches, which, it struck Lucy, seemed to roll off her tongue as if practised in advance. By the time the final award was played out, culminating in Emma's impression of a middle-aged Swedish male winner (not one of her finest), Lucy's mind had wandered and she was taken by surprise at the sound of her name.

'I asked if there was anything I'd forgotten', Emma looked at her with the familiar look of disdain and disappointment. 'What was I meant to remember?' she asked Lucy.

'I think that was everything,' Lucy smiled hopefully, trawling through her brain for anything she was supposed to be prompting her boss with. At that moment a commotion of suit carriers and blonde hair tumbled through the door, met with sniggers and a collective chorus of 'Oh, Warren!' from the Spectrum team sitting around the large table.

'Oh my GOD, I'm so sorry I'm late!' Warren did, in fact, look sorry enough that he might actually cry. A flamboyant, yet sensitive, character, Warren had been at Spectrum media for a couple of years before Lucy had joined, and had worked his way up to the coveted role of Entertainment Producer, meaning his job was to book celebrities to appear on the company's shows. Being

16

outlandishly emotional was apparently a necessary characteristic for anyone working on the Entertainment team, who dedicatedly lived up to their job titles and entertained the office with their many dramas, fallouts, reconciliations and public breakdowns. One of Warren's particular character traits was to seek Emma's approval at all times and at almost any cost. Arriving late to the production meeting of the biggest awards show of the year was probably up there with Warren's worst nightmares, met only, perhaps, by an international Dermalogica shortage, or his cleaner accidentally machine-washing one of his 'statement' cashmere jumpers.

Emma cast her eyes up and down Warren's body, from the toes of his gleaming patent loafers, to the highest point of his highlighted quiff, and Lucy recognised the flash in her eyes of something noted and worthy of comment.

'Warren,' she started, 'I can overlook the late arrival, given the fact it is entirely out of character and, I'm sure, due to circum- stances beyond your control.'

Lucy watched Warren half relax before sensing that the exchange was not over. 'What I can't overlook is the fact that you are the colour of an imitation mahogany table. What the HELL have you done to yourself?'

Now that she looked properly it was true that Warren had been a little heavy handed with the fake tan, but Lucy still cringed internally at the public remonstration, recalling their conversation a few nights ago in the pub, when he'd listed the many beauty treatments he was going to undergo in preparation for today. He had only wanted, Lucy remembered clearly, to look his very best for the occasion. She wanted to say something in his defence, but there really was no denying he looked totally, ludicrously brown the more she looked at him.

'It's developing,' Warren explained, 'I can't stop it. I don't know what to do. I've showered, I've exfoliated, but I'm sure it's still developing. I wasn't this brown an hour ago.' His voice wobbled at the end of this statement, threatening tears. Emma had already lost interest in this conversation, however, and was piling papers and pens into her oversized Prada bag.

Warren took the seat next to Lucy as Emma left the room, his big eyes searching for comfort.

'It's okay,' she lied. 'Don't worry about it, it's not that bad.'

It was dreadful. Up close, particles of tan were sitting in each pore, line and blemish; his face reminded Lucy of those olde-worlde maps you made at school by staining a piece of paper with instant coffee and burning the edges.

'I have the keys to make-up anyway,' Lucy offered. 'We can go and find some foundation.'

Warren held out his arms and grabbed Lucy in a bear hug. She patted him on the back and tried to wriggle down away from his face slightly to avoid any possible staining.

Awards ceremonies at the Metropolis were always fun; they had an atmosphere that Lucy never felt anywhere else. It was all about getting through the ceremony itself and then the party really began. Lucy had been allocated a role that only Emma's most valued staff were trusted with on the night; she was to be, yet again, a spotter. A spotter's job was perhaps the least dignified role you could be given at a glitzy event, consisting of crawling around on the floor with a camera crew, pointing out the beautiful people to be filmed. Each year when the roles were being handed out Lucy prayed that she might be spared, and each time she was painfully disappointed. In Emma's eyes it was such an important role that it needed to be carried out by experienced, responsible people like Lucy who had spent years working four-teen-hour days in hope of one day being taken seriously in the TV world. As Lucy changed into her short, black, bodycon lace dress and tried to fix her hair up with Kirby grips and hairspray, she raged momentarily at the absurdity of the 'cocktail dress' dress code for all Spectrum staff, and realised that the only thing less dignified than crawling around on the carpet all evening was doing so dressed as if you were expecting to be sitting at a table drinking champagne.

Lucy was surprised each time at how quickly two hours of spotting passed; it actually became quite addictive trying to make it round to the next table in the twenty-second VTs played on screen between each award. She was quietly delighted to have avoided being yelled at over the headset each spotter was wearing. Emma's scream of 'Sophie, that's NOT Paul Mulryan, that's a short-haired WOMAN', was probably a highlight for everyone on talkback except Sophie. In her defense, that woman did look a lot like crime writer Paul Mulryan; Lucy had checked afterwards when crawling past to get to the star of an International Series of the Year contender after the mishap.

The final award of the evening was the Lifetime Achievement award and the winner was Lucy's to find and get a camera pointed at in time. She was already at the right table, with her target in view, hanging back until the last minute so as not to give the game away. As the music fired up Lucy moved in with the camera crew following behind waiting for her instruction. As she reached the side of Mrs Dorian Briar, ninety years old, an OBE, writer of over fifty novels and twenty adaptations for the small and big screen, Mrs Briar spotted her and turned away from the table towards Lucy. Lucy tried to make herself invisible, the presenters were about to announce Mrs Briar's name and she needed to be looking up at the room, not down at Lucy on the floor. But Mrs Briar wouldn't give up. 'There's a girl on the floor!' she exclaimed remarkably loudly to the rest of her table, pointing at Lucy. 'Excuse me, young lady, are you okay down there?'

Lucy felt her face burn with panic. 'Fine thanks,' she mouthed, and prayed that this would appease the legendary author about to be honoured with the most prestigious award of the night.

'Would you like some wine, dear?' Mrs Briar leant across the table, picking up a glass of, surely someone else's, wine, and stretched down and sideways to try and reach Lucy on the floor.

'THE INIMITABLE DORIAN BRIAR', boomed one of the presenters, and Lucy felt the room around her, all 400 guests, getting to their feet with applause, as the big screen flashed to a live picture of Dorian Briar stretching away from the table, then falling off her chair clutching a glass of cabernet sauvignon, squealing in horror. The other guests at her table leapt into action, scooping her off the floor, horrified at the sight of this little old lady now drenched in red wine. Dorian was, to her credit, still smiling, but looked a little confused by the whole thing. Lucy moved, quicker than seemed possible on all-fours in a skintight dress, away from the scene, glaring at her camera crew with a look that she hoped conveyed 'let's never talk about what happened at that table'.

5

The production office's transformation into a fully laid-out dining room marked the end of the Spectrum team's working duties. There were already ten people scattered around the tables eating plates of roast chicken and vegetables, and pouring large glasses of wine. Lucy walked in with Warren and Sophie, fellow spotters, laughing about the Paul Mulryan confusion, and she placed a concessionary piece of chicken on her plate from the large silver warmer on the buffet table.

'Is that all you're eating?' Warren asked, filling his own plate with potatoes, carrots and chicken thighs before drowning it in gravy. Lucy didn't answer, but just smiled and took a seat at an empty table. Picking up a bottle of white wine that wasn't quite as cold as she'd have hoped, *I deserve this,* she thought, and poured out three glasses.

'What the hell happened with poor Dorian?' Sophie asked, her little brown bob tipping quizzically to the side, like a Cairn terrier, Lucy always thought.

'No idea,' Lucy took a first blissful swig of wine. It had dawned on her very quickly after the incident that no one else on the production team actually had any way of knowing why 'poor Dorian', as she was quickly becoming known, had fallen off her chair. Anyway, Emma had already been overheard rejoicing about what fantastic television it was seeing a national treasure tumbling to the ground in a fountain of red wine, so Lucy didn't feel too bad about keeping quiet about her role in the scene.

The room filled quickly with colleagues removing high heels and rubbing their feet between glasses of wine, and exchanging Emma stories in a sort of top trumps game of 'well you think that's bad, wait 'til you hear what she did in the green room when I was working on *Catch it, Cook it*, in 2010…'

Lucy retrieved her mobile from her bag and read a message from Scott sent an hour earlier: *Hey you, hope it's all gone well. You coming to mine tonight?* Lucy sent a quick reply saying she'd call him later; she half wanted to leave there and then and get back to his place. It would, she knew, be the most sensible thing to do; these nights always got so bloody messy. But the first two glasses of wine had slipped down easily and she was in that early wine daze, where everything felt slightly wonderful and it felt too early to leave.

Dinner was followed by the traditional 'sweep' of the ceremony room for bottles of wine that had been purchased by TV big-wigs to impress their tables, but which hadn't been drunk. Emma didn't like wasting money by, say, paying for wine for her staff, and the sweep was one of her ways of 'winning', as she saw it. Lucy hung back slightly after the incident last year where she and Natalie from the Entertainment team had swiped a bottle of champagne from the Sherbet TV table only to be stopped on their way out by the purchaser of the bottle on his way back to retrieve the fizz, who accused them of stealing: awkward didn't really cover it.

Emma was already deep in the after-party – Lucy kept catching glimpses of her up the stairs though the glass doors. She was working the room like a pro. It was a quality you couldn't help but admire; she was truly fantastic at making people listen to her and then give her what she wanted. She was also, Lucy knew, notorious for drinking far too much at events, and it looked like she was on her way already. She had changed into the red Donna Karan dress that Lucy had collected two days previously from Harvey Nichols and which Emma had taken great pleasure in telling the whole office the extortionate cost of. 'I suppose you could say that £1,800 for a dress is too much…' she'd mused loudly, before asking Lucy to bring it up on the Harvey Nicks website and show everyone just how beautiful it was. And it really was beautiful. Lucy had stroked it when she collected it from the store, before it was packaged with flair and precision into tissue paper, a box and then a bag for transfer back to the office. But Emma had a knack for making really expensive clothes look incredibly tacky. Lucy watched her move over to her next companion at the bar, clutching a glass of champagne in one hand and a fistful of the skirt of her dress in the other, struggling to work with the combination of billowing red fabric at ankle level and the high-heeled Prada shoes she'd opted for. It didn't look to Lucy as if Emma was wearing a bra, which made the dress sit strangely across her chest and gape slightly at the side. Lucy could already see the potential for another breast-based moment later in the evening. These had become something of a signature for Emma, who had fallen out of more designer dresses in public than Lucy could remember. She recalled the time, a few years ago now, that Emma had conducted an entire conversation with an author at a book launch with her left nipple sitting proudly outside the ridiculously strappy low-cut dress she was wearing. The author's eye had kept wandering down, and Lucy, standing next to Emma at the time, had wondered just how the hell Emma couldn't, at the very least, feel the difference between the right side – cloaked in All Saints (God, she was far too old to be wearing All Saints), and the left side – hanging out free as a bird. It had never become clear at what point Emma had finally noticed, and later on everything was back in place, but nothing was ever mentioned.

It was impressive how much wine could be swept from a room after an awards ceremony; the team was laden with bottles and bottles of red and white, and a few had found the ultimate prize – unopened bottles of champagne. As it was strict hotel policy that no wine should leave the room after the ceremony, the smuggling out to the after-party had to be conducted with confidence and poise to avoid any suspicion amongst the Metropolis's staff. Lucy considered herself an expert at this and took two bottles from Jenny, one of the runners, slipping one upright into her handbag, and the other under the flap of her black jacket before heading up the stairs and through the huge doors. Inside, the party was in full flow, a few merry authors and agents were dancing in the middle of the room while most people opted to continue their drinking and were gathered in groups around the edge of the dance floor, or sat in the crushed-velvet booths along the walls.

Lucy, Warren, Camilla and Katie stationed themselves at a booth at the far end of the room. Lucy skimmed across the plush fabric and sat next to the window, looking onto the twinkling car lights and street lamps of Park Lane. A stream of orange beams flowing one way, blinking red the other. An assortment of wine bottles was magicked onto the table and Katie passed around glasses. Lucy settled into the back of the cushioned bench, her back aching in appreciation of the support. Warren began his usual commentary on the scenes unfolding on the dance floor. A well-known screenwriter was performing an elaborate, and puzzling, finger dance, and an ageing agent, who Lucy had earlier seen stroking his neighbour's leg as she crawled past their table, was now dancing up against her in what was presumably intended to be an erotic style.

More wine was poured and Lucy shut her eyes briefly, remembering she had promised to call Scott. It was nearly midnight and the drinks were filling her with a warm sense of impending fun, so she pushed away the thought of her boyfriend waiting at home and finished her glass. She'd pop to the toilets in a while with Warren, who'd brought a supply for a few of them who were always ready for a party. She fancied a little pick-me-up.

'Dancing time?' she suggested, and the group, which had now grown to eight of the Spectrum team, left their bags and coats in ownership of the booth and moved a few yards into the room to start dancing to the R&B set the DJ was playing.

The noise in the room was growing louder with each song, more and more bodies joining them on the dance floor. Camilla appeared with a tray full of glistening shot glasses and the team expertly applied salt to the base of their thumbs, downed the sour liquid and squealed for lemons, which Camilla had forgotten to bring. Lucy slipped back to the table and downed a large glass of wine to wash away the taste. Her head spun as she turned and made her way back to the group, who were having a dance-off, throwing her hands in the air and shimmying in to join them. She flung her head back, laughing at Warren's moves, and feeling the rush from the alcohol.

6

Hideaway Bay, 2003

Nina and Kristian were on another break, and Nina could barely stand being in the same room as her on-off boyfriend of two years.

'I hate him, Lucy,' she whispered in Lucy's direction, eyes locked on Kristian and loud enough for him to hear her across the table. They were sitting on the small terrace at the back of the Beach Café, Tom's parents' place.

'I know, he's been a prat,' Lucy comforted Nina. She'd learned a long time ago that it wasn't worth pointing out that they were both at fault.

'I can hear you both,' Kristian said, pulling away from his conversation with Tom, probably about surfing. Tom grinned at Lucy, who tried to make a face at him that told him to look like he was taking this seriously.

'Oh why don't you text your little girlfriend about it, then, poor little Kristian,' Nina said mockingly.

'For goodness' sake,' Kristian rolled his eyes. *Not a good move*, thought Lucy.

'She is a friend,' continued Kristian. 'In fact, she's not even a friend, she had a surf lesson. She texted me to say thank you. You're out of your mind!'

This was not going to end well, Lucy realised. She made eyes at Tom to signify that they should extract themselves from the impending explosion.

'Oh you are SUCH A GENTLEMAN!' Nina shouted, causing other customers to stop their conversations and pretend not to look at them all.

'Hey, calm it down, okay?' Lucy tried to reason with them. 'It's not fair on Tom's folks to make a scene here.'

The café was their regular hangout and they'd already pushed their luck this summer with Tom's parents. Sarah and Neil were far more laid-back than any of the other parents, having recently forgiven them for breaking in one evening after a drunken barbecue on the beach. Tom had been instructed to pay for the broken glass by working an extra few shifts, and the embarrassment of Tom's mum looking at Lucy and Nina with surprise and disappointment had been the hardest punishment they could have been dealt. Sarah was wonderful, especially to the girls. Tom was her only child and she made no secret of how much she had longed for a daughter. She'd swept Lucy and Nina into their family within a few months of year seven and their friendship with Tom and Kristian. Lucy had known Sarah and Neil vaguely for years. They owned a few places around Hideaway Bay: the café, the fish-and-chip shop and the pub across the bay at New Hideaway. They were friendly with her parents and she'd heard Sarah's laughter ringing out over dinner-party chatter a fair few times. And then she'd met Tom. They had been at different primary schools; Tom at the private school half an hour away and Lucy at the village primary. Her dad didn't see the need to pay for primary school. It was when she joined Davenport Heights Independent at age eleven that they first met. Tom had been instantly friendly: Lucy terrified of the new surroundings and at a real disadvantage to the children who were already familiar with the senior school from their primary days. They both got the number 121 bus from the top of the hill to school, and each day Tom sat next to Lucy and asked her questions while she blushed, laughed and eventually looked up at him and realised he was rather lovely.

At sixteen they were best friends and totally in love. They felt unbreakable to Lucy, unlike Nina and Kristian, who had a relationship so volatile that Kristian sending a message to another girl sent them into a tailspin. Lucy often wondered whether Nina, her best friend since they were five, had been almost forced into a relationship with Kristian because of their proximity to her and Tom. Kristian was a lovely, lovely boy, but he was totally hapless when it came to managing Nina's fierce temper and tendency for jealousy. Even Lucy had fallen foul of Nina's wrath when it came to Kristian, although she had surprised herself at the ferocity of her defence when Nina once tried to imply she had flirted with Kristian at a party. The idea was totally absurd and had shown Lucy how bloody hard it must be being Kristian at times. She looked at him now, the same look of disbelief and confusion that she'd see on his face a hundred times before as he watched his girlfriend twist herself into a venomous tangle of rage over almost nothing.

'What are we doing tonight?' Tom asked, trying to break the tension.

'Can we come to yours, mate?' Kristian asked. 'A few beers, a game of pool, swim?' Tom's house was the largest not only of the group's but also in the whole town. Neil and Sarah were widely considered to own Hideaway, their house sitting at the top of the Bay, overlooking their business empire. Their landscaped gardens sprawled out from the back of the huge property, gradually sloping down to a lower level with a huge infinity pool, which looked straight out across the sea.

'Sure,' Tom replied. 'My dad will probably want us to help with something, though. You know what he's like.'

28

'That's fine,' Lucy said, perusing the menu on the table, wondering whether to order another coffee. 'It's the least we could do, really.' She didn't mind helping Sarah and Neil, and in fact she quite enjoyed folding napkins, helping Sarah to design sandwich menus, and deep-cleaning the pristine white coffee cups ahead of the impending summer high-season.

It was hot already in Hideaway, the sea just about managing to take the edge off the midday scorch. Lucy was tanned and happy; this was how she liked it. All of them together, good weather, lots of time and no school. GCSEs were done and she didn't need to think about her results for a while yet. The summer stretched out ahead of them, full of promise. She looked across at Tom and met his eyes. He smiled and winked at her. Kristian was out of his seat and had moved close to Nina, attempting to cuddle her. Nina almost gave in to him, before standing up and storming off, tears in her eyes.

'I'd better go and check she's okay,' Lucy said to Tom and Kristian. This was a familiar drill.

'Tell her I'm sorry,' Kristian called after her. Lucy stopped. 'What for?' she asked.

'Whatever she thinks I've done,' Kristian said, looking wounded. Lucy stepped back to the table and planted a kiss on Kristian's cheek. 'She's being a twat,' she said to him, quietly. 'I'll sort it out.'

7

London, 2010

Lucy woke to the sound of her alarm. She opened her eyes slowly, in anticipation of pain and suffering. Sitting up, she took in Scott's meticulous apartment, the crisp, white sheets, which had been ironed and smelled of washing powder; the tasteful, understated mahogany furniture; the delicate scent of vanilla drifting in from the Jo Malone diffuser that his mum had put in the lounge. She switched off the terrible noise bleeping next to her head and held her temples to try and soothe the throbbing. Scott had placed a glass of water by her bed before he'd left for work and her thirst came like a tidal wave at the sight of it. She finished the glass in five clumsy swallows, water trickling down her chin. Lucy glimpsed the mirror to her left and opened her eyes widely in the hope of waking herself up to survey this sight of herself. She was still wearing the lace dress she'd been in last night, and her make-up was smudged into two grey circles around bloodshot eyes. She looked like an extra from a low-budget horror film. She glanced down at her pillow and took in the black streaks and tidemarks of what must be a mixture of sweat, fake tan and foundation, which had seeped up the now-greasy white fabric in a hideous rainbow of dark brown to dirty beige.

Out of the shower, and after three sessions of tooth-brushing, gagging at each stroke to the back of her mouth, Lucy found the outfit she'd folded over the back of Scott's chair last week. She slipped on the black leggings, grey cashmere jumper and leather biker boots. She considered applying make-up, but her skin felt as though it was coated in some kind of hangover wax that no amount of scrubbing could remove and which make-up would merely sit on top of like scum on pond water. She sprayed herself with perfume from her handbag and looked again in the mirror. It was not a pretty sight, but it was an improvement, and probably passable for a post-awards day.

In the office, the people who had made it in on time were a scale of grey faces. 'I was sick on the tube,' Warren announced as he appeared at the top of the stairs, 'And it was pink.' Lucy's stomach lurched at the image.

'Oh God, Warren. That's terrible, have some water and eat some food,' she said. As a runner, the lowliest position at any production company, Jenny had been tasked with the early-morning breakfast run and had returned with a mammoth pile of greasy paper-wrapped baps and sandwiches, smelling of crispy fat and white flour. In a rare act of generosity, Emma paid for this post-awards ceremony tradition from her own wallet as she, like everyone else in the office, was always in need of fried breakfast items and carbs the morning after. Lucy cautiously took a bite from her bacon sandwich – white bread, buttered, brown sauce – offering it up as a gift to her stomach, aware it might be rejected. It tasted good, the salt kissed her cheeks and each chew released more and more smoky juice into her mouth. She could've cried at the pleasure of eating.

It was nearly lunchtime before conversations really started in the office. Everyone had made it in to work this year. There was normally one casualty who overslept, couldn't move or had woken up in another town and couldn't get in to the office. This was the ultimate crime at Spectrum. It was accepted, encouraged actually, to join in and party after a big event, to 'let your hair down' by drinking to excess. The only rule was that you made it in to work the next day. Regardless of what state you arrived in, you had to arrive, you had to be there, and you had to get on with it. Julia, an associate producer on *Make My Dinner*, Spectrum's long-running 'hilarious' celebrity cooking show, had been sacked last year after calling in sick the morning after the Food and Drink Awards, Lucy remembered. Perhaps that had helped to motivate everyone to get in today.

Stories from the after-show party were beginning to emerge as the communal hangover level was reduced from a solid seven to a more manageable three or four post-feed. It emerged that Charlie had told Emma she loved her, which was mildly amusing but not really news, as she did this each year, as far as Lucy could recall. More interestingly, and depressingly, Teresa, one of the runners who had just been promoted to junior researcher on a baking programme, had been caught kissing a recently engaged production manager and was vehemently denying the incident. Lucy felt sorry for her, as she seemed so desperate to make it not true with her refusals and protests. *That guy is a total creep*, she thought to herself. Everyone who worked at Spectrum knew what Matt got up to, and he had cheated on his fiancée at least five times that Lucy knew of: once, classily, in the disabled toilet at a wrap party. His post-incident tactic, and perhaps this was what was inspiring Teresa, was to flatly deny every single thing, regardless of who had caught, seen, or heard him and his prey, until eventually everyone pretended to forget.

It annoyed Lucy how it had become something of a joke amongst the team, and how there was now an eye-rolling sense of 'oh what's he like' about the whole thing. *A sleazy prick*, Lucy always thought, but didn't ever offer up. He somehow remained a truly popular and powerful member of staff. It was the girls who became the laughing stock each time, and they *were* bloody stupid to get involved, Lucy thought. She couldn't figure out how on earth he even managed to do it – what his appeal was. He was a balding, slightly overweight man, the wrong side of forty. She had concluded that it was simply because of the tiny number of men in TV and the huge amount of single girls. Nice odds for a midlife-crisis-wielding sex pest.

'And what about YOU?' Laura turned to Lucy with a devilish look of glee pasted across her wide, stupid, pale face. Laura, a researcher who'd really worked there long enough to have been promoted by now, was one of those terrible people who was always there on a night out, wouldn't miss it for the world, but who, judging by her chronic lack of hangovers, never actually drank along with everyone else, choosing instead to sit back and observe. She collected stories from drunken nights and loved drip-feeding them the next day.

'What?' Lucy asked, trying to think back through the evening to what she had done.

'You don't remember?' Laura trilled. This was the best-case scenario for a serial shamer.

'I don't know what you're talking about. Just leave it, okay?' Lucy replied, trying to sound casual and laid-back.

'Oh, this is hilarious!' Laura continued, and people from the other side of the office were listening now, sensing the shift in tone.

'Do you honestly not remember? That's amazing! You gave that guy a LAP DANCE!' Laura exclaimed really loudly, *unnaturally loudly*, Lucy thought. Lucy's face filled so quickly with blood she imagined she had turned purple.

'Don't be ridiculous, Laura. Just shut up, will you?' she snapped back, shocking herself with the force of her words.

'Touchy, touchy,' Laura sniggered, turning around to check her audience's reaction. The office was quiet. It wasn't just Lucy who couldn't stand Laura. She'd made herself an unpopular figure many times over for snitching on people and generally stirring up trouble so she could sit back and watch the fallout. Lucy racked her brain for any memory involving anything resembling a lap dance. And then it came, an image of herself, wine in one hand, the other outstretched over the shoulder of a man, seated on the edge of a booth, and her laugh ringing out over the music as she wriggled her hips and rippled her body over him as people watched and laughed. She turned to Warren, who looked embarrassed for her and gave just the slightest head movement that confirmed her fears. *Yep, you did.* Lucy stood and walked quickly to the toilets. Locking the door, she felt the tears come: big, hot, heavy tears that ran down her face silently and blocked her sore nose – and just would not stop.

I'm a total mess, she thought. *Why can't I just drink like other people? Have a good time, have some fun, then stop. Why do I always get myself to the point where I can't remember anything, where I do something stupid? Why didn't I just go back to Scott's, like he asked me to?* Lucy gasped slightly at the thought of Scott, choking on her tears. She cared about Scott, he was good to her, looked after her when she was tired from work, took her out to nice places, tried to make her happy. *And this is how I repay him,* she thought, hating herself for being the kind of girl who behaved like that when drunk. 'Making a spectacle of yourself', her mum would've said. *And God knows who saw – all those people in that room; people I work with, and work for, people who I need to respect me!* That one image she had of herself leaning over the as-yet-unidentified man, made her feel physically sick, not least because she couldn't finish the scene, had no idea of how it had played out. She didn't want to find out from Laura; she didn't actually want to find out at all. She'd never understood people like Warren and Charlie, who loved hearing about what they'd got up to on a night out. Lucy would rather never know, and wished there was some kind of code of silence about the whole thing. Laura was an utter twat for telling her, telling everyone, like that, but *she,*

Lucy, was the biggest fool, she acknowledged painfully, because this wasn't exactly a one-off. How many times had she drunk herself into this position? What, two or three times already this year? How did she forget this shame and terror each time?

What the hell is wrong with me?

She took her phone from her pocket and thought about calling Scott, before pressing cancel and letting more tears come at the realisation that he couldn't comfort her, and that it wasn't actually fair to expect him to.

Warren took her out for lunch on her own and tried to make light of the whole thing.

'You were joking around,' he told her, 'It really wasn't as seedy as Laura made it sound.'

But it didn't matter to Lucy, who pushed her pizza around her plate, struggling to make eye contact, filled with shame and self-hatred.

'What does this say about my relationship?' she asked, quietly.

'Nothing, babe,' Warren said gently, 'You were drunk; he was a hot guy. Really hot, actually… and you were just messing about. You didn't even kiss him. It was just a friendly thing.'

'Oh yeah,' Lucy smiled at Warren, 'Just your average friendly lap dance.' She almost laughed, but Warren reached across the table and took her hand. The tenderness of the gesture shocked her and she thought she might cry again. 'You're a good egg, Lucy. You could do with giving yourself a break sometimes, you know. You're not so bad', he said, looking her into the eyes and squeezing her hand in his. 'Chin up, missy.'

The pizza and a walk back to the office helped to ease the hangover and back at her desk Lucy made a deal with herself. *Just get through the rest of today and tomorrow everything will seem better.* She kept her head down, worked through a good chunk of her red-flagged emails and counted down to 6pm and home time. It was easy to keep a low profile as Emma was locked in her office all afternoon, which meant little conversation among the team, who were afraid she might be listening through the thin walls. It wasn't as paranoid a fear as it sounded. When the team had relocated to this huge office from a smaller warehouse building in South London, Emma had enquired about the possibility of installing some kind of 'listening tube' that would enable her to hear people at their desks from the comfort of her own office.

Laura caught Lucy's eye a few times throughout the afternoon and offered an irritating facial expression that Lucy thought was meant to suggest 'I'm slightly sorry for upsetting you, but hey, you did it!' She forced herself to smile back. *This is the last time I feel like this*, she vowed. *I'm not going to do this ever again.*

The office emptied at an impressive pace at 6pm. Lucy walked out of the door after a quick hug with Warren and the tiredness hit her all over again. The thought of getting on a bus felt like an epic mission and the black cabs driving past her with their orange lights on looked irresistibly enticing. Lucy put her arm out and a taxi pulled over. 'Balham please,' she said as she heaved her exhausted body through the door and onto the back seat. Her phone vibrated in her pocket; a message from Scott.

Are you okay? I'm working late, but I want to know if you are alright? it said.

I'm okay, Lucy typed, *I'm so sorry about last night. I didn't mean to get so drunk. I hope I wasn't as terrible as I think I might have been x.* She was relieved Scott was, firstly, still talking to her, and secondly, that he was working late. She didn't want to go to his perfect flat tonight; she just wanted to go home, run a bath, put on her comfiest pyjamas and take her duvet to the sofa. As the taxi turned the corner onto her road, a wave of familiar, pathetic, realisation hit her, *I want Tom*, she thought, *I just want Tom.*

8

Her wardrobe was a mess. Clothes had fallen off their hangers into heaps at the bottom. She reached through fabric until she felt the box. The shoebox was covered in wrapping paper: a garish pink-and-orange print she'd picked when she was thirteen, thinking it was exotic. Lucy carried the box onto the sofa and cocooned herself inside her duvet. Opening the box released the smell of paper and ink she only let herself take in a couple of times a year. She'd thought about throwing the box away as many times as she'd opened it, but always ended up shoving it back in the wardrobe. Amongst the letters, scraps of paper, notes passed back and forth by her and Nina in lessons, postcards from her older sister's travels, she found the wallet of photos.

There was Nina, all long limbs and beautiful long hair, running away from the camera towards the beach, being chased by Kristian. Then Lucy's childhood dog, Spencer, a big, fat Labrador, lying on the sand looking happy as her brother, Richie, crouched next to him, all of two years old, bucket in hand and a mischievous grin on his face. Photo after photo showed the view of Hideaway from various high points across the Bay. From Tom's palm-treed terrace, it looked almost Mediterranean, the sea a vivid greeny-blue. The photos from Lucy's garden, with the rugged cliffs in view, looked more traditionally Cornish. Her favourite photos of Hideaway were those she'd taken from the café. In these you could really see how the bay had earned its name. Once you were in the town you felt totally cut off from anywhere else – as if you were in a secret cove, unreachable from anywhere but the sea. The steep, winding road that linked them to the real world seemed to give up towards the beach, and from there it was just cobbled streets of tiny shops and cafés with stripy awnings. The view from the café always reminded Lucy of something from a *Famous Five* book: Keeper's Island sitting in front of them enticingly, but otherwise nothing but water and sand and the two cliffs either side closing them off from everywhere else, hiding them away.

She skipped past photos of Claire, feeling guilty about how long it had been since she'd seen her older sister. She didn't live all that far away and when Lucy had first moved to London, Claire had tried to hard to help her settle, to be friends. Lucy should have made more of an effort, she knew that, but it felt like it had been too long now, like she'd made an issue out of nothing by her inaction. Claire would be angry with her, anyway, like she always was when Lucy did spend time with her in those first few months in London. Claire was so bloody sensible and collected, and together, and Lucy just wasn't. The thing was, Lucy knew Claire's intentions were good and that she cared, but it physically hurt Lucy to be near her. The reason she'd left Cornwall was to escape the memories and seeing Claire brought them all crashing back in. And Claire knew too much. She could always see when Lucy was struggling and could never stop herself from bringing it all up all over again. Sometimes Lucy just wanted to pretend things were fine when they weren't. She didn't want to try and work through the fucking pain all the time – she knew it didn't work anyway. So she quickly shuffled the photos of Claire to the back of the packet of pictures, focusing instead on the hideous shots of her and Nina in some of their first trips into Plymouth, where they'd clearly tried to dress 'fashionably' but had fallen seriously bloody short of the mark. Nina was wearing an orange poncho with pom-pom trim and baggy jeans, Lucy didn't look much better in what looked remarkably like a ski jacket and denim skirt. They looked ridiculous and she laughed to herself at the sight of them.

Then, inevitably, she reached the glossy photo she'd tried to deny she would find.

Scruffy brown hair swept to one side, in surf shorts and a ripped t-shirt, Tom smiling at her, his blue eyes looking as though he was thinking something naughty, Lucy thought. She remembered standing there, on the beach, taking the picture. She'd thrown the rest away, but she could never bring herself to destroy this one, it was too perfect. It had been taken the summer before she'd left Cornwall, just a normal day on the beach, he'd been surfing all morning and she had taken the mick out of him for his scruffy t-shirt. He'd pulled her into him, 'You love it, Luce, I know you do,' kissing her neck and hair playfully. 'I love *you*,' she'd replied, kissing him back, and then she'd asked him to stand for the photo. Wrapped in her duvet, on her sofa in London, she could hear the seagulls circling the beach that day hoping for tourists' fish and chips. She could feel Tom's wet, salty skin on her body as he held her waist. She could smell the sun on his hair as she pushed it away from his eyes and kissed him. Lucy put the photo down and tipped her head back to stop the tears. *It was a long time ago*, she told herself, *a different life.*

This was why she shouldn't look at the photos, she remembered, as she put the box down on the floor and used the sleeve of her pyjama top to dab at the tears prickling the corners of her eyes. Why did he have to send her that email? Why did he need to bring it all back up again? She tried to blame the feelings on him reaching out to her about the summer, but of course she knew, really, that she was simply eternally trying to move on from him, from how much she had loved him. She loved him so much it had ruined anyone else for her, because no one was ever going to compare. And he was just a fucking memory, not even a real person in her life any more. He had let her leave; he had been fine with it. He had not spoken to her for five fucking years.

She tried to put him out of her mind and concentrate on her plan of action to make herself a better person. She decided she'd start running again, eat healthily, really focus on her career. She wasn't going to spend her life in London thinking about summers in Cornwall years ago, and she couldn't allow herself to think about Tom – it was just the tiredness – and that bloody email, that was all. *You can't be in love with a memory*, she told herself.

Even you're not that bloody stupid.

9

'Lucy? Lucy! It's Sophie.'

Lucy blinked slowly, her head throbbing with pain. She suddenly became acutely aware that she had no idea where she was.

'Sophie?' she asked. 'What are you doing here?' Her own voice trembled and sounded as if it was coming from someone else. Sophie was her next-door neighbour, a couple of years old than her – a primary school teacher who she sometimes had a cup of tea with when they bumped into each other. She outstretched a shaking hand and felt gravel. She tried to lift her head, but Sophie placed her fingers firmly on her chest and told her to rest. She was lying on the ground, she realised now, and the hard, stony surface beneath her felt suddenly uncomfortable.

'You just fainted, I think' Sophie said. 'It's okay, you're okay. Just lie down and get your breath back.'

Lucy opened her eyes again and looked down at her muddy running legs and running shorts. She remembered jogging from her house, to the park, feeling good.

'I was running,' she told Sophie.

'I guessed!' Sophie smiled at her.

'I'm okay,' Lucy protested, trying again to sit up.

'I'm not sure that you are,' Sophie said, kindly. 'Lucy, we need to get you home.'

'Yeah, I need to go to work—' Lucy started.

'You're not going to work, Lucy, I called your sister from your phone and she's coming to look after you. She told me once when you first moved in that I could call her if you ever needed her. I thought she was just being an over-protective sister, but it turns out you did need her after all!'

Lucy was suddenly, fiercely angry with Sophie for calling Claire. It was a ridiculous over-reaction. She began to argue again that she was fine, pulling her weight up with her arms, as she felt her heart pound and her eyes fill with sparkles, her head becoming heavy.

Lucy woke this time on her own sofa, wrapped in her duvet as she had been the night before. From the kitchen she could hear the sounds of cupboards being opened and closed, someone boiling a kettle, fetching mugs. Claire appeared in the room with two cups of steaming tea and Lucy felt tears running down her cheeks at the sight of her older sister.

'Hey you! It's okay,' Claire said, handing her a warm mug and sitting next to Lucy on the sofa. She smelled of expensive perfume. 'Before you start panicking, I've called work, they're fine. They know where you are and no one's cross, okay?' Claire blew over her tea to cool it. 'Lucy, I'm worried about you, fainting like that. And you're so thin. Is this why you've been ignoring my calls?'

Lucy knew she'd lost weight recently; her clothes were hanging from her collarbones and hipbones slightly but, if she was honest, she liked it. She saw it as an achievement; she got a boost from feeling hungry and thin.

'I can go in this afternoon,' Lucy began.

'It's 4pm, Luce,' Claire set her tea down on the stained wooden coffee table Lucy had picked up from a flea market in East London. 'You're not well. You need to rest now and later we'll talk about everything else.' Lucy didn't know what Claire was referring to by 'everything else'; she sipped her tea, closing her eyes as she drank.

'Scott,' she said, 'I need to call Scott.'

'Sophie, called him first,' Claire replied. 'After she saw you faint on the street, she came and helped you. You're lucky she was there, that she saw you. Anyway, Scott couldn't come, he's too busy at work, so she called me.'

Lucy saw Claire look away as she finished her sentence and sensed there was more to this story. It felt, suddenly, acutely clear in her mind. Scott didn't want to come. Scott had had enough of her dramas and wanted out. Her mind ran through the last few weeks and how badly she'd treated him. When she thought of his nice face and his sensible apartment, and his Jo Malone diffusers, she realised again that she didn't truly want any of it.

'He's coming over to see you this evening,' Claire said, and Lucy knew instinctively that it would be their goodbye. She thought about what things of his she'd need to pack up for him, ready for him to take away. Not much: a toothbrush, some clothes, a toy she'd bought him as a gift from her girls' holiday to France in the summer. She felt a pang of guilt at the thought of that holiday and the night she had spent with the handsome Frenchman after too many champagne cocktails. How she'd bought the silly toy the next day with a raging hangover and a familiar sense of shame at what she'd done. She'd not been a very nice girlfriend to Scott; it was time to let him go.

When Lucy opened her eyes again, it was dark outside her heavy cream curtains, and Claire had turned on a lamp by her sofa, sending a warm orange glow through the room. Scott was on his way over. Claire had spoken to him and told him Lucy would be ready for him at 8pm. Lucy looked at her phone. It was 7:45pm and she had four text messages, which she couldn't face reading. She got up from the sofa, her legs weak and her body aching slightly in a way she found strangely comforting, like proof of her own existence. In her bedroom she found a dress to pull over her underwear – Claire must have undressed her – and she felt momentarily embarrassed by the picture in her head of the scene. She pulled on thick black tights under the short, loose-fitting grey dress and pulled her hair up into a messy bun. She could see why Claire was worried: her face was drawn and gaunt and the hollows in her cheek, which looked pretty good with the right make-up, looked sickly now they were bare. Her eyes, she could see herself, looked sad, too big and grey. She swept foundation over her skin, then bronzer and applied mascara. The doorbell went and she heard Claire answer, greeting Scott as the stranger he was to her – they'd been together for almost a year and her older sister had never met him, Lucy realised.

'I can't keep doing this,' Scott said, after he'd checked she was alright.

'I know,' she said, plumping a cushion to avoid eye contact.

'I'm really sorry, Luce,' he reached out to put a hand on her leg. It felt unexpectedly patronising.

'You really don't owe me an apology,' she said, meeting his eye now. 'I just don't think we're quite right for each other.'

'Yeah, well, I tried,' Scott sounded bitter suddenly. 'Nothing I did was ever enough.'

He stood to leave. *Had he expected me to fight to keep him?* Lucy wondered, too tired to really care. The relief she felt at the sight of him making his way to leave was proof that this was the right thing.

'You'll be okay,' she said, hugging Scott at the door. She handed him the bag of his things.

'I'll drop your stuff off soon,' he said, pulling away from her. 'Look after yourself. Oh. And Lucy –' his face changed. 'It's really time you grew up and quit all this drama and nonsense.'

He didn't look back as he walked to his car.

Lucy knew that in time she'd miss him, miss the familiarity of his niceness, his solidness and his physical company – the guarantee of human contact when she needed it. Claire hadn't asked questions after Scott left. She'd run Lucy a bath and tidied the flat. She had obviously taken time off her own work as a barrister to look after Lucy and hadn't thought twice about coming to help her at a moment's notice. She was so kind, Lucy thought. *Kinder than me; I don't think I would have done it for her.* She found Claire in the kitchen, wiping the walls with kitchen roll and cleaner, a wisp of mousey brown hair fallen from her ponytail sticking to the back of her neck with the exertion.

'Thank you,' she said, 'for all of this, for everything...'

'It's nothing,' Claire smiled at her, 'You're my little sister, it's my job!'

Lucy tried, again, to convince her sister that she was fine now, that she didn't need her to stay. But Claire wouldn't agree and told her she'd sleep on the sofa and see how she was in the morning. Too tired to argue, Lucy made her way to her bedroom. Claire had clearly tidied it while she was with Scott in the lounge. The bed was made, her clothes folded away, and sitting on the chair at her dressing table was the box she'd been looking through the night before. On top of it there was an overturned photograph, which Lucy picked up. It was the image of Tom from the beach. Lucy thought back to the evening before and realised with plunging horror that she must have fallen asleep with the picture left out. Claire would have found it when she was clearing up and Lucy could imagine what conclusions she'd have drawn from that. *She must think I'm pathetic*, Lucy thought.

10

Claire stayed almost a week in the end. She took time off work as holiday and moved in with Lucy, cooking her massive carb-laden meals and watching her eat them. They drank sugary tea from Lucy's vintage harlequin-coloured, gold-rimmed teacups and watched their favourite rom-coms in the evening. In the daytime, with Lucy at work, Claire cleaned her flat from head to toe, polishing the bathroom bin, dusting skirting boards – the works. Lucy protested that she didn't need to do all this, that she should go home to her own flat, which she shared with her lovely boyfriend Tim in Harrow. Claire insisted, of course, that she wanted to stay. It was clear how worried she was, but she didn't ask any probing questions, and instead left it to Lucy to get back to strength, hoping she'd start talking at some point.

As Claire packed the few things she'd turned up with after Sophie's phone call on Wednesday morning, Lucy watched her and her meticulous ways with admiration. She was the most practical and careful person Lucy had ever known. She looked after everything properly, had bags that matched shoes and gave an impression of togetherness that Lucy envied but which made her feel chaotic by comparison.

At the front door, with Tim's car engine running, Claire pulled

Lucy in for a hug and checked for the fortieth time that she was going to be alright.

'You are in charge of your life,' she said to Lucy, seriously, 'And it can be whatever you want it to be.'

Lucy smiled at her sister's sentimental ideas and nodded in faux agreement. 'Lucy,' Claire implored, more seriously than before, forcing Lucy to hold her eye contact. 'I really mean it. And there's something I need to tell you,' she continued, with an expression now that Lucy couldn't quite place. Was it worry? 'I called Tom,' she said, matter-of-factly, but too quickly. 'I know what's happening this summer. I know he's asked you to be there. And I think you should go.'

With that, Claire disappeared into the darkness. The passenger door shut and the horn beeped a goodbye. Lucy stood on her front step, heart racing, tears threatening yet again, and a surge of anger, fear and something that felt like excitement trembling through her body.

11

Hideaway Bay, 2003

'Do you fancy a surf?' Tom asked from his seat in the sun on Lucy's decking.

'Could do,' Lucy said, considering whether she could be bothered with the walk back into town and trying to remember if she'd washed her wetsuit.

'It looks like there are some great waves,' Tom said, pointing to the sea as if Lucy needed the visual clue. She sat herself on his lap and kissed his hair.

'We can go if you like, or I might just sit and watch you. I don't think I want to get wet again and I need to write to Claire.'

'How is she?' Tom asked, slipping his hand around Lucy's waist and taking a sip of orange juice. 'Or where is she, more to the point?'

'Thailand now,' Lucy said, 'then she's off to New Zealand, though I'm not sure exactly when.'

'I don't really know why you'd need to go to Thailand when you've got this on your doorstep,' Tom said. It was an attitude that grated with Lucy; his lack of desire to leave Cornwall, seemingly ever.

'I think it's pretty important to see the world, Tom,' Lucy said, more sternly than she'd intended. 'I don't want to sit around here for the rest of my life.'

'I didn't mean that,' Tom said, rolling his eyes. 'I meant why would you go now, in the summer? You want to get away from this place in the winter, when it's bleak, when everything closes and everyone's miserable and there's nothing to do.'

'Oh, yeah, well, I guess,' Lucy said, standing up and stretching her arms up to the sun. 'It is pretty nice here at the moment.'

Tom and Lucy walked back down into town hand in hand, talking from time to time about the café and the season ahead. Bookings were looking good according to the hotel owners and the campsite was set to be busy. Lucy knew the café struggled over the early months of the season to cover its costs. It was a difficult call deciding when to open after the winter and plenty of days saw them make a loss. Lucy worked a shift there from time to time for a bit of cash and she felt guilty taking her wages at the end of a day when they'd only served half a dozen cups of tea and a handful of toasted teacakes. The summer itself was a different ballgame, of course. The whole town exploded into life from late June, especially when the weather was good. The campsite at the very edge of the beach brought in a university crowd, which spent plenty of money in the pubs and on surf-hire, while the upmarket hotels dotted along the cliffs, with their sweeping sea views and elegant furnishings, attracted the kind of guests that the town really needed, the guests that spent a small fortune on food and drink, souvenirs and clothes, hair and beauty appointments, and, well, just about anything. One of the most contentious issues in the town was that of development, with frequent proposals from huge corporations wanting to build super-resorts and massive hotel complexes in the green spaces that still existed around Hideaway's cliff tops. The divide of opinion was pretty simply split between the businesses who would profit hugely from the increase in footfall year-round and the business owners who feared their own hotels, B&Bs and apartments simply wouldn't match up to the new wave of developments. The latter tried to scare residents into believing that holidaymakers who came for the big resorts being proposed would simply sit in their complexes and spend all their money right there, that very little would trickle into the town. Lucy could see both sides. Tom was adamantly against the whole idea. His issues were more philosophical than the majority of the objectors' issues. He simply didn't want Hideaway Bay sold to the highest bidder. He didn't want the feel of the place changed. Lucy was coming round to his way of thinking more and more this year. The spring they'd just had in Hideaway had felt so blissful and easy, the town was in good spirits, the weather was amazing and the whole place had just felt positive since the New Year. It would be a shame for anything to compromise that.

'So has Claire met anyone?' Tom asked. He was nosey about people's love lives; it was a trait that always surprised Lucy.

'I don't know,' Lucy said, 'I doubt she'd tell me. Anyway, I'm sure she's far too busy using her time more productively. You know what she's like, she's already done a yoga course and some kind of meditation retreat. She's hardly living the gap-year dream, is she!'

Tom laughed. It was true that Claire was the more straightforwardly sensible of the two sisters. Even their mum wondered where her eldest daughter had inherited such a level head. Lucy's family were go-getters. Her dad could seem like a straight-laced finance-type, but that was just how he made his money. And boy, did Steven make his money. When he was in Hideaway he was always on the go – surfing, sailing, windsurfing, kayaking. And their family holidays were legendary. They never seemed to do anything anyone might consider normal. They'd be hiking some mountain with Richie strapped to Steven's back, or combining a safari trip with aid work in South Africa. Lucy, of course, considered this pretty normal – it was what she'd always known.

'I wish she would meet someone,' Lucy said, after thinking about it. 'It might lighten her up a bit. Even her emails are written like A-level essays. It sounds like she needs to drink a few cocktails and let her hair down.' She smiled to herself at the unlikely image.

'Maybe she'll surprise you,' Tom said, as they reached the beach. 'Talking of A levels, are you still sticking with your subjects?'

'Yeah, I think so,' Lucy replied, not wanting to talk about it. Thinking about going back to school in September did not fill her with joy.

'I've been meaning to talk to you about it all, actually,' Tom said, looking down at the floor. Lucy could sense his nerves.

'About what? A levels?' she asked. 'I thought you were set on sciences in case you want to do marine biology.'

'Yeah,' he replied. 'It's just, I've been thinking about it all and I don't really think it's right for me.'

'Oh, right,' Lucy replied. 'You seemed so set, I'm surprised. What do you think you'll do instead? I suppose you're good at English, maybe you could wait until you get your results in a few months and decide from there –'

'– no, I mean,' Tom hesitated, making Lucy nervous too now. 'I mean, I don't think I'm going to go back at all. I don't think I'm going to do my A levels. I don't think I need them.'

'What?' Lucy said, raising her voice in disbelief. 'That's ridiculous. Good one. Good luck convincing your parents with that.'

'They agree,' Tom said, kicking a line of sand ahead of them. 'I'm going to get more involved with the businesses. I'm going to help them out. They don't want to do all this forever and it will all be mine one day anyway, so –'

'– so you'll just give up on anything else at the age of sixteen and decide to stay here for the rest of your life? Are you fucking crazy, Tom? You'll have no options at all.'

'I know that's how you see it, Luce,' he said as she pulled her hand away.

'This isn't what we talked about,' she said, quietly, feeling foolish now. 'I thought we were going to get our A levels and then travel, you know, actually do something. Why did you let me talk about all that when you were planning to just sit here in Cornwall and work in a fucking café?'

'We can still do that,' Tom said, reaching for her hand again. She tugged it away from him.

'Yeah, or we can say that we will and then end up not doing it, because you'll never be able to tear yourself away from this place,' Lucy spat at him. 'You're pathetic sometimes, Tom, a massive fucking let-down.'

'Lucy!' he called after her as she walked away, rage burning her cheeks.

12

London, 2010

Lucy examined her freshly dyed, chest-length blonde hair, curled from the midsection, and reapplied her peach lip gloss in the mirror of the ladies' loos. The last show in this long-running series of *Cook My Dinner* really did feel like cause for celebration. The eighteen-week run had been a particularly stressful one, with fallouts between Spectrum and the broadcaster leading to plenty of unpleasant meetings and phone calls that Lucy was often caught in the middle of. The show was one of Spectrum's trademark productions and they'd been making it at their onsite studios for almost six years, with a variety of different presenters. The current 'talent' was a particularly difficult character, Gareth Bell, a former Michelin-starred chef who'd fallen into disrepute years before following a tabloid scandal involving cocaine and prostitutes, and who Emma had whole-heartedly believed she could rehabilitate onto daytime TV. He was also incredibly cheap to book, which was always appealing to Emma, but the relationship hadn't worked out quite as she'd hoped and his tendency for arriving on set half cut had caused some challenging production issues. He was sticking around for the wrap party tonight and Lucy had been tasked with checking this with him earlier in the day. From what she could tell, he was already halfway drunk and it was only 7pm. His speech would be interesting.

The show's daily guest was also due to stay for the celebrations. Warren and Charlie had gone all out for the last show in the series and had found someone who wasn't an obscure soap character, or someone Lucy needed to Google (you NEVER ask a booker who the name on the board actually is). Today's guest was Lawrence Shield, a member of chart-topping boy band The Team, and the most famous one at that. Emma was embarrassingly excited that Lawrence was staying for the party and hadn't left him alone. She was still fawning over him as Lucy left the toilets and headed to the bar. She ordered a pineapple martini, which came in a plastic glass, decorated in carnival-coloured circles and finished with an umbrella. She had hardly touched alcohol since the fainting incident and had expected to feel better for her abstinence. The lack of hangovers had been a nice break, but other than that, she just missed the taste of wine and cocktails; the pineapple martinis were going down well. Lucy felt a hand on her back and turned to see Helen from the edit standing nervously behind her.

'Hey, Helen,' Lucy smiled. 'You okay?' Lucy wasn't sure if she'd spoken to Helen properly before. She'd said hello a few times whilst she was up in the edit running errands for Emma, but couldn't picture Helen outside of the dark suites at all.

Helen had dressed up for the party and was wearing a calf-length leather dress and studded jacket. Lucy hadn't noticed her gothic style before.

'I'm, um, I'm a massive Teamer,' Helen looked at the floor as she spoke.

'Sorry?' Lucy replied. 'You're a what?'

'Oh,' Helen laughed nervously, shifting her weight from foot to foot. 'It's what we call ourselves, 'teamers', The Team's super-fans.'

'Oh, I see,' Lucy replied, bemused. 'That's cool.'

'I wondered if you think it'd be possible to get a picture with Lawrence?' Helen looked up at Lucy now, hopefully.

'Oh, of course!' Lucy replied. 'I can't see that being a problem. Just go and ask him, he's lovely.'

'I can't,' Helen's eyes returned to the floor. 'Please, would you ask for me? I'm too nervous.' Lucy looked at Helen and felt a patronising pity for her. She was a large girl, probably the only girl at the party bigger than a size ten; Emma oversaw the recruitment at Spectrum and heavily policed what she called 'the look'. Lucy wondered how Helen had slipped through the net and immediately hated herself for the thought. Helen had never been part of team drinks, team evenings out or any socialising at all as far as Lucy could remember. Maybe she'd never wanted to, but had she ever been asked? She'd probably worked there for a year now and Lucy had never spoken more than three words to her. She didn't fit in with the group Lucy hung out with and so Lucy had never made any effort to include her. Never invited her to join them.

'Of course I can ask him,' she smiled at Helen again earnestly and hoped suddenly that Helen didn't hate her for being the cliquey bitch she'd probably always seemed to her.

Lucy was used to politely interrupting Emma's conversations and edged her way in to the group Emma was talking to, waiting for an opportune moment to get her boss's attention.

'Emma?' she spoke quietly as the conversation continued among the rest of the group. 'Helen from the edit would love a picture with Lawrence. Can I borrow him for a minute?'

'Who?' Emma replied at full volume, not taking her eyes off Lawrence.

'Helen,' Lucy repeated, 'she works in edit one.'

'I have no idea who you mean,' Emma insisted, and Lucy recognised the rising irritation in her tone.

'That's her, over there, in the, er, black dress,' Lucy gestured towards Helen, who was still at the bar, trying to look away.

'Oh, dear God,' Emma turned back and looked at Lucy. 'How on earth did she get a job here? She doesn't have the Spectrum look at all.' Emma laughed at her own cruelty. 'She's a beast!' she exclaimed, causing the rest of the group to stop their conversations momentarily before laughing awkwardly.

'She is not to come anywhere near Lawrence,' she whispered fiercely to Lucy. 'She is not to speak to him, she is not to ask for an autograph. I will not have her embarrassing me. What the hell is she wearing? She looks like an S&M hippo!' This line gave Emma enormous pleasure and she began laughing again.

'Emma…' Lucy began, but Emma's attention had turned again to Lawrence, who she was giggling at now like a school girl. Fury burned on Lucy's cheeks. How could she walk back to Helen now? What was she supposed to say? She ducked back out of the group and walked in the opposite direction, away from Helen, who she knew must be looking at her, wondering what was going on. Lucy ordered another two pineapple martinis at the mobile bar, downing one on the spot. Out in the cool air of the car park, she took a cigarette from Charlie's outstretched pack. She told Charlie what had just happened with Emma and Charlie laughed, rolling her eyes. It wasn't the reaction Lucy had expected.

'It's awful, Charlie,' she said, seriously. 'What do I say to the poor girl? It's vile. I can't bear it.' Lucy could feel her pitch rising with frustration. 'Lawrence is lovely. He wouldn't mind at all,' she went on. 'Just because Emma is a nasty bitch, why shouldn't Helen have a picture with him? Because she's fat? Because she's not 'got the Spectrum look'?' Lucy couldn't contain the anger in her words. 'Woah! Calm down,' Charlie had picked up Lucy's martini and was holding it out for her.

'I don't want a fucking drink,' Lucy stood up, 'I want to work somewhere where this shit doesn't happen.' She walked back into the party, slipping though groups of drunk staff and found Helen still at the main bar.

'Lawrence,' Lucy tapped him on the shoulder and he spun

around with a huge grin on his face towards her, his nose stud glinting in the disco lights. 'Juicy Lucy!' he beamed and put an arm around her – he had clearly been making the most of the champagne top-ups. Emma shot Lucy a puzzled look, a nervous smile on her face. A mixture, Lucy imagined, of being impressed by her rapport with the celebrity, and jealousy that she was getting his attention. Then Lucy saw Emma spot Helen standing behind her before her face dropped to a thunderous look of disbelief.

'This is my colleague,' Lucy used her spare arm to pull Helen into the circle next to Lawrence. 'She's a massive fan, a 'Teamer', no less, and she'd love a photo,' Lucy continued, pulling her iPhone from her pocket, waiting for Helen to speak. Lawrence took his arm off Lucy's shoulder and turned to his super-fan. Helen was still looking at the floor and was now bright red and sweating slightly under the lights, her heavy black eye make-up smudged under her lower eyelashes.

'Absolute pleasure to meet you, um –'

'– Helen,' she finally spoke in a tremble, 'I'm Helen.'

'Well, the pleasure is all mine, Helen,' Lawrence took her hand and kissed it. Helen looked as though she might faint.

'Right, let's get that picture,' Lucy stood back and Helen and Lawrence looked at her iPhone as she counted down and hit the button.

'Beautiful, a keeper!' she exclaimed, as Lawrence removed his arm from Helen and promptly turned back to the group, duty done. Lucy purposefully avoided Emma's gaze, which she could feel burning into her skin, and walked away, heart thumping, with a giddy Helen.

Upstairs at her desk Lucy sat in her chair, her heart still pounding and her throat dry with realisation. She looked at her things on her desk and tried to work out how big a box she'd need for all her stuff. She couldn't allow herself to think about what she'd just done, how she had defied and undermined Emma. She knew her career at Spectrum was over. Tears ran down her cheeks as she opened drawers and removed notebooks, make-up, flip-flops and piled them on her desk. *What the hell have I done*, she thought, and held her head in her hands, alone in the production office, as the party boomed and cheered through the floor beneath her.

13

Hideaway Bay, 2003

Lucy sat in her garden drinking a glass of her mum's white wine;
a crisp, cool chardonnay that helped immediately to take the edge
off her anger. She glanced at the expanse of water on the horizon,
glittering in the sunlight, and wondered if Tom had gone surfing
after all. He probably had, she figured. Almost nothing could
keep Tom out of the water, certainly not an argument with her.
He'd surf right up until a minute or two before he was due at
work in the café. It drove his mum crazy – though Sarah never
really got angry with anyone and she would just tell Tom off
affectionately. The issue of their future plans had been simmering
for a while, really, Lucy knew that. She had always suspected he
intended to stay in Cornwall for the rest of his life, but she'd
never expected him to be so stupid as to write off any other
prospects at all by not even getting his A levels. She tried to push
the thought of it all from her mind as she felt her anger rise
again, her heartbeat quickening. She took another mouthful of
wine and reached for her phone to see the time. It was 3pm and
she had an empty afternoon ahead of her now, with no Tom to
entertain her. She wondered if she should call Nina, but remem-

bered she was back together with Kristian, fully loved-up and therefore wholly unavailable to anyone else for at least the next few days – until their next argument. She put her phone down on the cushioned sun lounger and lay back, closing her eyes and feeling the sun on her eyelids. She wondered when her parents and Richie would be home. She remembered her mum telling her about having people over for dinner this evening and needing to cook. Lucy worried momentarily whether the wine she'd opened was meant for this evening's guests, but sat up just enough to take another sip anyway.

The wine had calmed Lucy, as she'd hoped it would. A bead of sweat ran down her face from her hairline and she put her hand to her arm to check she wasn't burning. The sun on her skin felt good, healing somehow. The campsite at the bottom of the valley was already starting to fill up, more and more colourful tents popping up each day. Lucy could see a corner of the site from the bottom of her garden. She remembered the nights the four of them had spent camping there, the fun they'd had lighting a fire and drinking cheap wine into the night. Her parents had never caught her out on those secret nights away, when she'd told them she was staying at Nina's house. There was no way they'd have allowed her to stay with Tom in a tent when she was sixteen, and for good reason, as it turned out. Lucy remembered her argument with Tom all over again, but this time the wine fuzzed the anger and she felt something more like sadness. She picked up her phone to text him.

Sorry, shouldn't have said some of what I said. I was upset. I love you x

A car pulled up in the driveway at the front of the house. Lucy heard the gravel crunch and the car engine switch off. Her parents must be back, she thought, hoping her mum wouldn't try and rope her into helping with dinner preparations. She hated how her mum used her like a kitchen porter, only delegating the worst jobs and getting all shouty like a professional chef from TV cookery shows. She would make an excuse, she thought, say she had plans with Tom. In fact, she would go and see Tom. She'd apologise. She was more likely to convince him to stay on at college by being nice to him about it. She should have thought of that earlier. He was so stubborn once he'd made a decision; the more she fought it the more he'd stand firm. She was going to have to be cleverer than that.

'Lucy?' an unfamiliar female voice sounded from a few feet away, walking towards her.

Lucy sat up and turned around to see a man and woman in smartish office clothes walking towards her. She'd never seen them before.

'Yes,' she replied. 'Can I help you?'

She felt suddenly self-conscious in her shorts and bikini top and reached for her t-shirt to pull across her stomach.

'Lucy, is your sister here with you? Claire?' they asked, faces unsmiling. Lucy began to feel uneasy.

'No, she's in Thailand. Why?' she asked, her own voice sounding strange.

'We need to talk to you, Lucy,' the woman said, standing close to her now, looking like she might sit down on the lounger next to her. 'But we need to talk to you with an adult present.'

'Well my parents aren't home,' Lucy explained. 'They'll be back any minute, I guess, but I haven't heard from them.'

The woman glanced across at the man next to her, with an expression Lucy couldn't place.

'What is it?' Lucy said. 'I'm sixteen. What is it? You're scaring me now.'

The woman sat on the lounger next to Lucy and up close Lucy realised she was younger than she'd first thought. She could only be a few years older than Claire. Lucy studied her as she tucked a chunk of her short blonde crop behind her ear. Then the man, too, sat down awkwardly on the lounger.

'I'm Geraldine Slade,' the lady said, quietly but firmly, 'I'm a police officer and – would you like to go inside, somewhere a little more private?'

'This is private,' Lucy said, confused; their garden was huge, walled and not overlooked from any angle. What an odd thing to say, she thought.

'Your parents and your brother were sailing today, from Newquay,'

'I know,' Lucy said, as her mind raced. She felt suddenly that she might be sick.

'We don't know exactly what happened yet but there was an accident, Lucy, I'm so sorry –'

'What?' Lucy's voice shook, fear creeping through her body. 'What are you saying to me?'

'It was a very serious accident, Lucy. They're in the hospital now; they're doing everything they can for them.'

'What the fuck are you saying to me?' Lucy said, standing, her body shaking. This was the craziest, sickest thing anyone had ever done to her. She had no idea what was going on.

'It's a lot to take in,' Geraldine said calmly, ' And you need someone with you. Is there someone we can call? An adult?'

Lucy couldn't think. Everything was failing her; she thought she might pass out.

'My parents, my brother?' she said, slowly. 'Are they going to be okay?' The words sounded ridiculous. Of course they would be okay. There was no other option. The whole scene felt like an evil joke.

'I'm so very sorry. We'll know more at the hospital,' the man replied. 'We're here to help you in whatever way we can. But the first thing you need to do is call someone who can come and be with you here; someone you trust.'

'I need to speak to Claire,' Lucy said, numb, the words hollow in her mouth.

'We can arrange that,' Geraldine said, softly. 'Have a think about who I can call for you now, to come over here and travel to the hospital with you, or take you somewhere else – whatever you want.'

Lucy scanned through her brain for an appropriate response and found nothing. There was nothing in her that could cope with this. She couldn't even process it. The words kept repeating over and over and over. In the pit of her stomach a sense of doom settled; a fear that she was never, ever, going to be okay ever again. Nothing could ever be alright if something happened to her family. They just needed to come home, that's all that could happen. She just needed her parents and Richie to come home, like normal, and she'd be so grateful and it would all be okay. How could an afternoon so beautiful become such a nightmare?

She felt a hand on her arm and the reality crushed her all over again; her legs folded and she collapsed back onto the lounger.

'Call Tom's mum,' Lucy said, tears pouring from her eyes, her body stone-cold in the scorching heat, her heart threatening to stop beating all together. She just needed to get to the hospital and find out how they were going to make this all better.

'Call Sarah.'

14

London, 2010

Lucy looked around at the production office, which was a total mess. Clothes, make-up, and hair-straighteners as far as the eye could see – piled on top of papers, folders and keyboards. There were half-drunk glasses of champagne littering the desks and Lucy picked up the one nearest to her and downed the flat bubbles. She heard footsteps on the staircase and a saw a flash of black hair through the small pane of glass on the door. The door flew open, crashing into the wall behind with a terrible noise, even over the music from the party below.

Emma's face was expressionless and somehow more frightening than if she had been visibly angry. Lucy felt herself freeze and for a moment she thought she might wet herself. Emma strode towards her, stopping a few feet in front of her with a smile that didn't meet her eyes. Lucy didn't know what to say and she mumbled something incoherent before Emma raised a hand to her mouth in a 'shhh' gesture, dropping her smile. She pointed to Lucy's desk and took another step towards her.

'Take your things, and leave. Now!' she snarled at Lucy. 'You silly, silly little girl.'

Lucy watched her turn and walk away, still glued to the spot. Her legs wobbled slightly as the door closed again and Emma disappeared down the stairs. She took a heaving breath in and tried to compose herself. She pressed her hands into her eyes; she refused to cry here. There was a large woven shopping bag in her bottom drawer, from some launch she'd been to with Warren. 'Dream It, Live It,' the slogan on the side read. Lucy couldn't remember what the product or film, or whatever, had even been. She began putting the few personal things she kept at work into the bag. It wasn't like in films, she noticed. It didn't feel like the time for ceremony and she didn't have the kind of things that you'd pause and look at meaningfully, remembering good times or hard times – or whatever. She essentially had a filing cabinet full of pharmaceuticals to her name. She grabbed handful after handful of pill packets, deodorants, blister plasters, eye drops, and dried-up eyeliners and mascaras. There were lanyards that she'd been given at events, VIP access passes for concerts and festivals and photo-booth pictures of her and various Spectrum colleagues incredibly drunk at different parties.

She took the fire escape exit out to the car park, bypassing the party. She could hear Emma on the microphone addressing the crowd, people cheering her as if they adored her. The same people who, Lucy knew, in fact despised and feared her. But maybe it was more complicated than that, she thought, as she walked across the yard towards the main road. Maybe if she had the intelligence not to see everything in black and white, in good and bad and right and wrong, maybe then she wouldn't have just lost the job she'd worked so hard for. Emma was a bitch, that was certain, but she employed all these people, she was successful and she could be kind when she wanted to be, when it suited her. Had Lucy just thrown away a career because she didn't like her boss? Didn't that just make her the biggest idiot of them all?

On the Tube she tried to fight thoughts of what her life had become. She lived alone, had broken up with Scott, barely spoke to her sister and only seemed able to enjoy herself when she was almost totally out of it. She had singlehandedly lost herself her job tonight and she really didn't know what she had to wake up for tomorrow. She thought of Tom, and Nina and Kristian. Wondered what they were doing. Tom was probably drinking a beer and watching the sea, looking at the stars, like he always used to. 'Just magical, isn't it?' He always used to say at the sight of a glittering sky over the ocean. And she'd look at him, with his gaze fixed firmly up into the night, and study his beautiful, kind face in the moonlight, and think 'yes, it is, Tom, it really is magical'.

Back at the flat, she flicked her lamp on and sat on the sofa, suddenly tired from the evening's events. She looked at her phone; it was 10pm, probably not too late to call Nina.

'Hello?' Nina's voice answered. 'Don't tell me it's Lucy Templeton!' she feigned surprise.

'Hello,' Lucy replied, 'Don't moan at me. I'm sorry, I should've called you back ages ago but –'

'But you've been very, very busy being a London media daaaar-ling,' Nina said.

'I've been busy fucking everything up, actually,' Lucy replied, smiling with the relief of talking to her oldest friend.

'Well, you know what would make it all better…' Nina said.

'I know what you're going to say,' Lucy replied.

'And you know I'm right. I'm generally always right,' Nina said, seriously.

'I don't know if it's a good idea,' Lucy said, and she meant it. 'I don't know if coming back there, being around Tom – all the memories. I don't know if that's not just the worst thing I could do right now.'

Nina left a silence, forcing Lucy to continue.

'I just feel right on the edge, Nin. I seriously don't know what I'm doing. I've ruined everything up here and I've ruined myself, I think. I'm lost.' She was crying now and cursed herself for being pathetic.

'I think you do know what you need to do,' Nina said warmly. 'I think you need to stop running from everything, stop trying to escape it all and just come home. Let me and Kristian look after you for a while. Hell, let Tom look after you – who knows you better than him? Than us?'

Lucy couldn't reply.

'Lucy, what's the worst that happens if you come down here for a few weeks, take a break from London, breathe a little, get some Cornish sun, have some beach time with your very wonderful best friend – ?'

Lucy laughed.

'I mean it, Lucy. We'll be there, Tom's invited you. He wants you there. Did you know Claire called him too? Worried about you? It doesn't sound great up there.'

The reminder of Claire's massively cringeworthy call to her childhood sweetheart made Lucy's cheeks burn.

'Okay, okay,' Lucy replied, 'I'll need to sort things out here, the flat, my –' she realised she didn't actually have anything much to sort out at all. She'd wrecked most of it already.

'Come home, Lucy-Lu,' Nina said. 'It might be exactly what you didn't know you needed.'

15

The 13:06 departure to Penzance was boarding at Platform 4. Lucy had fifteen minutes until her train would pull out of Paddington and decided she had time to get a proper coffee for the journey. In Starbucks she ordered a tall skinny cappuccino and through the lightly steamed windows watched a group of young people with huge backpacks and festival gear laughing together as they headed for the platforms, and men in suits rushing past dawdling amateur travellers towards the Underground. Lucy sprinkled vanilla powder over the frothed milk in her warm cup and left the shop to head for her train.

Claire had paid for Lucy's ticket and had booked her a first-class single. In her squishy beige leather window seat, Lucy took the magazines from her case before lifting it into the rack above her single table. She'd walked past packed carriages of families off on their holidays and had inwardly thanked Claire for the foresight and generosity of upgrading her to this quiet, cool compartment. She would text Claire later to thank her again and to let her know she was on her way. Claire had offered to drop Lucy at Paddington this afternoon but Lucy hadn't wanted the fuss of a goodbye, the sense of ceremony of someone waving her off from London. She'd seen Claire last night instead, given her a set of keys and run through the things she might need to know about the flat. Anna, an old university friend of Tim's, was moving in in a week's time whilst on secondment to London from her Manchester office. The arrangement allowed Lucy to leave London for a while without having to move out of her flat. 'Keeping your options open,' Claire had said. *It's only a month*, Lucy had told herself.

Lucy loved her flat and had fought tears when she'd shut the door behind her this morning. But then she'd fought tears most days since leaving Spectrum. With her possessions packed away into cupboards and vacuumed into bags so that Anna had space for her own things, the flat had felt tidier and more organised than Lucy could remember, like someone else's place. But without accepting Claire's offer to cover her rent while Lucy looked for a new job, she'd have eaten her savings up paying to live in her flat within a few months. She couldn't afford London without a salary and spending her days in pyjamas wandering from room to room had begun to make her feel like a psychiatric patient in her own home. It seemed to Lucy now, as the train rolled out of Paddington, metal wheels screeching on metal tracks, that somehow, preposterously, Cornwall had actually become the most sensible option. Like Nina, Claire had unsurprisingly been in favour of the trip, of the time away from London. 'Healing time,' she kept calling it. It irritated Lucy how she kept inferring that Lucy was some kind of damaged woman who could be mended with sea air and brisk walks, like a mania-suffering Victorian lady sent to the coast by her desperate husband. But she was right, of course. Lucy did need some form of healing. She had spent day after day in bed, she still couldn't eat and she had lost more weight. She knew she looked horrible, but food felt like a reward she didn't deserve and her thin stature felt like a suitable reflection of her weak mind. A mind that had led her to have a mini-breakdown that evening at the wrap party.

She hadn't spoken to Tom. Nina was letting him know that she was coming after all. She'd never replied to his email and never asked Claire what he'd said when she'd phoned him that week she was staying with Lucy. The thought of that call still made her cringe with a physical shudder.

It was a beautiful day for a train journey. Bright-blue sky, vivid greens, sunlight glossing and glinting on houses and cars as they sped past. Lucy took her phone from her handbag and typed a message to Claire:

On my way, I'm okay. Thanks for the upgrade. I'll call you later x

The train driver was making announcements about stations and calling times; Lucy closed her eyes and rested her head against the window. Maybe she should email Tom. How awkward would it be arriving at Hideaway Bay in five hours' time without having spoken to him, she wondered? But the only way she'd been able to get herself to this point, to this seat on a train headed to Cornwall, was to not really allow herself to think about what she was doing. Images of Tom, the Beach Café, and all the memories she'd tried to pack away in the cobwebbed shadows of her mind, had started to force their way back and she pictured suddenly, with total clarity, Tom's parents' living room. Their old Labrador, Molly, spread out on the floor like a rug after a long walk, mugs of hot chocolate with marshmallows, made by Sarah, on the table. Neil and Sarah had been like second parents to Lucy. She'd lost them too when she left – not just Tom. They'd stopped writing eventually after she ignored too many letters.

The motion of the train beneath her in her safe, comfortable seat as she watched the countryside speed past her window was hypnotically reassuring. Lucy closed her eyes again.

When she woke, the view had changed dramatically. Lush greens had turned to striking reds and blues. The train appeared almost to be travelling through the water, waves lapping at the tracks on her left. Through the windows on the other side of the train red clay cliffs towered out of sight – it was as if a child had drawn this landscape, the colours were so bold. The train twisted through rocky caves and past Dawlish, a seaside town with crazy-golf courses on the seafront, rundown arcades set back from the road and shops selling holographic windmills and buckets and spades. A couple of families were playing on the beach and elderly couples were dotted around on benches eating cones of chips. It could have been a scene from a hundred years before, Lucy thought. Everyone becomes the same at the seaside, whatever their age, whatever the era, there was something naive and simple about these little towns. Checking her phone, Lucy realised she must have been asleep for almost an hour and she felt better for the rest. Her stomach groaned with hunger and she considered a trip to the buffet, but couldn't think of anything she might eat. She remembered the few times she'd been on the train in first class before, off to see Claire in London when she still lived in Cornwall, and how she'd try and drink as much free tea and coffee, and eat as many mini packets of biscuits as possible, to make the most of the perks.

She found Nina in a recent calls list and the call clicked through after the first ring.

'How are you getting on, lovely?' Nina's voice made her feel safe all over again, and glad to be just a couple of hours away from seeing her.

'We're on time,' Lucy told her, 'so I'll be at the station in about two hours. If you're still okay to come and get me? I can get a cab, honestly.'

'Don't be daft. I haven't known what to do with myself all day. I'll be there to pick you up – I'm too excited!' Lucy smiled at her friend's enthusiasm. 'Kristian's even insured me on the Audi – you have no idea what a big moment this is!' Nina continued. 'It's his baby, you know, honestly – boys.' Lucy pictured Nina rolling her eyes with a smile at this.

'I can't wait to see you either, Nin,' she said, genuinely. 'Right, I better get off before people in my carriage get cross with me.'

Lucy picked up one of her magazines: a hefty, glossy fashion publication, and tried to occupy herself. Her eyes kept being drawn back out of the window, to the seemingly endless views of rhythmic, glistening water. She hadn't seen the sea in five years, she realised suddenly. It was so beautiful.

16

As the train slowed into Bodmin Parkway Lucy spotted Nina standing by a black soft-top Audi in the car park. A wave of understanding of what she was about to do washed over her and she took a deep breath. When the door locks clicked off a bearded man waiting to board the train opened the door by Lucy. 'Let me get that for you, love,' he said, lifting her case out of her hands and down onto the platform, smiling.

'Thanks,' Lucy said, smiling back at his kind, tanned face.

'Luuuuuuuuucy!' Nina called as she walked towards her, arms outstretched. Lucy hugged her friend and felt her arms vice-like around her sides, squeezing her with real force. 'I'm so happy you're here,' Nina said quietly. 'Come on, let's get you in the car, let's get to Hideaway!'

Nina flicked through tracks on a Jack Johnson album, speaking over the intro to her chosen track. 'When in Rome,' Lucy laughed at the naff selection. This was the kind of music that tourists listened to on their campsites, sat around their fires with guitars, being all 'Corny-ish' as they used to call it. Music for the people who'd rock up in Hideaway with hundreds of pounds' worth of brand-new surf clothes and gear, only to spend their week's holiday on an old hired body board, too frustrated to continue when they couldn't stand during their first surf lesson.

'It's an art,' Tom used to tell Lucy, 'and I am a master!' He had always been beautiful to watch on a surfboard. The boys who'd grown up in the water moved differently to even really good latecomers to the surf. Lucy had tried a few times but wasn't much good and preferred swimming – but she had loved watching Tom. How many early mornings had she walked down the cliff path, still slippery with morning dew, opened up the Beach Café, made a coffee and taken it outside to sit and watch Tom in the water?

'I'm a better driver than Kristian, anyway,' Nina said. 'He thinks he's better, of course, but he just doesn't anticipate as well as me.' Lucy looked at her friend in profile. Nina must have cut her hair since she last saw her – it was just grazing her shoulders now and looked like it had lightened in the sun. She had never seen Nina without a tan and her honeyed skin looked radiant today, with the sun on her.

'You look good,' Lucy thought out loud.

'Ah, thanks,' Nina replied. 'You look thin. But good. You always look good.' She turned briefly towards Lucy.

'I haven't been too good,' Lucy conceded, with unusual honesty. 'I haven't got an appetite and I can't face eating anyway,' she admitted.

'Well,' Nina said, calmly, assuredly, 'It's a good job you'll be yards away from the finest eateries on Cornwall's champagne coast, my love. We'll have you eating crab sandwiches in no time.'

Lucy watched the roads become familiar and began to recognise even trees as they turned closer and closer to the coast, to Hideaway. With the roof down the smells of green and blue came in bursts of air.

'It's beautiful here,' Lucy said, still looking out to her left.

'It sure is,' Nina agreed, 'I still miss it. I still love it every time we come home.' Nina had been home at least twice a year since she and Kristian relocated to Bristol a couple of years ago. They were the most adventurous couple Lucy knew and were always travelling in exotic places, only coming back to the UK to work and save for a long enough to fund their next trip. Nina swung the car around a bend so fast that Lucy instinctively grabbed hold of the armrest and the Hideaway skyline unfolded in front of them. Lucy felt herself gasp involuntarily at the sight of her home town. Keeper's Island sat centre stage in the expanse of bright-blue water underlined with white-gold sand. The road wound down the hill into the town and Lucy looked on, like a stranger, at the same Spar shop she'd bought penny sweets from when penny sweets really cost a penny, the surf shop with the life-size mermaid model outside and the pasty shop with a snaking queue of sandy, damp tourists through its door.

'It's pretty much exactly the same, huh?' Nina remarked, looking at Lucy for a reaction, slowing the car to a snail's pace. Lucy didn't reply. She took in all the details: the way the sand from the beach had blown onto the tarmacked streets; the groups of children mesmerised by shiny souvenirs outside the 'tat shop', as they'd always called it. They turned another corner and Lucy looked to her right to see Sarah's and Neil's café in its proud position on the seafront. It looked new amongst these old shops and restaurants. It had been painted bright white and seemed to hold the sun in its walls, gleaming in the light. On the side facing the street, Lucy read 'Beach Café' in a large, italic, tasteful black font. To the back of the café, she could see a large area of light, driftwood-coloured decking stretching out towards the water. It looked almost nothing like she remembered – if it had landed in another town she wouldn't have recognised it at all.

'Ah, yes, now that *does* look a little different. Tom's done a lot of work on the place,' Nina said. 'He's gutted the inside too – it's really something. I couldn't believe it when I first saw it.'

'When was this?' Lucy asked, still staring at the café as it disappeared out of sight behind them.

'Couple of years ago now, I guess. Maybe more, actually,' Nina replied. 'I'll let him show you properly.'

Outside Tom's parents' house, Nina lent from the car and pressed the intercom at the gate. 'It's us,' she said to the metal box, which crackled in response. It buzzed and the gate began to draw open. Driving up towards the house, Lucy's heart began to race again at the prospect of seeing Tom.

'Five years, huh?' Nina said quietly, anticipating Lucy's thoughts.

'Yeah,' Lucy replied, her voice trailing into silence. The car stopped in the driveway – you couldn't really call it parking, the way Nina did it. The front door of the large Georgian property opened and Tom stood there, smiling at them, at Lucy. The sight of him made Lucy's stomach loop, her skin fizz. She smiled back at him without making any move to get out of the car. He was tanned, really tanned, and bigger than she remembered. He'd always had a surfer's physique, slim and toned, but he appeared to have broadened out at the shoulders and his arms bulged beyond the arms of his t-shirt. His dark hair was as messy as she remembered it, and he pushed it out of his eyes as he walked towards her, still sitting in the car. Nina made her way inside and Tom stood at her door, opening it for her.

'Luce,' he said, almost like a question, 'I'm so glad you came.'

'Of course, yep, great, good to see you,' Lucy said, too fast, realising she was still just sitting there like an idiot. Nina was already through the front door, calling to Kristian. She unclipped her seat belt clumsily and stepped out of the car. She didn't know how to greet Tom. Did they hug? Shake hands? He was the most familiar stranger she'd ever seen. Before she could decide what to do, Tom walked to the boot and took her case.

'I'll take you to your room,' he said, walking now in front of Lucy, towards the house. She followed him, stepping in through the front door before she was hit by the unique smell of his parents' house. It had always smelt like this, of washing powder and sunshine, and grass, Lucy thought. Tom took the staircase and Lucy trailed behind him, running her hand up the twisting wooden banister, remembering the feel of it on her skin. At the top of the stairs, Tom led them down the corridor to the larger bedrooms of the six-bed house.

'Nina and Kristian are in there,' he said, gesturing to his right, 'and you're in here – is that okay?' He swung the door ahead of them open onto what Lucy recalled as the nicest bedroom in the house. It was as white as a room could be and at the far end the French windows opened onto a balcony from which, Lucy remembered, you could see the sea. It was the balcony they had sat on many summer evenings during regatta week, watching fireworks, wrapped in blankets, drinking red wine. Kissing. Did he remember that?

'It's amazing – are you sure?' Lucy spun back towards Tom. 'I thought we'd be in the pool house?' she asked.

'Oh, no, my parents are away until October – we've got the whole place,' Tom replied. 'They've had enough of summer here, worked too many of them, I guess. They go to France for four months a year now, bought an old farmhouse that they did up.' Tom stopped himself now, and looked, was it slightly embarrassed, Lucy wondered?

'How lovely,' she said, quietly. 'I'd have loved to see them, though.' And she meant it. She'd imagined sitting with Sarah and Neil drinking champagne in the evenings, just like they used to.

'I'll let you settle in a bit,' Tom said. 'Bathroom's just through there, you probably remember.' He pointed to the en suite. He walked away towards the door and stopped, turning back to Lucy, who hadn't taken her eyes off his back. 'Thank you,' he said, 'Thank you for being here.'

Lucy made her way in to the garden, where the group was sitting around a large wicker table in the garden, reading papers and drinking coffee from a cafetière. Kristian got to his feet at the sight of her and swooped her into a hug when she reached them. 'Haven't seen you in forever!' he exclaimed. 'How you doing, Luce?' he asked. 'I'm okay, thanks,' Lucy smiled. She figured Nina would have explained what had happened in London and she didn't feel like going through it all now. She took a seat next to Nina, opposite Tom, who looked up at her from his paper and smiled. Putting his coffee down, he spoke loudly, addressing the group.

'So, what's the plan, guys?' he asked, waiting for a response.

'Was kind of hoping you had that covered' Nina replied, elbowing him. 'This was your idea, remember?'

'I just wanted a summer with all my oldest friends,' Tom said, 'and here you are. It's brilliant.' Lucy poured herself a cup of coffee and looked out at the view. From this elevated section leading out from the kitchen you could look down across the rest of the garden. The pool at the bottom glimmered in the late-afternoon light. The view of the sea was stunning. Lucy watched speck-sized boats bobbing across the water; a plane drifting white lines across the sky. The scent of jasmine lifted from the flowerbeds below them. Lucy closed her eyes, feeling the sun on her skin.

'I've got four weeks before I need to be back in London,' she said, to no one in particular. 'My sister's friend leaves my flat then and I'll need to go back and find a job.'

The thought of looking for a new job gave her a quick stab of panic, which Lucy tried to ignore.

'Well, we've got as long as you'll have us,' Nina chipped in. 'Our place is under offer. The sale should go through next week, so we are officially homeless,' she grinned in Kristian's direction.

'Will you stay in Bristol?' Tom asked. 'Or maybe I can convince you to come back here,' he jabbed Nina this time and she flinched.

'We'll see what happens with my job' Kristian replied, stretching back in his chair, stroking his blonde hair off his face.

'They'll make him permanent if he wants,' Nina rolled her eyes. 'He's just too stubborn to ask – he wants them to ask him first,' she laughed. Kristian had been working on short contracts for a management consultancy firm in Bristol. It paid enough to buy him and Nina a house and an Audi, while allowing them the flexibility of months off at a time to go travelling – a sweet deal by anyone's standards.

'Are you working, Tom?' Lucy asked. 'In the café?'

'Sure am,' he replied, 'but I've got most days covered for the next few weeks, so I'm all yours.'

Lucy took a sip of coffee and flicked through the stack of papers on the table, looking for a magazine.

'Great,' she said, almost looking at Tom, 'I can't wait to see it properly. We drove past and it looks fantastic.'

'I'll take you down there later,' he said. 'You can meet Tara.'

17

The afternoon had seen them slot back immediately into their easy dynamic as a foursome. It was so much like old times, so quickly, that it had really taken Lucy by surprise. Nina and Kristian still bickered and Tom still tried to catch her gaze as they did, smirking a little at their spats. Lucy, however, had barely been able to meet Tom's eyes. When he wasn't looking at her, she watched him. His mannerisms hadn't changed: his laugh was the same, the way his head went back as he grinned. He was definitely more gorgeous than she'd remembered, which she could've done without. It shouldn't have been a surprise to her that he was still just Tom, and yet it was.

Back in her room, Lucy stood at the wardrobe and looked at the very limited selection of clothes hanging in front of her. She'd not known what to pack and it now seemed she hadn't done a very good job of it. The plan this evening was dinner at the café and Lucy wanted to wear something relaxed but pretty. A dress with flat shoes would have to do. She settled on a short, black, loose-fitting dress with a dipped back, and gold sandals with bare legs. Sitting at the white, shabby-chic dressing table she listened to waves in the distance and Kristian's acid jazz playing downstairs, as she applied her make-up, examining her face with scrutiny. *I wonder how much older I look to him?*

She needed some sun on her face, she thought, as she swept bronzer under her cheeks and across her forehead. She liked her eyes, they were her best feature, and she defined them with dark-grey liquid liner at the corners and plenty of mascara. She pulled her long hair back into a ponytail and clipped strands in place with a Kirby grip from her wallet. Finally, standing in front of the full-length mirror, the finished result was not displeasing and she felt ready to step out into the night. She had meant what she had said to Tom about looking forward to seeing the café, but the mention of meeting Tara had unnerved her slightly – who the hell was she?

With everyone gathered on the driveway, Nina offered to drive them to the café. 'I'm not walking in these,' she said, lifting a high-heeled shoe to show the group. 'We can always get a cab back if I decide to get hammered,' she winked at Lucy. The evening sun was dripping orange across the pale sky and the town was busy with visitors looking at menus outside restaurants or carrying bags of meat from the Spar shop to be barbecued back at their holiday homes. Nina pulled the car up across two spaces to the side of a beach café, marked as reserved for staff.

'It's fine,' Tom told Kristian as he began to point out that no one else could now fit a car next to them on either side. 'No one drives to work,' he promised. The air was warm, a fine breeze carrying the day's heat over Lucy's skin as she walked into the café and up the stairs next to Kristian.

Inside the café, the smell of food, mixed with after-sun lotions and zesty perfumes, filled the large space with a heady scent. The place was beautifully laid out with stylish furniture and gorgeous lighting. The clientele seemed to consist mainly of youngish groups and couples, sharing platters of food on wooden boards. Tom led their group through the room towards the decking, checking with Nina that she wouldn't be too cold outside. He nodded hello at the waiting staff he passed on the way through. They looked like the usual mix of students and surfers, just like they had been when Lucy had been here as a girl. The large glass doors were folded back at the rear of the room, opening onto a large decked area that was bustling with diners and drinkers. The warm air hit Lucy's skin and she instinctively rubbed her arms, as she followed the group to the table that had been reserved for them. It was right on the water's edge and the wooden flooring helped to give the impression of being sat at the front of a boat on the ocean. The sounds of the sea rushed and pulled underneath them and Lucy heard it as if for the first time, its roaring and ceasing alien after all her years in London. Menus were handed out by a pretty blonde girl, who Tom introduced as Melanie. She smiled at everyone and Lucy thought she detected her pause slightly as she was introduced, as if trying to figure Lucy out, before checking herself and moving on. She was probably imagining it, she told herself. She'd had a few paranoid thoughts in the weeks since leaving Spectrum – all part and parcel of some kind of borderline breakdown, she figured.

'So, what do you think?' Tom asked the group, but looked directly at Lucy, smiling with the same smile from her photograph.

'It's absolutely stunning,' she answered, before thinking. It really was. The atmosphere was fun but relaxed, people all around them were clearly having a good time and it was busy, far busier than Lucy could remember it ever being before.

'It's all Tom,' Nina smiled. 'He's worked absolute magic with this place. So proud of you, dude.'

Lucy smiled at Tom and he caught her eye, grinning back.

'I didn't expect so much to have changed,' she said, honestly. She realised as the words came from her mouth how true this was. What had she expected? That everything would have stood still while she was gone?

Tom had turned the loveably scruffy Beach Café into a chic destination, and she hadn't had a clue. She'd imagined him surfing his days away, just getting by, with the café giving him an income. He had done more than she'd ever imagined, more than she'd given him credit for. The thought made her face hot.

'Well, when Mum and Dad decided they'd had enough, I realised I had a choice,' Tom paused to check the bottle of wine Melanie had brought over – an ice-cold prosecco that looked heavenly in its frosted bottle.

'I either plodded along doing the bare minimum or I took the chance to make something extraordinary,' he said as he poured glasses of fizz and handed them around the table. The phrase took Lucy by surprise. It was how she had always explained her plan to leave this place to Tom. 'I want something extraordinary,' she had told him as a girl. This place was never going to give her that chance. Because it never seemed to give anyone that chance. To Lucy, growing up here, Hideaway had seemed like a final destination for people who didn't have much ambition, who were happy to coast along. She'd been so angry that Tom couldn't see that, that he was happy to stay behind when she left, and it had made her think so much less of him.

'Well, it's extraordinary, for sure,' Kristian raised his glass in a toast and everyone clinked glasses. Lucy picked up a menu and perused the options, olives and flat breads, hummus and pickled tempura vegetables – the thought of it all made her hungry. Tom offered to order a selection to share and everyone murmured their agreement as they helped themselves to the homemade sundried tomato rolls Melanie had brought. Lucy wedged a big lump of butter into her still-warm roll and held it in her hand as it melted into the bread. Her free hand brought the glass of prosecco to her lips and she sipped the cold bubbles as she looked around at her friends. She felt, she realised, totally relaxed for the first time in too long.

As Tom opened the third bottle of prosecco, Lucy checked herself to make sure she wasn't feeling too drunk. Eating seemed to have helped the situation and she felt relatively confident that she was okay. Everyone was in good spirits and there had been a lot of laughing and reminiscing. It was a different kind of conversation to what she'd become used to. The familiarity she felt with everyone was so easy compared to her work friends in London. She loved some of the guys from the office and went out with them all the time, considered them proper friends. But how many of them could she have sat with, laughing like this for so long? And how many of them had bothered to ask how she was since she'd left? She'd heard from Warren and Katie, but no one else had called.

Kristian and Nina talked about their plans for their new home in Bristol. Reading between the lines, it sounded a lot like Nina was planning to spend an absolute fortune on doing an old place up, but Kristian didn't seem so keen.

'The thing is,' Nina said, looking at Kristian, 'if you're going to do it at all, you've got to do it well.'

'So I'm not going to scrimp on flooring and furniture, because we'll just need to replace it all in a few years. It's a false economy,' she finished triumphantly, clearly convinced her argument was watertight.

'The other thing is,' Kristian said, avoiding Nina and looking instead at Lucy and Tom, 'spending every single penny of our savings on a fucking floor feels really bloody stupid and rather depressing.'

Tom laughed. 'You're getting old, mate.'

'We all are,' Kristian said, squeezing Nina's arm and kissing her shoulder. 'I don't know why it seems surprising, given that it's the only way things go, but each year I can't believe I'm this old. I still feel like I'm sixteen inside.'

'But then he plays football on a Saturday and wakes up on a Sunday unable to move and remembers that he's a creaky old git,' Nina nudged him.

'That's exactly it, sadly,' Kristian said. 'And realising that I have a proper, grown-up job. Life was easier when I could just pick up a few shifts here and make some cash.'

'It sure was' Lucy said, remembering what it was like when they all worked here together over the summer. So much fun.

'Well, guys, we always need staff,' Tom smiled. 'Not sure I pay as much as your boss, though, Kristian, I haven't seen any of the waiting staff driving around in Audis recently.'

'Talking of work,' Kristian said, glancing at Nina as if to check before continuing, 'I heard about what happened with your boss, Lucy. She sounds a right piece of work.'

Lucy didn't really feel like talking about it and wondered what the bare minimum was that she could say before moving on.

'Yeah, well it was my fault too,' she said. 'I kind of lost the plot with it all. I don't know what I was thinking when I challenged her like that. That was just bloody stupid, to be honest. It wasn't brave. I wished I hadn't done it straight away.'

'But you stood up for someone who she was basically bullying,' Nina interjected, defensively. 'I think it was brave.'

'It was definitely stupid, either way,' Lucy concluded. 'I'm probably unemployable in my industry now – once people hear what I did. She'll make me sound unhinged. To be fair, I think I am a bit unhinged.' She laughed, but she meant it, and she felt embarrassingly like the fuck-up of the group. She wanted to move the conversation along.

'Well, selfishly, I'm just glad it meant you've ended up down here,' Tom said, looking at her briefly, then turning his gaze out to the sea. 'It's been too long.'

With the plates cleared away, Lucy looked at Nina's full glass of prosecco and told her to finish it up.

'I'm drinking you under the table,' she widened her eyes at her friend. Nina picked up the glass before handing it over to Lucy.

'Well, actually… I've been meaning to tell you,' Nina turned her head briefly to Kristian, who smiled at her encouragingly. 'I'm pregnant,' she said in a high-pitched voice Lucy didn't recognise.

'We're having a baby!' Kristian cheered, knocking over a water glass in demonstration of both how excited he was and how drunk he'd managed to get on the prosecco.

'Oh my God!' Lucy moved to hug Nina. 'That is just amazing, I am SO happy for you!' Lucy felt tears threatening as she held her friend and smelled her hair, as if to check she was still the same person.

'That's incredible, guys,' Tom raised his glass in a toast. 'You are going to be awesome parents.'

Lucy wiped a tear away and smiled at Tom. 'You really are,' she agreed, putting her arms around Kristian, who looked like he might cry too.

'Told you we're properly grown up' he said quietly to her, and another tear fell down her cheek

'Do you fancy a walk?' Tom appeared at Lucy's side as she leant against the railings looking down into the water.

'It's still pretty mild out,' he gestured towards the beach. Kristian had taken Nina home after she'd announced that as much as she loved watching everyone get pissed, she was done for the night.

'Sure,' Lucy said, turning towards Tom. They took the steps from the decking down to the beach and Lucy kicked her sandals off in the sand. Tom removed his flip-flops too and they left them there on the little wooden step as they made their way through the sand. The silence between them felt strangely normal and Lucy looked up at the moon without thinking about anything at all.

'Crazy news that they're having a baby,' Tom said, as if to no one in particular, and Lucy didn't answer.

'I'd have put money on us being the ones to have children,' he continued, and the words stung unexpectedly.

'Funny how things work out, I guess,' Lucy replied, without looking at him. As they reached the water, the cooler night air prickled Lucy's face and she hugged her arms around herself to warm up.

'Here you are,' Tom took his jacket off and handed it to Lucy. She took it and slipped it on.

'Thanks.' She looked at him now and felt her heart race. As she slipped her arm into the silk-lined sleeve, the smell of him seeped from the fabric and she felt like putting it to her nose just to breathe it in.

'Is that better?' Tom asked, and she nodded.

'Suits you,' he jabbed her playfully in the side. His touch made her jump and she wished suddenly that he'd hold her sides like he used to, pull her close and kiss her. She stepped away to continue walking as the sand became wet and the waves lapped at her toes.

'I really am glad you came,' Tom said, seriously now, 'And when you're ready to talk properly about London you just let me know. There's no rush, chicken.' His old pet name for her made her melt a little.

'Thanks,' she said, looking back at him as a wave of exhaustion hit her. 'Let's get back to the house. I'm really, really tired.'

Tom put his hand on the small of her back as if to steer her back towards the house. They walked in silence up the cliff path, Tom offering his arm at the trickier parts. Lucy looked up at the twinkling sky, inky blue now, and breathed the sea air deeply into her lungs as if it were medicinal.

Back at the house, Kristian was still in the kitchen, eating toast and drinking tea.

'Want a cup?' he gestured at Lucy and Tom to join him.

'I'd love one,' Lucy went to join him and looked over her shoulder for Tom to follow.

'I'm alright, thanks,' Tom dipped his head as a goodnight and headed up the stairs to bed. Lucy felt a little shunned and wished Tom had sat up with them for a while. Kristian seemed to sense her disappointment and after a brief pause he spoke gently and seriously.

'Tom looked knackered. He works too hard.' All these years later he was still covering for his friend.

Lucy sipped the tea Kristian passed her and he shuffled his stool up next to her at the counter, slipping his arm around her shoulder. He smelt very faintly of cigarette smoke and very strongly of aftershave.

'I'm going to be a Dad, Luce, me – a dad!'

Kristian was so happy – it was beautiful to see.

'You're going to be great,' she smiled at her friend, tilting her head onto his hand and closing her eyes.

'I need my bed,' she said, getting up to leave.

'Sleep tight, Luce,' Kristian was still smiling to himself, 'I've really missed you.'

18

Lucy woke the next day feeling fresher than she usually did after a night's drinking. It seemed eating really did help after all. Her crisp white room was flooded with bright sunshine pouring through the balcony windows. She had clearly forgotten to draw the curtains closed last night. Usually she liked to jump out of bed the moment she opened her eyes, but this morning she lay there for an extra few minutes, stretching and breathing in the fresh air, enjoying the weight of the duvet on her body.

In the bathroom she decided to run a bath, the free-standing tub looked too good to resist. She put on a fluffy white dressing gown and padded around the room, imagining she was the heroine in an old film. Lost in her daydream, she was startled by Nina appearing in her room, looking like she'd just come back from a run.

'Are you allowed to run?' she asked.

'Um, yes, my lovely, I'm pregnant, not ill' Nina laughed. 'Will you come with me tomorrow? I've got a new route along the cliff path – it's breathtaking up there.'

'Sure,' Lucy agreed, as her mind flashed back to her last run and the fainting incident.

'I just came to let you know we're surfing today, if you fancy it? Tom's got to work because someone's called in sick, so we're just heading to the beach with the boards. It is gorgeous out there today.'

'Sounds good,' Lucy replied. 'I'm going to have a bath and get dressed, but I'll see you down there.'

'Perfect,' Nina left, calling to Kristian 'Lucy's meeting us there! Where are you? HURRY UP!'

Lucy vaguely listened to the ensuing kerfuffle and waited for the sound of the door closing behind them. The peace was beautiful. In her bath, she slid under the water, enjoying the feeling of her weightless hair lifting away from her head. She suddenly remembered they hadn't met this Tara girl who Tom had mentioned, and the recollection made her feel uneasy. *It's probably his girlfriend,* she thought, wondering how she'd resist asking Nina and looking like a real sad case.

On her way to the beach, Lucy scoured the sand from the road above to spot Nina and Kristian. She located them in the corner they'd always preferred as teenagers, down by the cliffs in the patch of seemingly softer sand than the rest of the beach. Nina hadn't been wrong – it *was* another beautiful day.

I need to call Claire, Lucy thought, *I need to tell her I'm okay.* She promised herself she'd call her that night. She'd been so close to not coming at all, she thought, as she walked towards Nina, and now she was glad she was here. It had seemed like the maddest idea, but now she was back it felt like the only place she could possibly be now. She was so grateful to Claire for making her come back; she ought to tell her she was right.

'Ooh good timing. Can you zip me up?' Nina was half in her wetsuit and Lucy pulled the zip up her back.

'Nice, isn't it, that Kristian just runs off into the sea leaving me here like this? Urgh. I swear I'm getting properly fat already,' Nina sighed.

'You're not,' Lucy insisted, honestly, 'you're still tiny.'

'Right, thanks, lovely, I'm going in,' Nina gestured towards the water as she picked up her board. She really did look radiant; perhaps that pregnancy glow wasn't a myth.

'Are you okay to stay with the stuff for a while? I won't be long, my stamina's not what it used to be.' Nina draped the back of her hand over her forehead melodramatically as she said this and then grinned at Lucy.

'No problem,' Lucy said, unfolding the pink beach towel from her back and laying it on the sand. 'I'm just going to chill here and read some trash.' She pulled *Just Life* magazine from her bag, picked up en route from the shop where she'd once felt huge achievement when buying Marlboro Lights as a fourteen-year-old.

'Wow, that *is* some serious trash you've got there,' Nina barely concealed the disdain on her face.

'Enjoy the water!' Lucy called, as Nina headed towards the waves.

The beach was busy but Lucy had the relatively secluded corner almost to herself as she made herself comfortable on her towel. She reached for her magazine and looked at the cover with renewed embarrassment at having bought such junk. It always made her laugh how these boldly coloured, big-fonted, inanely grinning magazines were festooned with such horrible headlines. 'Sexually assaulted by my dog', 'I married my husband's killer', and 'My rosy cheeks were cancer', blurted the cover – 'that's *Just Life*' the title seemed to cheeringly shrug back, ridiculously.

The sun was high in the sky, and it was almost lunchtime now. Lucy had spent so long pottering around her room getting ready aimlessly. She found the pain au chocolat she had bought fresh from the oven in the bakery and took a big bite as she flicked through the magazine. She pulled off her top and wriggled out of her shorts, as she felt herself beginning to overheat in the sun. Finishing her pastry, she tossed the wrapper into her bag and reclined fully on the towel, holding the magazine to block the sun from her eyes.

'Luce… Luce?' it was Tom's voice calling her as she opened her eyes in a panic about where she was.

'Sorry to wake you up,' he said, leaning towards her and casting a shadow over her body. This handily blocked the sun's harsh light and allowed her eyes to focus.

'I must've fallen asleep,' she said – rather stupidly, she thought. *That's pretty obvious.*

'I've got someone here to meet you,' Tom said, stepping to the side, and Lucy became aware of a tall, slim, blonde girl now leaning over her where he had been. 'This is Tara,' Tom said cheerfully.

The girl held out her hand in Lucy's direction as Lucy pulled herself up, cursing internally at having fallen asleep in public. As she leant to meet Tara's hand, Tara pulled away from her suddenly

'Oh, you've just got something…' she rubbed an imaginary something away from the corner of her mouth and Lucy rushed to mirror her, looking at her hand and seeing chocolate. She brushed it off onto her bikini, leaving a horrible dirty mark.

'That's it, got it,' Tara said, shaking the non-chocolate-coated hand now and smiling at her with what Lucy took to be pity. Tara was absolutely, sickeningly, undisputedly gorgeous. She had that kind of blonde hair that looked good just twisted up into a messy bun, and her skin looked how Lucy always wished hers would look after a fake tan, and which it never did. Her big almond eyes were flicking up and down Lucy's pale body and she felt immediately vulnerable and mortified, overcome suddenly with a wave of hatred for this smug stranger hanging around with Tom.

'Nice to meet you,' she smiled in what she hoped was a convincing way and pulled her t-shirt over her stomach defensively.

'Tara's the café supervisor. She's the real reason we're doing so well.' Tom nudged Tara as she pretended to blush. Lucy groaned inwardly. *Such a fake.*

'What are you reading?' Tara leant down to pick up the magazine at Lucy's side and she had to stop herself physically restraining her. 'Nothing,' Lucy insisted, too fast, and too loud. *What a twat I am.*

'*Just Life*, wow. I haven't seen this in a long time – can't believe people read this stuff!' Tara stopped herself 'Sorry, I mean, it's just not my sort of thing,' she continued cheerfully.

Lucy couldn't have hated herself or Tara much more in that moment and could think of nothing to say.

'Well, we'd better get back to the café. Nina mentioned you were coming down so I just wanted you two ladies to meet,' Tom said, smiling at each of them. 'I knew I'd find you tucked away here in this corner.'

'I've heard lots about you,' Tara interrupted, *inanely*, Lucy thought. *There is no sensible response to that phrase.*

'Mmhmm,' she replied, like a moron. 'Nice to meet you too.' She felt a bead of sweat run down her cheek and over her lip. *Brilliant.*

'See you later on, Luce,' Tom called.

Lucy watched as they walked away and saw Tara loop her arm in Tom's, a sight that made her heart thud into her stomach. She dabbed at her face with her top and realised just how sweaty she was. She recalled the chocolate around her mouth and painted a picture in her own mind of a hideous wet, red face with brown stains around her lips and could have screamed with humiliation at the thought. As a thousand nasty thoughts forced their way in and tumbled around her mind she felt something like horror at the memory of how she'd wanted Tom to kiss her last night, how she'd almost allowed herself to think that he might. What a total fool. She wanted to cry. *He's moved on, he has a girlfriend, I am such an idiot. Thinking I can just come back here and pick up some childhood romance.* She still had her head in her hands when Nina returned, dripping and salty.

'You okay?' she asked.

'I just met Tara,' Lucy explained.

'I don't think I'd assume it was poo if I saw a brown smudge on your face,' Nina pondered seriously after Lucy explained what had happened.

'How and, more importantly, why, would you have poo on your face? It was obviously chocolate,' she reassured.

'Actually, my friend did once walk around with poo on his face for a morning, but that was because of some dodgy night he'd had when he met a guy off some app, got off his face on drugs, did God knows what, and headed home the next morning without looking in the mirror. But I don't think that's a normal situation.'

The casual way Nina reeled off this story left Lucy speechless, but slightly less embarrassed at her own misfortune at least.

'Um, thanks!' she laughed.

'Anyway, I don't care that Tom has a girlfriend – it's absolutely fine,' she insisted. 'It was just a surprise.'

'Oh come off it,' Nina looked her straight in the eyes. 'You are literally never going to be totally fine about Tom having a girl-friend – we all know that. He was your first love. It's fine *not* to be fine with it.'

'So she is his girlfriend?' Lucy replied, without looking at Nina, her heart beating fast.

'Actually, no, I don't think so,' Nina answered. 'They're really good friends, but I don't think there's anything more to it.'

Lucy remembered the way Tara had slipped her hand through Tom's arm and silently disagreed with Nina. *If there's not something going on already, she wishes there was.*

'I've heard so much about you,' Lucy mimicked in a bimbo voice out loud, without thinking about it,

'Oh yeah, you're totally fine with it, Luce, that's really clear,' Nina rolled her eyes and Lucy rolled her eyes back even wider.

'I'm going into the sea – your turn to look after the stuff,' Lucy said. She momentarily considered taking Nina's surfboard but figured there was only one direction her limited surfing ability could have gone in her six years out of the water and decided she'd swim instead.

'Swim away the tension!' Nina called. 'Deep breaths, poo-mouth!' She laughed loudly at her own joke and Lucy couldn't help laughing too as she headed for the water.

19

At the house, Lucy blow-dried her hair and straightened it with her GHDs. She'd forgotten how invigorating it was coming out of the sea into the sun and how glorious a long, hot shower felt after a day in the water. She applied a bit of bronzer on her slightly sun-kissed skin and swept some mascara over her lashes, pulling on a pair of leggings and a long gold top. She dialed Claire's number and went outside onto her balcony to speak to her sister.

'Lucy, it's so nice to hear from you, how are you?' It was good to hear Claire's voice.

'I'm good thanks, really good,' Lucy replied. She told Claire about her first few days in Cornwall and Claire asked whether she was taking care of herself, whether she was eating.

'And how is Tom?' Claire asked, trying to sound nonchalant, Lucy thought.

'He's good,' Lucy told her. 'He's transformed the café. It's amazing and it's good to see him.'

'I heard about the café,' Claire told her. 'You remember my friend Charlie who's still down there? He told me it's *the* place to hang out on the North Coast these days. Who knew our home town would become a hotspot, hey?'

'Yeah,' Lucy replied, 'he's done something special with it – it's pretty impressive.' 'And how does it feel to be back down there, with him?' Claire enquired, gently.

'It's nice,' Lucy answered truthfully. 'It doesn't feel nearly as strange as I thought it would. I've hardly thought about London. How is my flat, actually?'

'It's all fine here. Nothing for you to worry about at all. Tim's popping over there tonight to see how Anna's getting on, actually.'

'Okay, that's great. I suppose I'd better get going,' Lucy said. She could hear music playing, and pots and pans crashing around in the kitchen downstairs. They were cooking together this evening.

'Okay, Luce. Well I'm really really glad that you're okay down there,' Claire sounded a bit emotional. 'Do you think you'll go and see Mum and Dad, and Richie?' she asked.

'I… I don't know, I guess so,' Lucy felt panic rising at the thought of it. 'I've got to go now.'

'Okay. I understand it's difficult, but you should go,' Claire said. 'It's been a really long time. You should see them.'

'Knock knock,' Tom poked his head around Lucy's door with a smile.

'Hey,' she replied, putting her phone down, 'You okay?'

'I'm great,' he said, walking over to her and opening the balcony door. 'Have you checked out this view recently? Still special, huh?'

'It certainly is,' Lucy said, standing to join him in the fresh, sunny air. 'I'd forgotten how beautiful it is down here.'

'It's why I never wanted to leave,' Tom replied, looking straight ahead and smiling. 'I bet you still disagree with that, though.' He looked at her with a cheeky smile.

'I don't know any more,' she replied. 'You seem really happy, the café is amazing, so successful, and you live in an incredible house,' she paused, considering her next words. 'You've got a gorgeous girlfriend. Looks like it's all worked out pretty well for you, to be honest.'

'And you've had an amazing career in London,' Tom replied, ignoring her girlfriend comment and confirming her fears. 'Nina's told me bits and pieces over the years. It sounds like you've lived quite a life up there.'

'Yeah, if you mean screenings and parties and all that, then yes, I guess so,' she said, slightly annoyed by his naivete. She wondered how sincere he was, as she knew he'd have hated all that and probably thought it was all pretty silly.

'I loved my job – in lots of ways,' she said, feeling defensive. 'And I've got brilliant friends up there. I had a lot of fun.'

'But there's something missing,' Tom said, as a statement, as if he was so certain.

'What do you mean?' Lucy asked, looking at him. His face was thoughtful.

'Well, for all of that, it didn't make you happy, did it?'

'It did in some ways,' Lucy said, trying to sound convincing.

'Not in the important ways, though, maybe,' Tom offered, smiling at her again now, trying to be nice.

'I don't know. I'm sick of analysing it all, to be honest,' Lucy said, with a sigh. 'And I'm sick of feeling like I've messed everything up.'

'Well, you're here now and you can't mess this up,' Tom said. 'A summer with the four of us all together can only be a good thing.'

'Yeah,' Lucy agreed, remembering him and Tara and her heart sinking slightly.

'I don't want this to be awkward for you,' Tom said. Lucy didn't really know what he meant. Him having a girlfriend? How bloody embarrassing. *And yes, it's pretty awkward, so thanks a lot,* she thought.

'There's no issue, Tom,' she lied. 'I came down here for a break, for a few weeks away from London – with my *friends*. There's nothing more to it. So don't worry.'

'Okay,' Tom said, and he may as well have put his hands up

in an 'okay, sorry I mentioned it' kind of way as he made his way back in to her room and towards her door.

Lucy wondered how he managed to make her feel so stupid by being so nice to her. He'd always had this power over her – he was so stable and steady and confident. It sometimes made her feel like a total mess in comparison. And now here he was being the bigger person, doing the right thing and clearing the air before she could embarrass herself any further by getting silly ideas about him still harbouring any feels for her. She watched him leave her room and wondered whether this whole trip was such a good idea after all.

Tom stopped in the doorway and looked back. 'I meant to ask,' he said, 'if you want to go and see your family, I can come with you. If that would help.'

'Thanks,' she said, 'I don't think I can face it, but thanks.'

'Okay,' Tom said, looking resigned. 'The offer's there. Maybe you could think about it.'

20

Despite spending the following days trying to put thoughts of them out of her mind, keeping herself busy drinking wine, eating fish and chips and attempting to swim all the extra calories off, Lucy hadn't been able to shake the thought of her parents, of Richie. She'd woken this morning at 6am, unable to get back to sleep after another vivid nightmare about them all being stranded at sea together. Her mouth was bone dry and she had tears in her eyes; she realised it might be a better idea to just go and face them.

Once it was no longer too early to make a sound she left her room and went downstairs, creeping as quietly as she could out of the front door. There weren't really any solid plans for the day ahead. There had been loose talk of a beach day and a barbecue in the evening, but she wouldn't be missed for a few hours. She closed the door behind her and took the winding path down to the town, the morning air crisp on her face. The town was almost deserted at this early hour; the bakery's door was open, puffing out the smell of freshly baked bread and pastries, and people were pulling tables and chairs outside their cafés – but there were hardly any civilians up and about, apart from a couple of young dads who seemed to have been woken early by their kids and had brought them down the seafront for croissants and papers.

Lucy decided to walk the forty-minute journey rather than waiting for a bus. It was uphill and exhaustingly steep in parts, but the focus of her footsteps helped to keep her mind steady. The scent of the pink and lilac hyacinths she'd bought for her mum drifted in and out of her consciousness. Each time it took her back to her childhood home and the white vase her mum had always filled with hyacinths, her favourite flowers, in the lounge. She could hear her mum laughing, see her walking into the room with Richie in her arms. At the church, Lucy walked through the mossy, green and grey graveyard to her family's plot and read the three little names engraved in stone – Sandra, Steven and Richard Templeton.

Richie would've been sixteen this year, she thought. She put the flowers down and sat herself on the grass – at a complete loss. She should have come more often, she knew this, but she'd never been able to stand this place. It was so grey and stern and formal, and so unlike her family had been. Had she imagined her childhood into a fantasy of laughter and happiness with too much time and hindsight? She remembered how warm and loved she had felt as a girl, how much her parents had given them all, not just the big house and exotic holidays, but so much love and attention. Even her dad, who worked away so often, had doted on them as children, all of them, but especially Richie – his much-longed-for little boy.

The summer of the accident had been the happiest of Lucy's life and it had hit her like a tsunami of sorrow. She remembered Sarah holding her hand as they waited for news in the depressing little room at the hospital. How she'd held out a tissue when the doctor explained that not one of them had survived. Lucy remembered the room spinning as she took in those words, Sarah's grip on her the only thing that held her there and stopped her being sucked into the spinning nightmare and lost forever. The doctor had explained that they wouldn't have suffered, that it was all so very quick. That it would have been painless. And Lucy had wanted to believe him, but a part of her just didn't. Wasn't that just what doctors said to you about these things?

It had taken so long for the details to come out and half of what they learned came from the papers in the end. The local and national media had had a field day with the tragedy. They lapped up the picturesque setting, the glamorous family out on their boat, the fact her dad had been drinking. It felt like it went on and on – each time she caught a report on the TV or an article in the paper it had hit her all over again. And so much of it had been so wrong, or at least so misleading. Her dad wasn't a drinker – he'd had a couple of beers on the boat that afternoon. He could have legally driven them home. It transpired eventually that it was a 'freak incident', that they'd probably hit a wave at a bad moment, at too high a speed and whilst making too sharp a turn. It was a series of shitty judgement calls that led to a random catastrophe. Her mum and Richie had been thrown from the boat and her dad had jumped in to try and save them. Witnesses to the scene reported seeing the boat looping around them, in a tighter and tighter circle, until it struck them. There was nothing anyone could have done. It was a 'tragic accident', but that wasn't as exciting as suggesting it was somehow her dad's fault, that he'd been boozing at the wheel, and that he'd caused it all with negligence. Knowing the sensationalised reports were wrong didn't help Lucy at the time – each one hurt her to the core.

She and Claire had had no idea how to cope, how to react or who to turn to. Lucy had been lucky that Tom's parents were so incredible at knowing what to do. But the weeks afterwards had passed in a hideous daydream. Lucy remembered feeling nothing but anger at the funeral, anger at all the people there being upset, all the people still there, when her family wasn't. She hadn't cried – she wasn't sure if she'd said a word. Tom had been with her, of course. Had he spoken for her when people asked how she was doing? She couldn't remember – it was as if something had blocked the memories from her mind, filed them deep away, tried to bury them. She could have been on the boat too, and at times she'd wished she had been; the pain of being left behind was sometimes too great to bear. And then she felt sick at herself for not being grateful that she was still here, before she'd imagine what they went through when it all started going wrong. How much did they suffer? She'd spent eight years trying to block out the thoughts and they forced their way back in with a fresh terror each time.

Lucy knew that if she was in a film she would sit there and talk to her dead parents about her life, ask them for cosmic wisdom and leave feeling melancholy but somehow reassured. But she had nothing to say and sat there staring at the stone as if it were nothing to do with her or her family. The hyacinths she'd laid looked depressing against the granite. *Mum would've hated this*, she thought. *I should have brought the white vase*, her thoughts spiraled irrationally and she began to cry. She shut her eyes and wondered why she had come. The plot was neat – someone must've been looking after it. They were a popular family and her parents were sociable. It must be old friends still coming after all this time to pay their respects. Lucy wondered if her parents could see her sitting there – what on earth they would think of what she'd done with her life. She thought they'd be proud that she'd gone to London, but then hoped they wouldn't know what her life had been like there – the drinking, the boys, the drugs. Her parents would have killed her, she thought – they'd have been so disappointed.

Anger rose in her as she thought about how she'd had to leave Cornwall eventually, how the memories of this place had become too much to bear. She'd managed to finish her A levels. Even after Claire had left, Lucy stayed and carried on at school, like a good girl. If it had not been for the sanctuary of Tom and his family she was sure she might have ended it all one night. She had followed Claire to London because Claire was all she had once she left Tom. Like her teachers and friends, Claire had urged her to go to university, but Lucy felt she needed a different type of life. She wanted to work, to be a different person, to go somewhere she could be anonymous, not 'poor Lucy – do you know what happened to her family…?'

And like the good soul she was, Claire had looked after her, mothered her whilst she found her feet in the city. Then eventually Spectrum had taken the place of her family. Emma, in her weird way had become some kind of anti-mum, someone to try to impress, to put you down when you failed, to tell you you weren't really good enough but that she'd do you the favour of putting up with you anyway. And then she'd found the joy of drinking and drugs, and the shame that comes with that too. She'd pushed Claire away, ashamed of what parts of her life looked like, painfully aware of how much her sister would disapprove. She'd thrown herself into work; she'd done well. She was on her way to big things. Until she'd messed it all up.

Would she have ended up in London if her family hadn't been snatched from her that day? She thought she probably would have, eventually. But perhaps she'd have been able to stay long enough to convince Tom to come too. Or perhaps they'd have found their own way in Cornwall. Maybe she'd be a mum herself by now, rather than an underweight, borderline alcoholic, with anxiety issues and a coke habit. She almost laughed at the thought but choked instead on more unexpected tears, which came suddenly and viciously. It had started to rain, she realised disconnectedly. The bright- blue sky was somehow crying with her too, and the sprinkling of warm raindrops felt almost comfortingly miserable on a beautiful day. She wailed quietly; the sound wasn't human and she was panicked by the lack of control she had over it.

Lucy didn't know how long she'd been crouched on the floor when she became aware of footsteps behind her and she didn't turn around, assuming it was a fellow griever enduring their own ugly visit.

'Lucy,' she heard Tom's quiet voice. 'It's okay. I'm here. I'm here now, you're okay.' He crouched down beside her and wrapped her in his jacket.

'You're soaking wet,' he said softly, pulling her towards him, putting her head on his chest. She turned her face into his jumper and cried until the tears ran out as he stroked her hair and said nothing. Finally, embarrassed, she pulled away and apologised, wiping her eyes.

'How did you know I was here?' she asked.

'I was opening up at the café,' Tom replied, pulling her back into his arms, holding her there.

'I saw you come out of the florist with the hyacinths and I knew where you were going. When this much time passed and it started to rain I thought I'd come and check on you.'

'I didn't know you were even up,' she said, truthfully. 'I thought you weren't working today.'

'Change of plan,' he said softly, still holding her.

Lucy's breathing was slowly returning to normal as Tom stroked her head, holding her against his body.

'Thank you,' she said. She thought she felt him kiss her hair in reply. He held her for a few more minutes and then gently led her away to the car, which he'd pulled up outside the old metal gate.

Tom walked Lucy back into the house, like she was an old relative too frail to manage the stairs alone. He ran her a bath while she sat on the edge of her bed, and when she got out he'd laid her oversized white dressing gown out on the bed – it was warm from the tumble drier. He knocked on the door and came in to sit with her.

'I'm sorry about earlier,' she said, embarrassed at the thought of herself.

'There's nothing to be sorry for,' he said to her. 'What happened to your parents, to Richie, the way they were taken, it was awful, it was the saddest thing that I've ever known and it still gets me every time I go up there. They were beautiful people and they loved you so much. They should be here now to see you grow up and they're not. They're not here to see what a beautiful young woman their daughter is and that's heartbreaking. I know time heals and all that, but, well, it doesn't really, does it? That never gets any easier to bear and I wish you didn't have to bear it.' Tom stopped himself to look at Lucy for her reaction to his clearly unexpected monologue.

'You always were the only one who ever really got it,' she said, and it was true. When she'd left Tom behind, she'd lost the only person who really knew what she'd been through and who she was. It felt so obvious now that it was a mistake to have left the only person who truly understood.

'Do you really still go up there to see them?' she asked.

'About once a fortnight or so, yeah,' he said. 'I just make sure it's all nice up there for them. Your mum would've hated it all scruffy, and I like remembering them, remembering what life was like when they were around.'

Lucy looked at Tom. All this time she'd been in London it had never crossed her mind that he would've been visiting their graves. She hadn't been for six years and he'd been looking after things for them; she'd underestimated him in so many ways.

'You've had a rough morning,' Tom said, standing up. Lucy didn't want him to walk away – she wanted him to lie down with her, to hold her in his arms.

'You ought to get some sleep.' He folded the duvet back and gestured for her to get in. It was a strangely intimate feeling, him helping her into her bed and she felt naked. He smoothed the duvet over her and lent down to kiss her hair once more. *He just feels sorry for me*, Lucy thought sadly.

'I'm back off to the café. We're fully booked and I don't want Tara struggling there on her own.' Lucy was shocked at how jealous this sentence made her – it was an ugly emotion to feel.

'Of course. Thanks for everything, Tom, I'll be fine here,' she promised as he left the room, pulling the door shut with a smile that made her feel fifteen years old.

21

Kristian sat Nina at the large round table in the bay window and headed towards the bar to get the drinks in. The Ship was one of six pubs in Hideaway, and the most popular with the younger crowd. They had live music in the summer months and a band was sound-checking at the far end of the room; squeals, beats and guitar riffs sporadically interrupting conversation.

'This place hasn't changed,' Lucy noticed out loud. It was exactly as she'd remembered it from their days of underage drinking.

'Even the staff,' Nina said, nodding towards the guy carrying a tray of empties past their table. Lucy recognised him vaguely.

'I'm going to be so jealous of your gin and tonic,' Nina said, sighing. 'I'm drinking a fucking Appletiser on a Friday night, woo!'

'Well it'll all be worth it, won't it?' Lucy said, trying to encourage Nina to focus on the reason she wasn't drinking.

'Oh I know,' Nina replied, shifting in her chair. 'I just wish my parents were a bit happier about it – that's been pretty depressing.'

'What have they said?' Lucy asked. It was hard to imagine Nina's parents being anything other than lovely and supportive, as they always had been of their only daughter.

'Mum's pissed off that we aren't married,' Nina replied. 'Like we're Victorian or something – like it really matters.'

Lucy could see the hurt in Nina's eyes. Her mum's disapproval wasn't something that didn't affect her, however much eye-rolling she was going to do to try to seem casual.

'What about John?' Lucy asked. Nina has always been close to her dad.

'Oh, well, he's just bloody mute on the subject,' Nina said, looking down at the floor. 'He's barely mentioned it and when I bring it up he just changes the subject. Do you know, I really thought they'd be happy for us. It's pretty gutting.'

'Yeah, well, that is shit,' Lucy agreed, reaching her hand over to Nina and giving her a squeeze. 'They'll come round, though, just doing the annoying parent thing. Try not to focus on it. We are all delighted! I am so excited!'

Nina looked up and smiled, genuinely buoyed by Lucy's enthusiasm.

'Here we are,' Kristian leant across Lucy, placing drinks on the dark, stained wooden table.

'Can I smell your gin?' Nina asked Lucy.

'Um, yes I supp –' Nina took the glass from Lucy's hand and stuck her nose right in to inhale.

'Classy,' Tom laughed, sitting down with his beer. 'Really classy, Nin!'

'Tara!' Kristian called out, looking past Lucy's head. She spun around towards the door and saw Tara in a tiny black dress and flip-flops, hair loose around her shoulders, in perfect bloody beachy curls.

'Hey!' Tara called over. 'Can I get anyone a drink?'

Lucy turned back towards the table and made eye contact with Nina.

'We're all good, thanks,' Nina called back to Tara, 'but come and join us.' She began moving her chair to make room, before looking back at Lucy with a sheepish look on her face.

Great, Lucy thought. She felt suddenly self-conscious with her crap hair scraped back into a ponytail and wished she'd put a bit more make-up on.

Tara made her way back with a bottle of beer and pulled a chair towards the table. Tom leapt from his seat to help her, sending a wave of jealousy so powerful through Lucy she had to physically turn away. Tara sat between Tom and Nina, right opposite Lucy. She looked her straight in the eyes and smiled at her, forcing Lucy to smile back. *So smug,* Lucy thought, cringeing again at how pathetic she was being.

The pub was busy and they'd been lucky to get a table. A large crowd was standing towards the so-called stage, which was, in fact, just a gaffer-taped section of dirty wooden floor covered in instruments and scruffy-looking band members. Kristian chatted to Lucy about the day's surf and about their plans for tomorrow. Lucy tried to focus on their conversation, agreed with him about heading to one of the bays further along the coast, and reassuring him that she'd try and make sure Nina was okay about her parents' current attitude towards their pregnancy. But her eyes kept drifting across the table to the increasingly cosy scene between Tom and Tara. Tom was leaning back in his chair, with his arm slung around the back, reaching around to Tara's chair. Her body was angled towards his and she kept leaning into him as he spoke, pulling her hair away from her face and giggling. Tom looked happy, Lucy realised. Tara made him smile. It reminded Lucy of how they used to be, when they were young. Before she threw it all away and left.

She downed another gin and tonic so quickly that even Kristian noticed. She stood to head to the bar, and offered drinks to the table. Nina gestured at her Appletiser with a sad look on her face and Kristian raised his full beer. 'Go on, then, I'll have another,' he said, as Nina gave him daggers.

'I'm fine, thanks,' Tara shouted over the music, still smiling. *Of course she's one of those sensible girls who just enjoys one leisurely drink,* Lucy thought, *the smug cow.*

Lucy made her way through the crowd, dodging sweaty bodies and pints of beer. She stood behind the mass of people waiting to be served, trying to decide whether to make her gin and tonic a double. A hand reached around her waist, making her jump. She turned around to see Tom. He leant into her and said something she couldn't hear.

'What?' she said, leaning back into him. She could smell aftershave on his neck and shampoo on his hair.

'Just came to give you a hand,' he shouted, as she held her a finger in her other ear.

'Oh, thanks,' she smiled at him. His eyes lingered on hers and she had the overwhelming urge to kiss him. His hand was still on her waist, she realised, and she stepped out of his grasp to try to escape the feeling of his hands on her.

He took another step closer to her as she ordered the drinks, his body pressed against her; his physical closeness made her want to cry.

Lucy passed him Kristian's beer and asked him if he wanted one. He shook his head. She took her gin and tonic and they pushed and weaved their way back through the room towards the table.

'Here you are,' he spoke loudly into her ear as he pulled his own chair out for her at the table. 'You sit here for a bit. I'll go and chat with Kristian.' He slipped around to the other side of the table and passed Kristian his beer, sitting down in what had been Lucy's seat.

Great, Lucy thought, as she sat next to Tara, who turned around immediately and began chatting to her.

'I love your top,' Tara said, grinning. 'It's a lovely colour.'

'Thanks,' Lucy said. 'It's from London.' She wondered what the fuck had just come out of her mouth. Her top was from Topshop. They had one of those in Plymouth – about forty minutes from here. It was hardly some exotic purchase.

'Oh, well, it's very nice,' Tara said. 'I think my dress is too short.

I'm glad I'm sitting down!' she giggled, nervously, Lucy noticed.

'You look lovely,' Lucy said. 'I wouldn't worry.'

The band started up louder than ever and a cheer erupted from the crowd. The shaggy-haired lead singer was energetically bouncing around and sticking his microphone out to the crowd for the chorus. It was too loud to do anything other than listen to the music, which suited Lucy just fine. She sat back in her chair and tried not to think about anything. She glanced over at Tom to see him watching Tara, then mouthing something to her that looked like 'are you okay?'.

She couldn't bring herself to look at Tara, so forced her gaze straight ahead again at the band. The pub was the same, but tonight showed just how different almost everything else had become. She was going to need more gin. She missed her London friends, she realised, sitting there feeling like a total twat, she missed the outgoing social girl she'd been in London. She reached into her handbag and found her phone. She typed a message: *fancy a trip to Cornwall?* and hit 'send' to Charlie and Warren.

22

'Lucy!' The girl's voice came from the kitchen and Lucy turned to see Tara peering around the door as she unloaded a tray of scones onto a glass cake stand.

'Hi,' she called back, unsure whether she was supposed to stop and talk.

'How are you doing? Tom's not here at the moment,' Tara continued cheerfully.

'Oh, okay,' Lucy replied.

'Sit down. Do you fancy a coffee?'

'Um, yeah, sure, thanks,' Lucy answered, before thinking about it.

'It's going to be a busy day,' Tara carried the scones to the counter before filling the coffee machine.

'You seem busy here every day,' Lucy pretended to read the menu on the blackboard behind Tara, feeling awkward. Tara shrugged a reply and began frothing milk under steam.

'Cappuccino sound good?' she raised her voice over the hissing machine.

'Sounds great,' Lucy replied, watching Tara make her coffee. Although she'd been struck by how pretty Tara was the first time she met her, she'd not fully appreciated how striking she was, she realised now. She was one of those effortlessly attractive girls, who seemed at ease in her own skin. Watching her flit around behind the counter, Lucy could see why Tom would like her. She smiled at Lucy a couple of times as their eyes met and Lucy realised she must be staring at her.

'Tom's surfing, of course,' Tara said, and Lucy felt stung at the obvious familiarity, as if Tara was staking her claim with her knowledge of him.

'So, how long have you known each other?' Lucy asked, as Tara placed a frothy white coffee in front of her with a smile.

'Ooh, a few years now, I guess,' Tara replied.

'We met in Exeter on a night out, would you believe?' It didn't seem that unbelievable a story to Lucy.

'We started hanging out a bit…' Tara trailed off and Lucy felt the familiar burning jealousy start to take hold. 'And then Tom needed someone to help out here, I needed a job. It all went from there, really. You're so lucky to have grown up down here. It's great.'

Lucy nodded and her gaze drifted out the window to the beach. It was a clear, bright morning, promising a day of sunshine. The first few families were making their way on to the beach to stake their claim to a patch of sand and make elaborate windbreaker fortifications around their plastic spades and sandy towels. Lucy could hear Tara in the kitchen now, unpacking boxes and bags, humming to herself. Lucy drank the cappuccino and it slipped down her throat, leaving a silky, sweet taste and provided comfort Lucy hadn't known she'd wanted. She took her phone from her bag and texted Nina: *in the café, fancy brunch?* She reckoned the probability of Nina being keen was around the ninety-nine per cent mark, her appetite had definitely become even healthier with pregnancy.

Lucy still couldn't quite believe she was old enough to have a best friend who was having a baby, but Nina was taking it all in her stride as if it were the most natural thing in the world to be having Kristian's child. And it was, of course. Lucy knew that really, it just made her feel so far away from being ready to become a mum, and somehow a little bit, what, sad? Her phone beeped with Nina's reply: *Sure thing, be down in 10.* Lucy smiled to herself; she hadn't spent enough time with Nina on her own since being down in Cornwall. Everything had ended up being a group event, which was great, but she loved talking to Nina one on one and she wanted to hear all about the pregnancy.

Tara appeared back behind the counter. 'How's the coffee?' she called over, and Lucy looked down to see that she'd finished it.

'Great, thanks, really nice,' she said, genuinely.

'Good stuff. Want another?'

Tara's phone beeped and Lucy watched her examine the screen, her face changing as she read. Tara reddened slightly, then seemed to go pale. She looked upset as she put the phone back into the pocket of her apron.

'Sorry,' Tara said, turning to Lucy again, flustered, 'did you say yes to another coffee?'

'Maybe in a bit,' Lucy called back, 'Nina's coming down for brunch.'

'Oh great,' Tara's enthusiasm made Lucy feel jealous again and she cursed herself inwardly for being so pathetic. 'She's MY friend', a childish, mocking voice whispered in her head.

'Menus!' Tara placed two A4 pieces of cream paper, printed with the day's brunch menu, in front of Lucy and stood for just a moment too long for it not to feel awkwardly like she wanted Lucy to start a conversation with her. *About what*, thought Lucy, *eggs and bacon*? Lucy turned back to the window and scanned the surf, wondering if she could still recognise Tom from this distance. It had been a game she played with herself when she worked here; once everything was set up she'd stand outside with the salty air breathing life into her, usually hung over, soul, and try and pick out Tom from all the wetsuited bodies in the water. She'd follow her chosen figure as he rode, then as he left the water, and more often than not, if she remembered correctly, as he turned into a full-size Tom walking up to her, wet hair dripping in front of him, hands reaching out to her for a kiss and cuddle before he showered and joined her at work. Lucy could hear Tom's mum calling out to him to clean up before coming to the café, but it had never made any difference. Tom had always come and given Lucy her kiss fresh from the water, and even though he left her needing to wipe sea water from her face, she'd always been glad of that moment. A daily dose of pure happiness, she supposed now, as she realised she couldn't pick him out any more.

Nina arrived in a fluster, complaining about Kristian hiding her hair-straighteners. It felt an unlikely story, but Lucy nodded along sympathetically as her friend calmed herself down and ordered a decaf latte from Tara.

'Absolutely hate decaf coffee,' Nina sighed, 'but I'm not drinking no coffee at all, so what can you do? Anyway, my dear, how are you doing?'

'I'm fine, thanks,' Lucy replied. 'No plans at all today, which feels quite nice. Still getting used to this pace of life again.'

'Yeah, bit of a change from London, right?' Nina hadn't asked her much more about what had happened, and Lucy wondered what Tom had told them after Claire's call to him.

'It was too much for me there in the end,' Lucy said. 'Just the job, really, I think. It was a negative place to be and I was partying too hard to try and feel better.'

'Which, of course, only actually makes you feel worse,' Nina looked Lucy in the eye and she nodded in agreement.

'All I wanted was a promotion, to get on with my career and really prove myself. But Emma wouldn't let me move out of that role because, as vile as she was to me at times, she liked me as her PA. It was a horrible job,' Lucy realised she had hardly thought of Spectrum in the last few days. It made her feel a bit panicky even talking about it now.

'When I go back to London I'll look for a job in a bigger, more professional, company with proper structures in place,' Lucy continued. 'It'll be exciting.' But she didn't really believe the last part herself and she didn't want to look at Nina as she knew she'd know that too.

'Good,' Nina replied. 'That's good to hear. It never sounded a great place for you, Luce. I was worried about you. You just went off grid – I hardly heard from you. And then when we spoke you had that fraught tone to your voice that you used to have at school around exam time. Except this was all the time, as far as I could work out.' Lucy knew what she meant.

'Do you know,' she replied, 'I really miss some of my work friends. I spent so much time with them, and then suddenly it's all gone and I'm not part of it any more.' Nina leant across the table and held her hand in a way that only Nina could pull off without it feeling incredibly patronising.

'On the positive side, of course, it brought you back here, to me!' Nina grinned now at Lucy. 'And that is pretty damn awesome, as I know you rather well, and I am so wonderful that I will even buy you brunch. Now, what are we having?'

When Tara appeared with the plates of bacon and eggs on toasted muffins, Lucy's stomach rumbled.

'Thanks, love,' Nina smiled at Tara. 'This looks a-mazing.'

When Tara was out back in the kitchen Lucy asked Nina, without looking at her, 'so you're friendly with Tara, then?'

'Uh huh,' Nina nodded as she pronged bacon into her mouth. 'She's lovely, you'll really like her.'

Lucy smiled, in what she hoped appeared to be casual agreement.

'You will, Lucy, honestly, give her a chance,' Nina replied, knowing her too well. 'Anyway, about tonight, Kristian wants to do a 'massive' barbecue on the beach, for old times' sake. What do you think?' She raised her fingers in quotation marks for the 'massive', indicating that Tom and Kristian would go and blow a bloody fortune on food and drink.

It had been one of their group traditions; strangely elaborate now she came to think about it, barbecues on the beach with seafood, great burgers, lots of wine. What precocious teenagers they'd been.

'That sounds lovely, who's coming?' Lucy hoped this hadn't been Nina's way of telling her Tara was joining their little group; that wasn't what she'd signed up for. 'Just us four, like I said, for old times' sake. Although obviously I can't get drunk and run into the sea naked, so it won't be quite like it used to be.'

Lucy laughed at the memory. It was something of a party trick of Nina's to be more drunk than anyone else incredibly quickly, then pretty much naked, and then in the sea. It was probably quite dangerous, Lucy thought for the first time now, though it had never occurred to her at the time.

Lucy wondered what she would wear tonight and what she would say to Tom. They hadn't really spoken alone since the day at the church, and Lucy had wanted to thank him properly. She needed to try to get past the Tara situation

Tonight would be the perfect opportunity.

23

Lucy waved Nina back up the hill to the house and walked through town in search of the hairdressers. Her hair was the longest it had ever been and all the sea water had taken its toll on the ends. She'd resorted to tying it back into a ponytail every morning. There were two hairdressers in the town: one had always been the old ladies' salon and the other was run by the glamorous Emily and Juliet Tweed, who were always identifiable around town by their fashion-forward catwalk-inspired hairstyles. Lucy remembered how they'd introduced the two-tone-dye look down here, a long time before it was actually fashionable, and how awful it had looked on everyone apart from the Tweed sisters, who could pull off almost any look.

She turned the corner at the bottom of the hill, taking the winding mews path lined now with fashion boutiques and a more tasteful selection of Cornish gift shops than had ever been imaginable back when she was growing up here. *Not a seashell- encrusted beach hut lamp in sight,* she thought.

Talking Heads had kept its prime spot just before the seafront, though its sign was new, a striking logo in steel and plastic. It looked smart. Lucy could see Emily Tweed through the window at the reception desk. She looked good, Lucy thought, trying to do the maths and work out how old she must be now. Forty? Her sleek blonde shoulder-length bob swished about as she talked animatedly to a younger girl using the computer. Lucy pushed the door open and walked into the warm smell of hairspray and shampoo, the roar of hairdryers almost drowning out the radio. She hadn't expected Emily to recognise her, she had forgotten about the infamy of being one of 'those poor girls'. Even after all this time. She could see Emily vaguely recognise and then struggle to place her, her face did the sudden drop Lucy had hated during those last few years she lived down here when people worked out who she was.

She arranged an appointment for later in the week.

'That'll be with Liv,' the receptionist said, nodding towards the row of salon chairs. 'Sounds good,' Lucy replied. 'I'll see you then.'

As she turned to leave a hand touched her back, taking her by surprise.

'Lucy? Is that you?' Lucy turned to see a grinning face so close to hers she could smell her chewing gum.

'Yep, that's me' she replied, trying desperately to work out who the pretty, petite girl was. She didn't even look familiar.

'It's me, Olivia,' said the grin. 'Oh, you won't remember me. I was a few years below you at school and we all used to come in to the Beach Café when you worked there. You've been gone for ages! You look great.'

'Oh, thanks,' Lucy smiled, struggling for anything more to say. It was unnerving how the grin hadn't dropped even momentarily throughout the exchange.

'Well,' said Olivia, standing now at the desk looking at the booking chart. 'Looks like I'm seeing you on Friday for, what is it…' her finger scanned along the line. 'A full head of highlights, wash, cut and blow-dry – fab!'

Lucy smiled at Olivia, trying to match her enthusiasm, and beginning to dread the appointment.

Back on the street, she wandered past a couple of boutiques and paused at the window of a pink shop, her eye caught by a coral dress hanging on a green velvet hanger. She could see the price tag from where she was, marked £139. *Hideaway Bay really has gone up in the world*, she thought. A hand knocked on the glass from the inside, making Lucy visibly startle. The stark lighting in the window meant she could only see a silhouette, beckoning at her to come in. Confused, she opened the door and stepped cautiously inside, looking to her left to see who it was calling her in.

'LUCY! It IS YOU! I knew it!' *Not another one*, Lucy thought, before her eyes adjusted to the dim light and she realised who it was.

'Oh my GOD, Annabel? I didn't know you were still here,' Lucy ran over and hugged her. Annabel still smelt like her childhood home – Lucy couldn't believe the clarity with which she remembered the smell. Annabel was one of Claire's best friends at school and had been Lucy's idol growing up. She thought she'd left years ago – Claire hadn't mentioned that she still lived here.

Annabel made tea in the storeroom while Lucy looked around the store, answering Annabel's shouted questions about what she was doing back in Hideaway, and about life in London. 'And Tom?' Annabel quizzed, as she walked over with their tea and a packet of biscuits.

'Oh yeah, it's fine. It's great to see him again,' Lucy said, honestly.

'It must be so strange for you, though,' Annabel pressed a biscuit towards Lucy's hand. 'I mean, you guys weren't just some childhood thing. We all thought you'd get married.'

'Yeah, I know, it's weird that it's not weird, if you know what I mean,' Lucy said. *I sound like a moron*, she thought. 'We hadn't kept in touch, so there's been a lot to catch up on.'

'I bet,' Annabel said. 'The Beach Café is amazing. It's going into the Condé Nast Traveller's guide to the best beach bars in September, you know. I couldn't believe it when Tara said. Quite the golden couple, aren't they? Tom's her knight in shining armour, lucky girl.'

Lucy felt her face flush, though with what, she wasn't quite sure. Embarrassment?

'I didn't know that,' she tried to sound casual. 'But it doesn't surprise me.' She wasn't sure if she was referring to the beach bar's imminent fame or the confirmation of Tom and Tara as an item. Lucy put her cup of tea down on the counter and looked at her phone.

'I really need to go, so sorry,' she clumsily pushed her phone back into her pocket and smiled at Annabel. 'It's been lovely to see you.'

'Oh, you too, Luce. Hang on a minute, will you? I saw you looking at that dress.' Annabel was reaching into the window, grasping in the direction of the coral, silk, backless, Lucy noticed now, dress, slipping it off its hanger and inspecting its label. 'Yeah, thought so, it's a size eight – looks about right for you. Here you are.' She pulled out a brown bag, opened it up and wrapped the dress in tissue paper in one motion, handing it to Lucy with a kind smile.

'I can't take that,' Lucy protested, confused by the generosity.

'You can and you will,' Annabel's hand remained outstretched. Lucy took the bag. 'I loved growing up with Claire – I loved going to your house. Hanging around with all of you. Your mum…' she paused, looking at Lucy, who smiled back at her.

'Yeah, they were great days,' Lucy said, her mind flicking through images of the Annabel, Claire and the gang having sleepovers in the lounge, her mum making them popcorn and nachos, laughing with them all.

'They were golden days,' Annabel replied, her mind wandering through the memories too, Lucy suspected.

'I'd love you to take the dress,' Annabel said, bringing them back to the room. 'You'll look drop-dead gorgeous in it, and there aren't many people in this town who could pull it off. Far too many washed-out pastel-coloured sailing clothes around', Annabel rolled her eyes and smiled mischievously at Lucy.

Lucy laughed and opened the bag to feel the silk in her hand. 'It's beautiful, thank you so much.'

'You're more than welcome. Just make sure you come and see me okay?' Annabel opened the door for her to leave. 'And send my love to your sister, will you?'

Lucy promised she would, kissed Annabel on the cheek and stepped back out onto the sunny street, as goosebumps rose on her arms.

24

It was warm enough at 8am for breakfast on the terrace. Every evening the TV news was full of reports of the 'hottest summer' in living memory and the hosepipe ban looked imminent now. It had made Tom's huge garden and pool the main hang-out for the four of them, as the beach was invaded daily by an ever-increasing number of sweaty red tourists.

'I'm going to start a campaign,' Nina announced, as she placed a wooden board piled high with pastries and strawberries onto the glass table.

'Oh God, here we go,' Kristian muttered, reaching for a handful of berries, and offering Tom one from his hand.

'I want a sign as you enter the town. You know the 'welcome to Hideaway Bay' ones we've got at each side of the valley?' she waited for affirmation from her audience.

'Well, I'd like them to say underneath 'Please remember, just because you can get it on, it doesn't mean it fits.'

Lucy laughed. 'You are terrible,' she said, helping herself to a croissant and tearing it in two.

'It's just good advice,' Nina continued. 'I mean, honestly, there are all the signs about feeding the seagulls, why can't we have something to protect my eyes from the monstrosities walking through town every day the sun shines?'

'I'm with you, mate,' Tom said, folding a pain au chocolat into his mouth. 'They come into the café, sandy feet, burnt, hairy beer bellies, it's pretty grim.'

'It's pretty grim watching you talk with a mouth full of pastry,' Lucy snapped.

Tom looked at her with slight confusion, before visibly shrugging and turning back to Nina. Lucy felt rage rise in her chest.

'So who's driving today,' Tom asked pointedly in Nina's direction.

'Oh, obviously me' she replied, cross at her newly awarded role of designated driver.

'Well, we'll be having a few beers,' Kristian confirmed.

'I'll drive if you like,' Lucy offered. 'I'm not drinking, I don't mind.'

'I thought we were taking you for a champagne cream tea, Luce.' Tom looked at her, but she refused to make eye contact.

'Your all-time favourite, champagne queen,' Kristian nudged Lucy. 'Don't be a bore.'

'I'm not really in the mood,' Lucy replied to Kristian, trying to sound soft rather than stern. She'd been so embarrassingly angry with Tom since her conversation with Annabel, she'd tried to stay out of his way. But the trip to Freetown had been planned for over a week.

'Yeah, thanks Luce, but I'm not having that,' Nina said. 'You SHALL go the Old Quay House for champagne!' she announced in the style of Cinderella's fairy godmother.

'Right, well, that's decided, then,' Tom said. Lucy was sure he was still looking at her but pretended not to notice.

'I'm going to go and change my shirt, it's boiling' Tom said, walking back to the house.

He was right – it was sweltering already. So hot there was a haze hanging over the bay, like the sun's heat was fizzing out into the sky. Lucy felt a bead of sweat trickle down her back and thought she ought to change her dress – black was a ridiculous choice.

'I'm changing too,' she called as she ran off up the steps to the kitchen.

'Oh fine, I see, I'll drive AND clear all this up,' she heard Nina shout to her as she stepped in to the cool white hallway, heading for the stairs.

'Lucy,' it was Tom, halfway up the stairs, holding on the banister.

'Are you okay?' Lucy asked. He looked breathless.

'Yeah, I'm fine, he replied, 'I just tripped. I didn't think anyone else was in here – embarrassing!' he laughed.

Lucy felt hugely awkward after the pained exchange at the table.

'Okay, well I'm just changing too. I'm too hot in this dress.'

'Very hot,' Tom smiled at her. He reached out and touched her arm, which she pulled away from him, the intimacy of the simple act taking her by surprise.

'Um, okay,' Tom looked confused and leant down to stroke his ankle instead. 'Hurts a bit,' he said, inanely, before looking back at the floor.

'I'll see you at the car,' Lucy said, hurrying up the stairs to her room and closing her door. She stood on the wooden floorboards, clenching and releasing her fists, so frustrated at herself and at Tom. What was he playing at? Did he think he could bring her here, ask her to leave London, to stay at his house, so he could introduce him to his girlfriend and then flirt with her on the stairs? What the hell?

Freetown was a twenty-minute drive, and a fifteen-minute foot ferry, away. Lucy smiled as the old man walked around the flat deck, four cars deep by five cars wide, collecting the same little colourful card tickets that they'd always used on the crossing. Freetown was an arty little town, full of winding streets packed with antique shops and art galleries. It had been ahead of its time with its food scene and was home to Lucy's favourite dining spot in Cornwall, The Old Quay House.

As the group approached the large stone building, Lucy remembered walking hand in hand through the wooden doors with Tom so many times. Kristian had booked a table out on the veranda, overlooking the quayside. Lucy walked through the cool corridors, past the well-dressed waiting staff with their polite smiles and ironed napkins, and stepped out onto the terrace, shielding the sun from her eyes with her hand. Their table, blissfully, had a huge parasol and was tucked in a corner, where a slight breeze from the water drifted over them from time to time. The terrace was busy with glamorous ladies drinking tea and one family with slightly fraught-looking parents possibly regretting bringing children somewhere so smart.

Tom ordered for the group – four cream teas, one with champagne, two with Doombar, the local beer, and one with peppermint tea. Nina and Kristian sat on one side of the table, their chairs pressed together so that Kristian could reach his arm around Nina's shoulders. He pulled her in to kiss her head at random moments throughout the conversation without even thinking about it, Lucy noticed. Nina's hand was on his thigh and she traced patterns with her fingers on his khaki shorts as she spoke.

The champagne was ice-cold and felt like a tonic in the day's heat as Lucy sipped it from a frosted glass. Nina was telling the group about her first scan, pulling a black- and-white picture from her bag. Tom did a good job of looking interested, Lucy thought. Kristian glowed with pride as he pointed out hands and feet, 'definitely a sportsman's physique', he said.

'We don't even know if it's a boy!' Nina protested.

'I do,' Kristian insisted. ' I can tell. It looks like a boy.'

Lucy examined the photo in detail with Nina, while the boys moved on to a deep discussion about surf conditions for the next few days. Lucy still couldn't quite believe that Nina had a new life growing inside her and that she seemed so relaxed about the whole thing. It helped that Kristian's job was so flexible and well paid, of course, but still, their life was about to change forever. Even in the few weeks that they'd been together in Cornwall Lucy thought she had watched Nina's belly begin to grow, though she may have been imagining things.

'I think I can feel some little movements now,' Nina told her one morning, a smile Lucy had never seen before creeping across her face – a completely new kind of love growing.

Kristian had taken his hand off Nina's shoulders and placed it on her belly now, his fingers stroking her gently as she reclined slightly in her chair, fanning herself with the scan picture. It wasn't a great summer to be pregnant, Lucy could see.

'Always thought it would be you two, I suppose,' Kristian said, addressing the whole group now.

'What's that?' Lucy asked.

'You two.' Kristian gestured with his free hand at Tom and Lucy. 'It always looked like it would be you two that did the whole baby, marriage, forever thing. Funny how it's worked out.'

Lucy thought she could see Kristian regretting taking this path, as Nina turned to him with a possibly angry, definitely warning, look on her face.

'Yep, funny how things work out,' Lucy replied, trying to think of a way to change the subject.

'Well, who knows what would've happened if you'd stayed,' Tom took Lucy by surprise with his words. They hung, starkly, in the silence of the group.

Lucy picked up her glass and took slightly too large a mouthful of champagne, struggling to swallow the bubbles.

'Or if you'd come with me,' she answered back, without looking at Tom, wishing immediately she hadn't said it. That she had some sodding self-control.

Nina sighed at Kristian in a 'look what you've done' manner

and picked up a menu, reading the sandwich selection aloud and adding her own commentary on the relative pros and cons of each option, while everyone else sat in silence, drinking their drinks and spreading jam and cream onto warm scones.

Tom picked up the bill when it arrived and Lucy decided to go for a walk around some of the antique shops she'd always loved. Nina and Kristian were off to a surf shop to look at boards for Kristian, 'which he doesn't need', Nina had pointed out as they practically skipped off. Glad to be getting away from the tension, Lucy supposed. She didn't know what Tom was going to do. He'd probably sit and watch the boats, she thought. He'd always done this when they'd come to Freetown. He loved reading their names and wondering who owned them, where they'd been, where they'd go. He was a dreamer, Lucy thought to herself. He used to be, anyway.

The cobbled streets were even smaller than Lucy remembered, and there were fewer shops than in her memories. Quite a few premises were boarded up, empty and the town didn't look quite as high-end as it used to. The financial climate had hit Cornwall hard, she'd known that, but seeing Hideaway, an exception to the rule, had shielded her from the reality. Freetown looked tired and bleak. The pastel-coloured fishing cottages looked like they needed a fresh coat of paint and the gift shops had been invaded by the tat that spelled trouble for most towns.

Lucy walked into an antiques shop that had been there for as long as she could remember, a bell ringing as she opened the door, but there was no sign of any staff. She walked through the tiny shop, piled high with trinkets made of metal, glass and wood, and stood at one of the large glass display cabinets full of jewellery and knick-knacks. She was angry with herself all over again for how she'd reacted back at the table. She just felt so stupid and her face reddened now at the memory. The bell on the door rang behind her as she examined a pretty silver box engraved with a hunting scene.

'You should never have left me without saying goodbye,' Tom was standing behind her. She didn't turn around.

'I know,' she replied, quietly. 'I just didn't know what to do. I didn't know what was fair.'

She turned around to face him. He looked tired, hurt maybe. 'It wasn't fair to just go, to never look back,' he trailed off without finishing the sentence. Lucy's heart hurt. 'But anyway, that's the past and I don't want to argue with you.' He stepped next to her and looked into the glass cabinet.

'Remember that necklace I bought you here?' he said. 'An amethyst heart, wasn't it? Classy!' he said lightly, smiling at Lucy.

She met his eye and smiled back.

'I'm sorry,' she said. 'I didn't mean to snap at you back there. There's just a lot going on with me at the moment and it's weird being back here. So much is exactly the same and some things have changed too much.' She could hear herself talking in clichés and it made her cringe inwardly.

'I know,' Tom said. 'It must be really weird, especially staying at mine and seeing how the café's changed, and...' he stopped again. *Seeing you with your hot blonde girlfriend*, Lucy thought. *Yep, pretty damn weird.*

Lucy's phone buzzed in her pocket – she pulled it out to see a message from Scott. She instinctively turned her phone away from Tom slightly as she scanned the screen:

Hi Lucy, hope you're good. Bit awkward, but I need my key back please. Can we meet up? Or you could just post it through the door. I'm seeing someone, and she doesn't like you still having a key, so I'd appreciate it if you could return it. Cheers, Scott x

Lucy had totally forgotten the key. She'd only used it once or twice; it had never had any significance for her. She was pleased for Scott that he'd met someone else, but felt a bit sorry for the girl who cared that his ex had a key. Why had he even mentioned it to her? How odd. It was probably someone from work, she thought, maybe Cindy – the girl who used to text him when she was drunk. She realised she really didn't care. She'd text him back later and tell him she'd send it to him. She hoped it was somewhere sensible amongst her things.

'Anything important?' Tom asked, still looking at the display cabinet.

'Not at all,' she replied. 'We need to go back to the ferry soon.'

'Fancy ten minutes looking at the boats first?' Tom asked, looking out of the shop towards the harbour.

'Sure,' Lucy replied, making her way towards the door, the weight of her amethyst heart necklace, which she'd worn every day for seven years, weighing slightly heavier than usual around her neck.

25

Sitting in the hairdresser's chair, Lucy explained to a very excited Olivia that she just needed a few inches off her hair and a few highlights through it.

'Going to look ab-so-lute-ly awesome,' Olivia assured her. Lucy was confused by just how excited Olivia seemed to be about the whole thing.

'So we'll just get that washed and then we can have a good old natter,' Olivia said, patting Lucy's shoulder as if reassuring her that she wouldn't have to wait too long for this much-anticipated treat. Lucy shut her eyes as a junior girl washed her hair and massaged her scalp. She thought about the last time she'd had her hair done, in a salon by the studios, after a boozy lunch with the entertainment team. She'd taken cans of gin and tonic with her to share with the hairdresser, so unable was she to stop drinking after a few glasses of prosecco. She shuddered slightly thinking about it, remembering how she'd eventually met up with Warren to carry on 'partying', picking up an obscene amount of cocaine they'd planned to keep for the next few weeks. They'd finished it that same night.

Back at the mirror, Olivia began sectioning her hair and weaving the pointed silver prong through it before applying dye to the selected strands, packaging them up in foil. Lucy made polite conversation with her about the town, about school and the teachers. Olivia was very sweet, but there didn't seem to be a lot going on upstairs, Lucy thought. She told Lucy at length about her boyfriend, Ben, who worked as a lifeguard on the beach and animatedly explained how jealous she got of all the girls in bikinis who spent their days 'trying to get his attention by struggling in the water'.

'You know you're desperate if you're drowning yourself to try and pull,' Lucy offered, but Olivia had moved on to the next topic: how difficult it was packing for a holiday when you didn't know what the weather was going to do. It was going to be a long couple of hours in the chair.

'Oh my God,' Olivia whispered, glancing towards the reception desk. Lucy looked up from her magazine to see a tall, blonde surfy-looking guy standing at the desk chatting to Sarah. 'That's Olly,' Olivia said in the loudest, least-subtle whisper Lucy had ever heard. 'What I'd give for a lesson from him.' Lucy puzzled at Olivia's sudden forgetting of her boyfriend. 'He's a surf instructor,' Olivia continued, almost salivating, her eyes fixed on what Lucy had to concede was a fine example of a man. 'He's teaching Emily's son,' Olivia explained. 'He comes in here every week so she can pay him. Highlight of my week.'

She sighed, looking back at Lucy's hair and folding a little silver-foil packet up to her scalp slightly too tightly.

Lucy continued to look at Olly, his blonde hair still wet from the water. He looked about her age. She definitely hadn't seen him before. He probably knew Tom if he was on the beach every day. He had a truly beautiful face, too beautiful really – he almost didn't look real. His smile revealed perfect teeth and Lucy realised with a shock that he was smiling at her. She smiled back and looked away, embarrassed. She'd been staring and he'd seen her – how mortifying. When she dared to look back at the desk he'd gone.

Olivia was drying Lucy's hair, freshly trimmed and newly dyed, before she plucked up the courage to say what she'd clearly been desperate to say from the moment Lucy had sat down.

'I was in Richie's class,' she offered, hesitantly. 'That's how I know you. We used to come in to the café after your –' she stopped herself '– when you lived on your own. My parents used to talk to you about your parents, about Richie.' Lucy could see how hard it had been for Olivia to tell her, and she smiled at her to let her know she was okay.

'Oh right,' she said. 'Who are your parents?'

'Mel and Steve', Olivia replied. 'My mum's the florist.'

Lucy thought she could vaguely remember them. 'Oh yes, of course,' she said.

'I just wanted to say, I hope you don't mind – that Richie, he, he idolised you. He loved you so much. I just don't know whether he ever would have told you that, being so young, but I remember how much he loved you. I've never forgotten – ever since it happened. I've thought about it a lot. I'm sorry, I'm rambling. I just thought that I'd want to be told that, if it was me. But I don't know what it's like, I suppose, so I'm sorry,' Olivia didn't look at Lucy as she trailed off, her grin a distant memory now.

'That's lovely,' Lucy said gently. 'That means a lot, thank you. I thought the world of him too. I'm glad you said that, thank you, Olivia.'

The whirr of the hairdryer drowned out any awkward silence. Lucy sat and allowed herself to remember her brother, vividly, for the first time in years. That mop of brown curls, his cheeky grin, the annoying way he'd hide her things 'as a game', for her. She realised she was smiling at the memories. He should be Olivia's age. What would he have been, she wondered? *He was kind*, she thought, *he'd have done something good*.

Olivia had done a great job of Lucy's hair. It was still long, down to her chest, but had sun-kissed highlights running throughout it now. It looked good, Lucy knew as she inspected it in the mirror. She paid at the reception desk and gave Olivia a hug as she left, thanking her as she said goodbye.

'Hang on a sec, shall I book you in for six weeks' time?' Olivia asked, stopping Lucy at the door.

'Um, no thanks. I won't be here then,' Lucy replied, 'I'll be back in London.'

Lucy called Claire as she walked along the beach back towards the house, carrying her flip-flops in one hand, the sand almost too hot for her feet. The midday sun was scorching and she felt as though she could see her tanned limbs darkening before her eyes. Claire answered after two rings, happy to hear from her sister.

'I wanted to speak to you about your flat,' Claire said.

'Oh yeah, is it all okay?' Lucy asked, realising she'd hardly thought about it since she'd left London.

'It's all fine,' Claire replied. 'It's just that you've been gone for almost two weeks now. Anna's only meant to be there for another fortnight. Are you coming back?'

'I am coming back,' Lucy said, slightly cross at Claire's tone. As if she would be thinking about staying down here.

'I might be a bit longer than a couple of weeks, I suppose, if Anna wants an extra few weeks there?'

'Okay, that would be really helpful, I think, thanks,' Claire said, sounding like her patience was being tested. The call was irritating Lucy too; she wanted to get off the phone before they fell out.

'Okay, well let's say another month for Anna and then she'll need to leave so I can come back.'

'Have you got a job to come back to?' Claire asked

'I'm working on it,' Lucy lied. She hadn't even started to contact anyone yet about possible TV roles, the thought of it filled her with an unspecified but definite dread.

'Great, that's great news,' Claire said, slightly patronisingly, Lucy thought.

'I'm not a total fuck-up, Claire. I'll sort it out,' she said, before she could stop herself.

'I didn't say you were. God, Lucy, stop being so fucking precious all the time. I'm on constant fucking eggshells around you and I'm sick of it. All I ever try and do is look out for you. You could be more grateful sometimes, you know. I'm running around sorting out your fucking flat.'

Lucy had never heard Claire swear before – certainly not at her, like this. It made her feel like she was going to cry.

'I'm sorry,' she said, quickly, 'I'm being a brat, I'm sorry. It's just hard being down here, remembering it all.'

'You weren't the only one who lost everything,' Claire said bluntly.

'I know' Lucy said, embarrassed by her selfishness.

'You do realise I've not been back there either; it's weird for me too. The whole damn thing. And now you're there hanging out with Annabel Carmichael, sitting in the Beach Café, walking the cliff path, while I'm up here trying to pretend everything's just fine all the time. Holding it all together. It's hard for me too sometimes.'

Lucy didn't know what to say. Of course, Claire was right, and she'd been so selfish not to even think of her this whole time.

'You're right and I'm sorry' she said. 'I'm coming back, Claire. I just have a few plans for the next couple of weeks and then I'll be back.'

'It's still home, isn't it?' Claire said.

Lucy was confused. 'What do you mean?' she asked

'Hideaway – it's still home. You keep saying you're coming "back", not "home", "back". Because you *are* home.'

'That's nonsense,' Lucy said, irritated again now. 'Stop being dramatic about it all. I'm coming back, okay? In a fortnight, I'll be back, or home, or whatever, Claire. I've got to go.'

'Just try and behave like an adult, Lucy,' Claire said, coldly. 'And watch out for Annabel, don't fall for her, she's a total bully.

There's a reason we haven't kept in touch, not that she'll tell you that.'

Lucy was sick of Claire's lecturing, her nagging, her total insistence that she was the grown-up and Lucy was an idiot child. She hung up the phone, feeling absolutely terrible.

26

That evening Tom and Kristian carried the barbecue down to the beach and bought enough meat from the butcher to feed an army, while Lucy and Nina got ready at the house. Nina was in Lucy's room, doing her make-up at her dressing table, while Lucy walked around in a towel trying to decide what to wear.

'The coral dress!' Nina said, suddenly remembering it. 'What a jammy cow you are – getting that for free!'

'Isn't it a bit dressy for the beach?' Lucy said. 'I mean it's backless and short. It might look a bit tarty.'

'Says the girl who once rocked a white leather skirt and green snakeskin top,' Nina replied. Lucy shuddered at the image, but it was true, she had been that girl.

'Ha ha, very funny,' she said, 'but I'd be careful what you say, I have photographs of you in a one-sleeved diamante-studded tunic somewhere, my lovely.'

Lucy took the coral dress from her wardrobe, and held it against her, as if it might give her an idea of its suitability, seeing it crumpled over her towel.

'It's the one,' Nina whispered in a cringey American accent.

Lucy had to admit it looked good on. It suited her tan and lit up her face. She'd worn so much black in London. She slipped on her gold sandals and waited for Nina to free up her dressing table.

'I'll look like a fucking elephant next to you,' Nina complained.

'You will not. You look like a radiant pregnant goddess,' Lucy said, truthfully. Nina looked so beautiful, she always had done. Kristian was a lucky man.

'Now hurry up so I can do my make-up,' she gently nudged Nina, who grabbed her hand and pulled it to her stomach.

'The baby's kicking!' Lucy whispered loudly. 'Oh my God.' Tears formed in her eyes before she could stop them and she let them fall, placing both her hands on Nina's belly, waiting for more. Nina smiled at her stomach and then at Lucy, wiping away her tears and putting her arms around her.

Lucy helped Nina down the last few rocks to the beach. She'd refused to take the path, insisting on the shortcut, even though it involved climbing the final section down to the sand. There were a few groups gathered on the beach as the orange sun melted into the sea. Lucy could see Tom and Kristian in the distance. They had already lit a campfire and were sitting on the sand, beers in hand, she was sure.

'How many times have we walked down here, do you think?' Nina asked

'Hundreds, thousands maybe,' Lucy replied.

'When did we get so old?' Nina continued. 'I used to feel like I could do anything I wanted, like everyone always told us we could, all those teachers, our parents. But it's not true really, is it? I mean, look at us. I'm having a baby, you don't even have a job, sorry, you know what I mean. We can't do anything we want.'

Lucy made an agreeing noise.

'I think it's more a case that, if you're lucky, you have a period of your life when you're young, when the choices you make totally affect, if not define, how your life's going to pan out. They ought to make that clear to you at the time. Maybe I'd have done things differently.'

'Aren't you happy, Nin?' Lucy asked. 'Looks like you've done alright to me.'

'It's not that. I am happy, of course I am. It's just life feels smaller to me than I expected it to sometimes. I think my head was filled with the idea that I could be, or do, or achieve anything. And it's almost like just having this normal, happy life is a bit underwhelming.'

Lucy thought about what her friend was saying and she agreed with her.

'I mean, I had dreams, you know. I wanted to be Britney Spears,' Nina finished, seriously, and Lucy laughed.

Kristian looked like he'd already had a fair few beers as he staggered over and bear-hugged Lucy and Nina. 'Girrrrrrrls' he said, lifting their hands to spin them around. 'Oh God,' Nina replied, 'You're hammered.'

Lucy slipped her hand away, leaving Kristian to pull an unwilling Nina in for a kiss, and walked over to Tom as he lit the barbecue.

'Wow,' he said. 'You look, just, you look absolutely incredible.' He looked up at her, from where he was crouched down on the sand.

'Thanks,' Lucy blushed, stroking her dress nervously. 'How's the barbecue coming along? Need a hand?'

Together they got the flames going and Tom passed her a beer to celebrate. 'Cheers,' he clinked her bottle, looking out at sea. It was almost dark now, the stars were extraordinary tonight, Lucy realised, following his eye line.

'To the most beautiful place on earth,' he said.

'Cheers,' she replied. And in that moment, she agreed with him completely.

There were a few groups of people on the beach, a couple of guitar-playing Jack Johnson wannabes were holding court to their left, mesmerised girls swaying to their distinctly average efforts. The four of them were circled around the rather impressive campfire eating burgers and drinking beers, laughing as they tried to define ten categories of people that came on holiday to the north coast.

'What about the sloaney ponies who've come down here to "escape London"?' Nina said. 'There's a lot of those – needing to get away from their days of shopping and nights of clubbing, poor little things.'

'They come under "posh London twats",' Kristian explained. 'If we broke that category down into its component parts we'd be here all night. This place is teeming with them these days. Mainly because of this idiot's posh beach bar,' he elbowed Tom to show he was at least half-joking.

'Guilty as charged,' Tom said, 'But I needed to make some bloody money and sausage rolls and teacakes weren't cutting it.'

'It's absolutely brilliant for the town,' Nina said. 'You've done amazingly well. Your parents must be so proud.'

'Yeah, they are,' Tom said, looking back out to sea. 'It's meant they can travel, you know, get away from here from time to time. It's given them some freedom, my taking it on as my own. And I'm bloody lucky to have had the chance.'

Lucy finished her beer and wedged the bottle in the sand. 'Does anyone fancy a cigarette?' she said, before apologising quickly to Nina, who insisted she didn't mind.

'I'd bloody love one,' Tom said. 'Shall we go to Spar and buy some? Marlboro Lights for old times' sake, right?'

'Yeah,' Lucy said. 'That'd be nice.'

Tom held out a hand to help her up and her head rushed with the beer. She managed to style out her slight stumble and they walked away from Nina and Kristian towards the lights of the town.

Lucy still felt like a fifteen-year-old buying cigarettes; guilty and excited. She giggled as they walked out of the shop together and Tom pulled her into him, cuddling her.

'I love that laugh,' he said, kissing her head. She felt momentarily like she could turn to him and kiss his lips – and she wanted to, so much. Then she remembered Tara, and remembered it was just a friendly hug. She squeezed him back and pulled away.

'Can we go to the house?' she said, without thinking about it. 'I'd like to see it.'

'Are you sure?' Tom said, looking at her, serious all of a sudden. 'I don't know what state it's in. Has anyone been back?'

Lucy wasn't sure. She knew Claire had paid a company to pack everything up sometime during Lucy's first year in London, when it became clear she wasn't going back. They'd boxed everything and fenced the place up – put some kind of security system in to protect it from intruders. She'd not heard any more since then. They hadn't wanted to sell it, even though they both could've done with the money at that point.

'Yeah, I'd like to go together,' Lucy replied, surprised that she meant this.

'Okay,' Tom said, taking her hand now. They turned away from the beach and walked up the road, past the campsite, awful karaoke blaring from the bar, and took another left, up Avenue Road, Lucy's old address.

The house was indeed fenced off, potentially too securely for them to get in, Lucy thought.

'Over there,' Tom said, pointing at a lowered part of the fence. 'We can get over there. If you're sure.'

Lucy walked ahead towards the fence and Tom lifted her up so she could climb down the other side. It was difficult in her silk dress. Before she could ask Tom how he was going to make it over, he landed next to her, on his feet, as if he'd just done it in one clean jump. He looked quite pleased with himself before he looked up at the house, and his smile dropped. Lucy followed his gaze to the house. It looked exactly as she remembered it, but bigger than she remembered, perhaps. It was a huge house, she could see now. Its white walls looked grey in the darkness of the night, and probably masked the years of neglect. It looked quite beautiful, standing alone in the night. They walked silently to the front door and Lucy hesitated before trying the handle. It was locked, of course, but thankfully no alarm went off. Tom walked to the living-room window and peered in. Lucy joined him, putting her hands on the cool glass. The room was full of boxes, white sheets draped over oak furniture.

'We've had so many offers from developers,' she said to Tom, unprompted. 'But we can't sell it. It's stupid, isn't it?'

'Not stupid at all,' he said, looking at her now. 'It's your home.'

'Was my home,' Lucy corrected him, the words catching in her throat.

'So many memories,' Tom said quietly. 'Our first kiss over there,' he pointed at the French windows.

'Yep,' Lucy smiled. 'Lots of memories.'

Tom put his hands on her face and she froze, unsure what he was about to do. He examined her, studiously, his face soft but unsmiling. He bent down slightly and kissed her forehead. 'We ought to get back.'

Lucy wasn't sure if she could walk, her legs had become jelly after the feeling of his lips on her skin.

'Yes,' she said. 'We ought to go before someone comes and shoots us for trespassing.' Her attempt at humour sounded inane.

Tom helped her back over the fence and they headed towards the beach. Nina and Kristian would be wondering where they were, Lucy knew. Nina would want to know what had happened. What had happened? She wondered herself. Tom took her hand again as they walked. *Does he feel this too?* She wondered, desperately. *I love him. I still bloody love him.* The total truth of it terrified her.

At the edge of the beach, where the concrete gave way to grass then sand, Tom dropped Lucy's hand.

'Tara!' he called to a silhouette walking out of the café. She was still in an apron, her hair messily tied on the top of her head.

'Just locked up,' she smiled at them. 'Great night. Fifty covers!'

'Brilliant' Tom said, looking at her with the affection he'd once looked at Lucy with, before hugging her.

'Do you want to come and join us on the beach? We've got beers,' he offered.

'No, no, I can't thanks. I'll leave you to it,' Tara replied, unconvincingly, Lucy thought.

'Don't be daft,' Tom protested. 'Come on, Nina would love to see you.'

The jealousy made Lucy feel pathetic all over again. She was determined not to let it show.

'Yeah, come on, it'll be fun,' she said to Tara, who looked suddenly pleased by Lucy's offer.

'Okay,' she smiled at Lucy, 'I'd kill for a beer, actually.'

Lucy sat down on the sand slightly away from the group, leaning back on her elbows and looking up at the sky. She remembered that she'd meant to call Warren tonight, to arrange their trip to Hideaway. He and Charlie had been excited at her invitation and she'd arranged for them to come and stay in a week's time for the Bay's biggest event of the year, the Sundowner. She was so glad that they were coming, hoping that a glimpse of her London life might help to drag her back to reality, snap her out of the nostalgic dream she was falling for here, and which threatened to break her heart all over again. Warren's phone rang out to answerphone; he was probably out. She wouldn't bother calling Charlie, as she never, ever answered her phone. Putting her phone back in her bag, she looked over to Nina, Tara, Tom and Kristian, a happy foursome. She'd been replaced, she realised. She'd been gone too long. She finished her beer and had a word with herself, plastered a smile on her face and walked back to join them. She wasn't going to make a fool of herself any more – she was going to be fine with it all, with the reality of the situation. She wasn't in love with Tom because she didn't really know him any more, and anyway, he had moved on. She would enjoy her last couple of weeks, look forward to the Sundowner and she'd get her act together and find herself a job to go back to in London. She needed to prove to Claire, to herself and to everyone, that she could make a go of it all.

Tom and Tara were sitting close to each other on the sand. She was leaning in to him, talking conspiratorially, and Tom looked concerned. Lucy tried to speak to Nina about their plans for tomorrow, but kept glancing back over. Tom's arm was around Tara's waist now and he was talking right into her neck as she looked at the sand. It was an intimate scene, but they looked unhappy. Tara visibly pulled herself together, in a way Lucy recognised, before giving Tom a kiss on the cheek and standing up to walk over to her and Nina, grabbing another beer on the way.

'Are you okay?' Nina asked. Tara nodded. Tom walked over and placed one arm each around Tara and Lucy. She could smell the beer on him and Tara pulled away, laughing.

'I'm going to head off,' Tara said, making to leave.

'Hang on a sec,' Tom said, 'I'll walk you.'

Lucy smiled goodbye and watched them walk off towards the town.

'It's not what you think,' Kristian said.

Lucy stopped him. 'It's none of my business,' she told him. She kissed them both goodbye and walked back to the house alone.

27

When Lucy checked her phone the following morning there was a message from Tom: *Hey Lucy, hope your head's okay this morning. I wondered if you could do me a massive favour and help out in the café this morning? I'm two staff down, and you know the ropes. Don't worry if not, but I'd massively appreciate it if you can? Tx*

Lucy wasn't sure that she did still 'know the ropes', but the thought of working in the café was actually quite appealing. She didn't have any plans for the day and the cash would be helpful. She texted Tom back.

Sure, no problem. I can be down at 8:30, see you there x

His reply came immediately: *I'm not around this morning. Tara will meet you there. Thanks so much! Tx*

Down at the café Tara was already pulling chairs out onto the terrace, singing along to the radio, unaware that Lucy was now watching her.

'Morning,' Lucy said, looking around for an apron. 'What can I do to help?'

'Lucy, hey, thanks so much for this. Could you start filling the cake stands? They're out the back. Molly's at the bakery, she'll be back with everything any minute.'

'No problem,' Lucy said, heading for the kitchen, finding a

stray apron behind the counter and tying the navy-blue fabric around her waist. She caught a glimpse of herself in the glass partition as she walked. She looked like her sixteen-year-old self, dashing around with an apron on. *Just without Tom chasing me with a tea towel*, she thought, smiling to herself.

The café was quiet for a Friday morning. The day was hot and the tourists seemed to be buying things to take away and eat on the beach rather than sitting inside. The terrace was buzzing, though. In fact, it had seemed eternally busy out there since Lucy had first arrived back in town. It really was one hell of a spot, Lucy could see, as she went out to top up coffees and check the tables were happy. The view out to Keeper's Island was crystal clear this morning, the haze of the past few days having lifted overnight. The water glittered with sunshine and Lucy could feel a cool, fresh breeze bouncing off the waves as she stood looking out to sea.

'All okay out here?' Tara asked as she approached Lucy from the café, standing by her side and admiring the view.

'Perfect,' Lucy replied. 'Everyone's happy.'

'Great stuff,' Tara tucked a loose strand of hair back up into her messy bun. 'God I feel quite hung over after all those beers last night.'

'It was fun, wasn't it?' Lucy said.

'It was really fun,' Tara said, still looking out to sea. 'Have you ever been over there?' She pointed to Keeper's Island.

'Yeah, we went on a school trip once, and the four of us swam over a few times,' Lucy said. 'It's a wildlife reserve now, I think. They used to run boat trips in the summer.'

'Yeah, I've seen them go out there,' Tara said. 'I'd really like to see it. It looks so mysterious from here, like something from the *Famous Five.*'

'That's exactly what I've always thought of it as,' Lucy said, turning to Tara. 'Like it should be full of secret tunnels and treasure maps, right?' Tara nodded in agreement.

'It's a shame, it's actually just really, really dull,' Lucy said, remembering the disappointment of that much-anticipated school trip, the endless signs about birds that lived on the island, the lack of underground tunnels.

Tara laughed. 'I love it here,' she said. 'You're so lucky to have grown up here. Tom never stops going on about what you all got up to back then.' She hesitated before continuing. 'It's really nice to finally meet you.'

'You too,' Lucy said, feeling guilty for how nasty some of her thoughts had been about Tara. She was a nice girl and they weren't that dissimilar, truth be told.

'Right, well I had better go and help Molly make the cream teas. That girl is a disaster with clotted cream,' Tara rolled her eyes and made her way back across the terrace. Lucy kept her gaze on Keeper's Island. *I'll take Tara over there*, she thought, surprising herself.

Lucy was pleasantly surprised as Tara counted out the tips at the end of the day. £30 each was a lot better than it had been back in her day working there. She'd ended up staying on to help out in the evening, when it got increasingly busy as the sun faded. Stefan the chef's lobster roll special had proved a real hit with diners and the atmosphere had been really fun. Lucy had enjoyed herself.

Tara had changed out of her work clothes into a loose white-linen dress and let her hair down. It was the first time Lucy had seen it loose and she looked gorgeous.

'Thanks again,' Tara said, struggling with the bags of washing she was taking to do at home.

'Here, let me help you with those,' Lucy said, taking two carrier bags. 'Where are you heading?'

'Oh, don't worry, it's fine,' Tara said, trying to take the bags back, seeming a little flustered. 'It's not far.'

'Honestly,' Lucy said, 'I'm helping you home with these, which way are we going?'

Tara looked Lucy in the eyes and conceded that the help would be good. They headed up the hill, saying goodbye to Molly as she turned off at the end of her road.

'Where has Tom been all day, anyway?' Lucy asked, as they climbed further up the hill.

'I'm not sure,' Tara replied. 'I think he had to go to Plymouth for something. He was supposed to be back this afternoon.'

'You two seem really close,' Lucy said. 'I'm glad he's got someone like you to help him with the café. It's pretty full on there.'

Tara took a few more steps before replying. 'Yeah, it's so busy, it's crazy really. I never expected to stay here for so long. It was just meant to be a temporary summer job, but here I am.' Tara shrugged.

'I heard about the Condé Nast listing,' Lucy said. 'That's amazing.'

'Yep, it's been his dream. He's worked so hard for it,' Tara said, pausing to catch her breath and sweeping her hair away from her face. Lucy felt the familiar pang of jealousy that Tara was the one who knew his dreams now.

'Well, it looks like he couldn't have done it without you,' she said, pausing too now.

'He thinks the world of you,' Tara said, out of nowhere.

'Oh, um, well, we have a lot of history, I guess. Ancient history, really,' Lucy said, feeling awkward suddenly.

'I don't think it's ancient history for Tom,' Tara said, not making eye contact, beginning to walk again.

'It's very strange being back,' Lucy said, honestly. 'I didn't really think about it before I got back here. I was just fucking everything up so badly in London, I needed to escape and Tom emailed, and it all just fitted together. I shouldn't have been so surprised that it feels odd being back here, or odd that it isn't odd at all, if you know what I mean.' She realised she was rambling.

'I can't really imagine what it's like,' Tara said, slowing down as they approached what Lucy assumed must be her apartment block. 'But I know how much it meant to Tom that you agreed to come, so I'm really glad you did. I'm really pleased to be getting to know you,' Tara said, reaching for keys in her pocket.

Lucy didn't reply.

'Thanks for these,' Tara said, taking the bags from Lucy as she propped the door open with her foot. The apartment block was newly built since Lucy had left the town; she'd not seen it before. It was smart and slightly soulless.

'Do you want a hand taking them upstairs?' Lucy asked

'No, no, it's fine, honestly, thanks,' Tara insisted.

Lucy said goodbye and turned to walk back down to the town. Tara was a nice girl. It was becoming increasingly clear why Tom liked her so much – how could he not? She reminded Lucy of herself before she'd left for London.

A silhouette walked towards Lucy as she neared the town, raising a hand in a wave to her. She instinctively did the same. As the figure got closer she recognised the guy from the hairdressers – Olly. He was wearing a shirt now and looked like he'd brushed his hair – he looked ridiculously hot. Lucy smiled at him and he smiled back.

'Evening, miss,' he said, bowing his head slightly as he passed her.

'Evening,' Lucy blushed, feeling ridiculous for her girlishness. She picked up her pace and made her way into the lights of the main street, still busy with late-night drinkers with red faces.

Lucy felt in her pocket and found the packet of cigarettes she'd bought with Tom. She made her way to the beach, finding a patch of sand away from the groups of teenagers still hanging around. She lit a Marlboro Light and blew smoke into the night sky. She wondered whether she should text Tom to check if he was alright. She hadn't heard from him since the morning. It wasn't like him to go missing for a day like this, or at least, it never used to be like him. She typed a message on her phone:

Hi Tom, hope you're ok? All good at the café today, had a great time. Let me know how you're doing x

She hit send, wondering whether he was already back at the house, sitting out on the decking with Kristian, drinking more beer.

She gazed at the stars as she smoked, hugging her legs with her free hand. It was getting cold. She thought about what Tara had said, about how much it had meant to Tom that Lucy was coming back. What did that actually mean? Tara didn't speak as if they were a couple, but Lucy knew girls, and she knew that Tara had feelings for him. Why else was she hanging around working at his café? It wasn't as if the money was great or the prospects exciting. *I wonder if his parents love her*, she found herself thinking, *I bet they do.* The thought of Tom's parents made her feel old suddenly. She wished they were here; she'd have loved to see them. His mum would have been able to give her some sensible advice about moving back to London – what to do. She'd tried talking to Nina and Kristian about it, but they were just adamant she shouldn't go back to TV, seemingly oblivious to the fact that she wasn't qualified or experienced in anything else. Tom wouldn't really engage with her on the topic. He'd asked a few questions about Spectrum and what it had been like working there, but it seemed to make him uncomfortable talking to her about her London life, and Lucy hadn't exactly been eager to go into it with him anyway. She should probably talk to Claire about it all, she knew, but after their last conversation, her sister was the last person Lucy felt like calling. She felt embarrassed at the thought of how that call had gone. What a selfish brat she'd been. She tried to imagine what Tom's mum would say to her. *She'd ask what would make me happy*, she thought, *but I really don't know any more, I just don't know.*

She stubbed her cigarette into the sand and brushed sand from her legs. She checked her phone but Tom hadn't replied. It was late, she realised now, and she ought to get back. Her phone beeped and she expected to see Tom's name, but it was Warren from Spectrum.

Hey Luce, I've got news for you, call me. Lots of love xxx

28

The garden lights were still on as Lucy approached the house and she could hear laughter coming from the garden. Tom was back. She let herself in the front door and contemplated going straight to her room and to bed. She felt exhausted after a day on her feet at the café.

'Lucy?' Tom called from the garden. 'We're all out here.'

Lucy sighed to herself and walked into the kitchen, where there was a bottle of prosecco in an ice bucket on the side. She poured herself a glass and made her way into the garden. Music was playing from Kristian's speakers on the patio and Nina was sitting on his lap on the decking, his arms wrapped around her with a blanket. 'Oh, you guys,' Lucy said, rolling her eyes. 'Would you just quit being so bloody happy?' She smiled at Nina and raised her glass to her.

'I've only just seen your text, Luce, sorry,' Tom said, beckoning her to sit down next to him at the table. 'Thanks so much for helping out today. Tara said you were brilliant.'

'It was fine, not a problem, I enjoyed it,' she said, sitting down next to him. He shuffled up to make room for her, but left his leg brushing against hers, and she felt her skin tingle.

'Do you fancy a few more days this week?' he asked. 'You can say no.'

'I'd love to,' she replied, honestly. 'I'd be happy to.'

'Can you believe we've been here nearly a month?' Kristian said, raising his beer to his lips.

'It's gone so quickly,' Nina said, sadly. 'I don't want this summer to end. It's been the best.'

'It has,' Tom agreed. 'You can all stay, you know, as long as you like. My parents aren't rushing back from France any time soon.'

'I'd love to, mate, but I've got this thing called work,' Kristian said. 'Pain in the ass, really.'

'Yeah, I know,' Tom said, finishing his beer and reaching for another from the coolbox beside him.

'Kristian's taking the full-time position,' Nina said. 'We decided for definite yesterday and he's accepted the role today.'

'That's amazing news,' Tom said. 'So you'll only be a few hours away: awesome. That's great, mate, seriously. Good call.'

'Yeah, well, I figured a bit of consistency would be good, given the baby and all that,' Kristian said, looking at Nina. 'We're probably not going to be jetting off to India any time soon, are we, my angel?' Nina smiled at him and rubbed her stomach protectively.

'What about you, Lucy?' Tom said, turning to her now, his leg still resting against hers.

'Oh, I'm going back to my flat,' she said, feeling pressured by the shift of attention to her. 'Then I need to find a job. Actually, I had a message from Warren at work. I need to call him. He might know of something coming up.'

'I thought you weren't going back to TV,' Nina said, looking concerned. 'It's obviously not a great fit for you.'

Lucy felt defensive. 'It was fine, actually. It was my problem,' she said. 'I messed it all up. I actually had a good job – it wasn't bad there. I just got carried away with it all.'

'No you didn't,' Nina replied quickly. 'It got on top of you, because you worked for a fucking awful woman at a terrible

154

company that bullied and belittled people. Don't rewrite history now, Lucy.'

Kristian looked uncomfortable at Nina's outburst and tried to pull her in closer to him to stop her talking.

'No, I'm serious,' she continued. 'You turned up here after months and months of no contact, looking absolutely awful. You looked ill. And now you're talking about going back to it all? That's ridiculous, and you know it.'

Lucy was taken aback by Nina's anger. 'I hadn't even said I was considering that,' she said, firmly. 'But it is my decision what I do. I was an idiot to just drop everything and come here like this. Don't try and make me feel stupid for wanting to pick up the life I'd been building myself for years in London. What other option do I have?' she said, more loudly than she'd intended to. Tom had moved his leg away from hers and was looking away from the group, as if trying to extract himself from the conversation.

'You could stay,' Nina said, quietly now. 'You could stay here.'

The conversation had made the remainder of the night uncomfortable. Lucy had finished her glass of prosecco and made her excuses to go to bed. She'd said goodnight to Nina and hugged her to let her know there were no hard feelings. She knew she was just looking out for her, but it was pretty galling listening to her sanctimonious lectures about what was right. It was so easy for Nina; she had Kristian, a baby on the way and a perfect job lined up for Kris in Bristol. She'd probably never have to work again. Lucy was jealous at the thought.

In her bedroom she changed into her silk pyjamas and waffle dressing gown, opened the balcony door and stepped outside. The night air was cold now, but it felt good on her skin. She looked at the time and decided it was probably okay to call Warren – he was most likely out in town somewhere, given that it was a Friday night. The phone rang and rang and he answered just as she was about to hang up.

'Luce!' he exclaimed. He sounded drunk.

'Hey, Warren, how are you?' she asked.

'I'm great, how are you?' he slurred

'Yeah all good here, thanks, I got your message. Is now a good time? I can call back.'

Lucy could hear Warren moving through crowds, muffled laughter and shouting in the background, then relative peace.

'No it's fine. I'm outside now. I'm out with the gang from the office. I'm shitfaced, to be honest with you.'

Lucy could tell.

'So, I spoke to Emma earlier,' he said. 'She was asking about what you're up to now. I think she wants you back.'

Lucy didn't know what to say. It didn't feel like the big news he'd made it out to be.

'I doubt that,' she said, dejectedly, not sure she'd even want Emma to ask her to come back.

'I know, right, after what you did at the wrap party we all thought you'd become one of those people no one can ever speak of again in the office. But Emma's not found anyone to replace you and she's started mentioning you quite a bit, in a nice way, and then today, like I said, she asked me if I knew what you were up to. What *are* you up to, actually?'

'I'm working in the café,' Lucy said, without thinking.

'Oh God, Luce, I'm sorry,' Warren said, as if she'd told him the sorriest tale he'd ever heard. 'That is so sad'.

Lucy laughed, 'I'm bearing up okay, Warren,' she said, 'I'm coming back to London in a few weeks anyway. And you guys are down here next week, so it'll fly by.'

'A-mazing scenes,' he replied. 'Do you want me to tell Emma you're coming back? I'll leave out the café part if you like, that just sounds tragic. I really think she might offer you your job back, you know.'

Lucy didn't know what to say. She hadn't expected Emma to ever forgive her, let alone consider wanting her back. And knowing

Warren, there was a fair chance he'd got it all twisted up anyway – he was hammered, after all.

'Um, no, don't say anything, thanks' she said. 'I couldn't come back after everything that happened.'

'You were great at your job, Luce. You shouldn't just give up on it all because of one mistake. If she gives you the chance to make it all okay again, I think you'd be an idiot not to take it.'

Lucy went to reply, but he'd hung up the phone. She made her way back into her warm bedroom, closing the curtains behind her. She took off her dressing gown and got into bed, feeling lost.

Kristian was in the kitchen frying bacon when she made it downstairs in the morning. 'Nin feels terrible about last night,' he said, used to apologising for her, it seemed to Lucy.

'She just cares about you – we all do,' he said. 'But she's not the most tactful, sometimes.' He gave Lucy a knowing look and she smiled.

'I know. I was being a cow anyway,' she said. 'I just feel so stupid, like everyone thinks I'm an idiot.'

'They don't' Kristian said, cracking eggs into the pan now. 'I wanted your help with something, actually. When Tom gives you a day off from your new job, can I borrow you?'

'Of course,' Lucy said. 'Is everything okay?'

'Yep, I just want your opinion on something. Tom said you might be working the next few days, but if you're free on Wednesday, I could use an hour of your time.'

It was news to Lucy that she might be working for the next few days. She needed to speak to Tom about what was going on with that.

'Sure, that's fine' she said. 'I'll help you with whatever you need.'

'Cheers, Luce. Want a sandwich?' he gestured at the pan.

'I'm alright, thanks. Got to get to work or my nightmare of a boss will bollock me,' she said. 'I'll catch you later. Tell Nina we're okay, please?'

'Of course,' Kristian called as she left the house.

29

Tara had ended up being the one to ask Lucy to work for the next few days. Tom had more business to do in Plymouth. He'd not even been around in the evenings when Lucy had come home from work.

Things were, much to Lucy's relief, fine again with Nina. With Tom away, they'd sat up most evenings talking about the future. Lucy promising to stay in touch this time and not to 'be a prat', as Nina so eloquently put it. Kristian had been acting strangely, Nina confided in Lucy, and she didn't know what was up with him. Lucy thought back to their conversation in the kitchen, and his request for her to help him with something, but decided not to mention it to Nina. She had a good idea about why he might be acting strangely in light of that. They talked, too, about Tom, about how odd it was the way he'd absented himself for the last few days, especially given that it was almost the end of their time together. Nina had a theory that he was buying another property in Hideaway; the Beach Café was doing so well, and he had mentioned wanting to set up a gourmet sandwich bar as a sister company. It made sense, Lucy thought, and that would be Tom's style, to want to keep it all quiet until it was signed off and a done deal. He'd always been proud like that, never wanted anyone to see him mess anything up.

'There has to be something big going on,' Lucy had said to Nina. 'His board's not moved for days. It takes something serious to keep him out of the water.'

'You're still in love with him,' Nina said, a statement, not a question.

Lucy didn't have the energy to deny it.

'When you talk about him you go all soft,' Nina said, 'like you always did.'

'It really doesn't matter how I feel,' Lucy said, looking at her friend. 'I'm going back to London soon. And he has Tara here.'

'You know that doesn't mean anything,' Nina said gently. Lucy could see how hard she was trying to be careful with her words.

'It means something to me,' Lucy replied. 'I came down here, I don't know what I was expecting, but I guess I just wasn't imagining a Tara on the scene. And I really like her, she's great, I can see why they get on so well. But, I don't know, there've been a few moments where I thought he was going to grab me and kiss me and make everything alright again, but that's not going to happen. I feel pretty pathetic that it's been so long and I haven't really moved on, not like he has.'

Nina didn't say anything in reply. *What was there to say to that? So embarrassing,* Lucy thought to herself.

Lucy took the long way to work, skipping the shortcut and walking through the winding street past the arcade. The fashion and interior stores were shuttered and dark, and she caught sight of her reflection in the windows. She smiled at the image of herself, after all these years, heading in to the café to work a shift. As she approached Annabel's boutique she remembered Claire's words about her old friend and wished she'd asked her what she meant. She'd never thought of Annabel as anything other than one of her sister's oldest friends, certainly not a bully. She was surprised to see a light on in the shop, so she tried the door and it opened into the shop.

'Lucy, hey!' Annabel beamed at her from a rack of pastel scarves.

'Morning,' Lucy smiled back at her. 'You're open early.'

'Oh, not actually open,' Annabel said, turning back to the fabric and beginning to reorder them. 'Just had some new stock in, so wanted to get that out before the day starts. It's been so busy that I haven't done half the things I meant to do. Anyway, what are you doing up and about at this hour?'

'I'm working, would you believe?' Lucy shrugged her shoulders. 'I'm helping Tom out at the café.'

A strange squawk of a laugh escaped from Annabel's grimacing face. 'What? How bloody awkward is that!?'

'It's fine,' Lucy said, feeling slightly uneasy – and remembering Claire's accusations. 'I actually really enjoy it.'

'But you must be working with Princess Tamara,' Annabel scoffed, still pulling a strange expression.

'Tara?' Lucy asked.

'Oh yes, sorry, we're not allowed to refer to her by her *real* name. Poor little wounded princess.' Annabel looked positively venomous now. It shocked Lucy, who'd never seen this side of her.

'I've only ever known her as Tara,' Lucy said, trailing off, wishing she hadn't come in now.

'Yes, well, you get the official Hideaway Bay press-release version. Everyone's very accommodating of her precious demands. I don't know what the bloody fuss is about with her. I find her totally, unbearably smug.'

Lucy reddened slightly at the memory of her own similar feelings towards Tara. She'd come to really like her. Working together had let her see what a great girl Tara was and she didn't like hearing her spoken about like this.

'She's lovely,' Lucy replied. 'I really like her.'

Annabel rolled her eyes. 'Another convert,' she sighed, moving to a display of sunglasses and shuffling them around aimlessly.

'I'd better be off,' Lucy said, pleased to be able to leave.

'Sure, well come in later if you like. We can have a glass of 'wine and a proper gossip,' Annabel had cheered up and returned to the version of herself that Lucy had always liked.

'Okay, yeah, maybe,' Lucy said, knowing she wouldn't be going back there this evening. She left the store and felt like she could finally catch her breath back out in the fresh air. Annabel's hatred of Tara had made Lucy realise that she considered Tara a friend. It wasn't what she'd expected, but it was true. She tried to pick out the content from the spite – it had sounded strange, what Annabel was trying to imply about Tara. What did she mean? Lucy had the distinct feeling she couldn't ask Tara directly about it – there was obviously some seriously bad feeling there. She'd have to find out what was going on by other means.

Lucy arrived at the café to find Tom behind the counter examining the glassware.

'Oh, hi,' Lucy said. 'I wasn't expecting to see you here.'

'What, working in my own café?' Tom smiled. 'Sorry I've been MIA for the past few days. I had loads of stuff to sort in Plymouth.' He placed a smeared wine glass down by the dishwasher. 'Can't get the staff,' he sighed, jokingly, at Lucy.

'It's fine,' Lucy said. 'It's been fun the last few days. I feel like I've really nailed this whole waitressing thing all over again. Maybe I've finally found my calling.'

'Well, if you want a job, it's yours,' Tom said. 'We don't shut 'til October – I make that a whole two months before you'd need to think about anything else. Actually, we might not shut at all this winter. Tara thinks if we change the menu a bit we could run right through; although she might just be trying to keep herself in a job, now I think about it.'

'Sounds like a good plan, if you ask me. Tara knows what she's talking about,' Lucy said.

'A good plan you staying?' Tom said, with what sounded like a hopeful tone to his voice.

'No, you staying open all year,' Lucy said, embarrassed by the confusion. 'I've booked my train back to London. I leave next week.'

It was strange, but fun, working with Tom again in the café. He was so popular with the locals and the tourists, and it was a pleasure to watch him charm everyone so effortlessly, so genuinely. Liv, from the hairdresser's, came in for a coffee after work. She, like every other person who recognised Lucy at the café, seemed surprised to find Lucy waitressing.

'I'm just helping Tom out,' Lucy explained again, feeling like a broken record.

'Oh, how lovely!' Liv said, over-enthusiastically. They both watched Tom take an order a few tables away, making the ladies laugh at something.

'I'm going back to London in a few days,' Lucy said, turning back to Liv and trying to emphasise, for her own benefit, the short-term nature of the arrangement.

'That's a shame,' Liv said, looking at Lucy again now. 'It's been nice having you around again.'

Lucy smiled and walked away to make Liv's latte. The café was filling up with the afternoon tea rush: old ladies eating toasted teacakes, kids making ridiculous scones piled with jam and cream. They were selling everything so fast it looked like someone would need to go back to the bakery for more cakes.

Lucy asked Molly to pop out to the baker's and frothed the milk for Liv's coffee. She still loved using the coffee machine; there was something so pleasing about the process. Stefan called from the kitchen that one of her tables' orders was ready. She finished the latte and popped it on the table in front of Liv, who was now engrossed in a magazine. She collected the plates of mussels and fries from the pass and began walking them over to the terrace table that had ordered them, a pair of youngish-looking dads who had offloaded their kids on the beach – just about in their sight from the deck.

'Hello again,' Lucy turned to see Olly walking through the

main door, scanning the café. He was smiling at her, flashing those perfect teeth and looking like something from a surf magazine in his bright board shorts and open shirt.

'Hi,' she said, unsure whether to stop and chat. 'Are you looking for a table?'

'Um, hi, no,' he said, making eye contact now. 'Tara's not here, is she?'

'Nope, it's her day off' Lucy said. 'I just need to run these outside.' She nodded at the steaming plates of food on her tray.

'Of course,' Olly said, flashing that perfect smile again. 'I'll have a coffee over there when you've got a min.' He pointed outside at the free table by the wall.

'Okay,' Lucy said, walking towards the decking, cursing herself for blushing simply because she was talking to a good-looking guy.

'What kind of coffee would you like?' she asked Olly, now sitting leaning back in his chair, looking out at the view.

'Oh, just a normal one, cheers,' he replied.

'An Americano?' Lucy asked

'A what-o?' Olly said, smirking slightly. 'Whatever you recommend, er, sorry, I don't actually know your name – I'm Olly.' His effortless charm reminded her of Tom.

'I know,' said Lucy, before her brain could catch up with her mouth. She lifted a hand to her face instinctively, as if to hide the embarrassment.

'I'm Lucy,' she said. 'Nice to meet you.' She held out a hand, which Olly shook firmly.

'Very formal. I like it, Lucy. Nice to meet you too,' he said. Lucy suddenly felt like she'd been standing at his table too long.

'I'll go and make that coffee,' she said, turning to walk away.

'Thanks, babe,' Olly said as she left, and she smiled to herself at the sound of his voice.

There were no clean mugs at the coffee machine, so Lucy went to the kitchen to retrieve some fresh ones from the dishwasher.

Stefan was cursing at something on the hob, so she steered clear of him, heading around the other side, past the storeroom instead. She heard a noise from behind the corner of the door and popped her head around to ask Molly if she needed a hand unpacking the cakes. It was Tom, sitting on a chair, slipping a small bottle into his pocket.

'You okay?' she asked. 'What are those?'

'Painkillers,' Tom said, patting his pocket, which rattled. 'I picked up an injury in the water last week – nasty ligament tear. It kills, actually. I can't surf for another week at least. It's driving me crazy.' He looked up at Lucy and puffed his cheeks.

'You looked cozy out there,' he said, turning away.

'What?' Lucy asked, confused.

'You and Olly. I should have figured you'd like him. The ladies can't resist Olly, it seems.' He had a mocking tone to his voice. *Is he jealous*? Lucy wondered.

'I've just met him,' Lucy said, truthfully. 'I don't *like* him, for God's sake, Tom, we're not fifteen.'

'It certainly looked like you like him,' Tom said, refusing to drop it. 'Not that it's any of my business. Anyway, you're going next week, aren't you? So it'd just be a casual holiday fling, or whatever. You go ahead, enjoy yourself.'

Lucy couldn't believe what she was hearing. He couldn't be serious?

'Are you kidding me?' she said, looking at Tom sitting there. 'You're going to try and make me feel bad about talking to a guy I'm serving at a table? Are you insane?'

'Sorry,' Tom said, standing up and making to leave the room. 'I'm pretty shattered and my leg hurts. I shouldn't have said that.'

Lucy turned and walked out ahead of him. He had no right to be jealous, but she kind of liked the thought that he was. However unfair that was. *God, I need to grow up*, she thought to herself as she picked up the tray of clean mugs and made her way back to the coffee machine.

Molly was practically dragging the large bags of cakes into the café and Lucy went to help her in with them.

'Oh Olly's in,' Molly said, looking out at the terrace. 'Have you texted Tara?' she asked Lucy.

'No, why would I text Tara?' Lucy replied, confused.

'Oh, no reason. He just normally asks for her, that's all. I normally let her know when he's in.' Molly replied, looking slightly flustered. 'I'll go and get these out,' she said, rushing away with the cakes.

Olly was chatting to Tom about the surf forecast when Lucy delivered his coffee. Tom was complaining about his leg and Olly seemed genuinely upset for him. 'Man, you're gonna miss some epic waves. That sucks,' he said, looking devastated at the thought.

'Cheers, babe,' Olly turned to Lucy, winking at her as she placed his Americano down on the table. Lucy felt embarrassed in front of Tom and didn't know how to reply.

'So this is the famous Lucy,' Olly continued, addressing Tom now. 'I thought it might be, when I saw you around town with Nina and Kristian.' He looked back at Lucy. 'You've got quite a hold over this one, I gather. Fair play, Tom. I can see why. You're a beauty,' he said, smiling again. Lucy had never met anyone with so much confidence.

Tom attempted a laugh. 'Yep, she's going again soon, though. Back to the big smoke,' he looked at Lucy, holding her eye for a little too long to be comfortable.

'Shame,' Olly said, 'I was hoping to get to know you a bit better.' He seemed to stop himself from saying any more, taking a sip of his coffee instead as Tom and Lucy walked away together.

'So he's your friend?' Lucy asked Tom back inside the café.

'Kind of. Well, we both surf every day. I know him. He's alright.'

'He's so cocky!' Lucy laughed. 'Is he friends with Tara? He was asking for her when he came in?'

'Yeah, they're friendly,' Tom said. 'They were both new to town a few summers ago. Kind of helped each other through, I think.

You know what it can be like here – not the friendliest place for new arrivals.'

'Sure,' Lucy said. It could be a cliquey place, North Cornwall; suspicion of outsiders was an ingrained trait.

Tom watched Lucy make a coffee, leaning against the counter, looking her up and down. 'You're still the best barista we've ever had,' he said to her, playfully. 'Sure I can't tempt you to stay?'

The truth was Lucy was tempted, not so much to stay there, but just to not go back. London life felt so far away after the last few weeks, she'd barely missed anything. She'd certainly not missed any*one*, which seemed to say rather a lot. Warren had texted her a couple of times about Emma. He was convinced she wanted her back at Spectrum and he was excited about their trip down to see her in Cornwall – missing his drinking buddy, Lucy guessed. She thought back to the nights she'd spent after work, drinking herself into oblivion, almost always ending up in the toilets doing coke. The mornings afterwards, so hard, so depressing. She'd done it for months and months, years even, she realised. If she was going back, she was going to have to do things differently. And she'd meant what she'd promised Nina – she would stay in touch this time. They had a baby on the way, for God's sake, she wanted to be a part of its life. She wanted to feel good again. *Like I feel now*. But, of course, she couldn't stay. She'd given it enough thought. It wouldn't be difficult to let her flat go, to move back down here, if she wanted to. But it wasn't the right thing to do – and anyway, things were so confusing with Tom, it would be pathetic of her to just hang around him now, when he so clearly wasn't interested in her in the way she was in him.

Back out in the café she watched him again from the counter; he had the cheeky look on his face that she remembered from school. He was always such a happy person, but he was sensitive too. She knew that about him, but plenty of people didn't. She began polishing cutlery, ready for the evening service. It was looking like a busy one; they'd taken almost every reservation available already. She was glad she was handing over to Jen for the late shift. She checked her watch. She had one hour until she was due to meet Tara.

30

Tara was dressed in a green shift dress as she walked towards Lucy, waving at her slightly manically.

'Hey,' she called to Lucy. 'Sorry, I'm late. I couldn't decide what to wear.'

'You look lovely,' Lucy said, truthfully. 'I didn't have time to change, so I'm still in my café stuff – bit grim.' She looked down at her black playsuit and brushed away imaginary coffee grounds.

They walked together down the street, in and out of the glowing lights of the shops that stayed open for the warm evenings. The town felt calm tonight, as if the cumulative effect of the scorching heat had started to catch up with the visitors and locals. People seemed to be walking slowly around the streets. There were people stopped in groups, talking about their days, their plans for the rest of their holidays. An ice-cream stand was serving what were surely its last customers of the day. The sun was almost setting, Lucy noticed, its orange light beginning to seep across the horizon above the calm sea. They chatted about the café, about the shops; easy, low- key chatter with lots of comfortable silences. It made Lucy start when Tara stopped suddenly, frozen to the spot, her face anxious, gaze fixed straight ahead.

'You okay?' Lucy said, instinctively placing a hand on Tara's shoulder.

Tara didn't answer. She looked away from the spot ahead and then back to it as if to double-check. Then she turned to Lucy.

'Sorry,' she said, forcing a smile. 'I'm fine.' She started walking again and Lucy joined her, unsettled.

'Did you see something?' she asked, confused.

'No, no, I thought I saw someone I knew, but it wasn't them. I'm always doing it.' Tara tried to laugh, but it shook slightly. Lucy decided not to pry. She'd speak to Nina about it later. Maybe there was something she didn't know about Tara. Given what Annabel had said about her in the shop, it seemed that there was a back story that Lucy was not aware of. She knew from her own experience that there are some things not to drag up without being invited to, so she let it go for now.

When they reached the harbour side, Lucy looked around for Louie. She'd known him since she was a girl, working in the café the first time around. He used to come in every day for a bacon sandwich and a 'proper coffee', to take out on his glass bottom boat with him. He was a nice guy, Lucy remembered, a proper salt-of-the-earth Cornishman, but one with a real business brain. He'd started with just one boat, as a teenager straight from school, and was now the owner and manager of a fleet of eight that sailed from the harbour each day, for fishing trips, dolphin-spotting and glass- bottom boat rides.

Tara had been so excited when Lucy had suggested they take a trip over to Keeper's Island, which had taken Lucy by surprise. In fact, it had taken Lucy by surprise that she'd asked Tara to take the trip with her in the first place. Nina had pressed Lucy on what she made of the situation, but the truth was, she liked Tara, it was that simple. And as long as they steered clear of the topic of Tom, something they seemed to have silently, mutually, agreed, they got on really well.

Louie was helping customers into the boat as they joined the small queue at the 'Princess of the Seas', their vessel for the evening. The sunset glass-bottom boat tour didn't promise much in the way of spectacular sea life, given that the light was going, but it would take them to Keeper's Island.

'Evening, girls,' Louie took Lucy's hand, helping her into the boat.

'Hey, Louie,' she smiled at him. He looked so much older than she'd remembered, but then she figured she probably did to him too.

'This is Tara,' she looked back at Tara as she struggled with her footing, giggling and reaching for Louie's arm.

'I know Louie,' Tara said. 'He's in every day.'

'Never thought I'd get her out on one of the boats,' Louie said, looking slightly bemused by Tara's total lack of coordination. 'You said you were scared of the water.'

Tara looked embarrassed as Lucy walked back over to try to help her from the boat, offering her arm, which Tara took, nearly pushing them both to the floor as she finally landed on the deck.

'Not scared, exactly,' she said, to Lucy rather than Louie. 'More, concerned.'

'Well, never mind, here you are,' Louie said, scanning the harbour for any stragglers before doing a final head count. 'Think we've got everyone.'

Lucy and Tara found a spot at the back of the boat. The tour couldn't have been even half-full, there was so much space.

As the boat pulled away from the harbour, Lucy watched the town turn first into a picture postcard of itself, and then eventually just a cluster of warm lights. The boat could really move. Her hair blew in the wind, and a slight spray of salt water hit her face when they clipped tiny, choppy waves. It felt exhilarating. Looking over at Tara, Lucy felt like a girl of fourteen again, on her first trip over to Keeper's Island. She'd gone with her family, all of them, on a rare weekend when her dad was home. Her mum had packed a picnic and they'd taken their own boat over. It had been a brilliant, sun-shining, happy day.

'How are Nina and Kristian getting on with their house hunt?' Tara asked, bringing Lucy back to reality. They'd gone to Bristol yesterday to look at a couple of places, and Lucy realised now that she hadn't heard from Nina yet about how they were getting on.

'I'm not sure,' she said. 'There was one they were really keen on, so hopefully that's gone well. I ought to call her later.'

'So grown up,' Tara said loudly, over the sound of the wind and the engine. 'Buying a proper family home. They're a really good couple, aren't they?'

Lucy found it a strange way to describe her friends. They'd been together almost as long as she'd known them, but their relationship had certainly not started out with great promise of becoming a real love story. She thought about the endless nights she'd spent counseling Nina about it all, listening to their ridiculous arguments and watching them dramatically make up again – so many times.

'I guess they are,' she smiled out at the sea. 'They certainly think the world of each other. I don't think anyone else could put up with either of them, so thank goodness they've got each other.'

Tara spent the rest of the boat journey talking to Louie about his dog, Minty, a beautiful border collie that went everywhere with him. He was sound asleep by the wheel and Louie rubbed him with his foot as he steered. 'Love of my life,' he said to Tara. 'Never met a woman as loyal,' he laughed.

'What about Susan?' Tara asked. 'I thought there were was something going on there.'

'God she's nosey, this one,' Louie rolled his eyes for Lucy's benefit. 'Bet she's grilled you non-stop since you got back, hasn't she?'

Lucy smiled, feeling slightly awkward.

'I'm not nosey. I'm interested,' Tara clarified. 'There's a difference.'

'If you say so,' Louie replied, looking like he'd had enough of the conversation, and of Tara, possibly.

'Here we are, ladies and gentlemen,' he announced to the group spread around the boat. 'Keeper's Island. If I can have everyone back on board in an hour that'd be grand.'

The island's landing spot was an idyllic-looking sandy beach. Lucy and Tara walked through the shallows to the shore from the boat, Tara shrieking slightly as the water splashed at the backs of her legs.

'Are you really scared of water?' Lucy asked – it certainly looked that way to her.

'Only a bit,' Tara said, definitely embarrassed. 'I know it's stupid, I've just never been around the sea much, until now, obviously, and it's so bloody big.'

It wasn't stupid, Lucy conceded. She knew only too well how scary, how dangerous the water could be. Somehow, what had happened to her family had never put her off the water. If anything, in a twisted way, it had made her feel even more in awe of its power.

She held her arm out to Tara, who took it gratefully, as they made their way on to the still-warm sand. The peace of the island was startling. Birds called loudly from the trees and unidentifiable squeaks sounded from hedgerows, but there was no buzz of streetlights, no hum of industrial fridges, no chatter of tourists – it was blissful. Not wanting to spoil it, Lucy and Tara walked in silence for a while, losing the rest of the group quickly, as they took a turn into a more densely forested area. Evening light dappled through the trees, illuminating clouds of gnats that they batted away as they walked.

'It's just up here, I think,' Lucy said, somewhat uncertainly.

'Ah, yes, here, here it is,' she said, as the incline began to level off and she recognised the pair of trees that framed the view ahead of them, the finest view of Hideaway Bay. The sight was breathtaking.

'Oh my God,' Tara whispered. 'This is stunning.'

'Yeah, it really is, isn't it?' Lucy agreed.

Stretching out before them the sea glistened and glimmered with orange sparks, and on the horizon the town glittered with street and shop lights, the beach speckled now with freshly lit campfires.

'This is what I wanted to show you,' she looked at Tara, who was still totally transfixed by the scene before her.

'It's amazing, Lucy, thanks so much for bringing me. I love it,' Tara's face was lit by the disappearing, golden sun and she looked beautiful.

'No problem' Lucy said, looking back out to the sea. There were a few figures down by the landing spot, congregating for the journey home. The breeze was carrying random words up the hill to where they sat.

'Oh and look,' Tara was on her feet walking over to one of the two huge oak trees that bookended the viewpoint. 'It's covered in engravings.' She stretched a hand out as she reached the tree, tracing letters with her fingers.

'It's the finders keepers tree' Lucy called over from where she sat, watching Tara looking from initial to initial, boxily carved heart to clumsy ampersand.

'It's amazing' Tara said. 'Some of these are really old, they're dated.'

'From World War One,' Lucy confirmed. 'That's when the tradition started, when the men started going to war. Couples came over here and carved their names, for posterity I suppose. To make their mark on the world before they were separated.'

Every inch of the tree was covered in carvings, so many more than when Lucy was last here.

'I just want to know all their stories, what happened to them all,' Tara continued, dreamily. 'Look, J&R 1920 – what happened to them?' she asked, as if Lucy might know.

'It's supposed to bring good luck to the couple' Lucy said,

walking over to join Tara, taking in the carvings at close range now. Tara was right – it was a beautiful oddity.

'I think we need to make a move,' Lucy said, glancing at her phone for the time. She had a missed call from a London number.

'Okay,' Tara said, keeping her hand on the tree until the last possible moment, as if being drawn to it by some magnetic force.

'I just love it,' she said, by way of explanation. 'I think it's utterly beautiful. I'm going to come and engrave my initials here some day.' She stopped, as if she'd said too much.

Lucy watched her finally pull away from the tree. If Tara had just run her hand a little lower, down towards the back of the trunk, she'd have found a tiny L&T, scribed with a compass one blowy, autumnal afternoon when they should've been at sixth form. *It didn't bring us much luck*, Lucy thought.

The temperature had dropped significantly for their crossing back to Hideaway. Tara looked freezing in her little green dress and Lucy pulled her cardigan tightly around her legs, trying to trap some heat. She had to call Nina, she remembered, to find out how the house-hunting had gone and whether they were back tonight or tomorrow. She took her phone from her bag, remembering the missed call.

'I just need to phone someone,' she said to Tara, stepping away to an empty area. Minty was spread-eagled on the boards beside her. She hit 'call' and listened to the ringtone give way to a long beep and a voicemail message

'Hi, this is Lydia Pearce, Office Manager at Spectrum Media. I can't take your call right now, but if you leave a message I'll get…'

'Hello?' the voice took Lucy by surprise.

'Hello,' she replied. 'It's Lucy, Lucy Robertson. I had a missed call.'

'Lucy, hi! It's Lydia. I thought it might be you calling me back. Did you get my message?'

'No,' Lucy replied. 'I just saw your call. I didn't recognise the number.'

Lydia laughed, 'It's not been that long, has it? Look, Lucy, I know Warren's already given you the head's up on this. Emma wants you to come back. She's asked me to make it happen. All is forgiven, would you believe? You are quite the exception, let me tell you.'

Lucy pictured Lydia, sitting there working late like she did almost every night. She was nice enough, but had that edge of bitterness that some of the older, single women working in TV had about them; that ever-present capacity for casual nastiness to the younger girls.

'That's a surprise,' Lucy said. 'I thought Warren had probably got it mixed up somewhere along the line.'

'Apparently not,' Lydia said, sounding bored now.

'So?' she waited for Lucy's reply.

'I don't really know what to say,' Lucy said meekly. 'Can I think about it and call you back?'

Lydia made a slightly theatrical spluttering sound. 'Okay, Lucy, that's fine. But I seriously wouldn't push it, if you know what I mean. You are incredibly lucky she's giving you another chance. It's only because she can't find another assistant.' She paused, registering what she'd said. 'I mean, look, no offence, but I thought we'd seen the last of you. I think this is one hell of an opportunity, if you're serious about making it in the industry. She can make your name mud, you know. You won't get another job, not anywhere decent.'

Lucy knew she was right. It was why she'd been dragging her heels about looking for a new position; the minute they checked her references it would all come out. It was such a small bloody world, run on boozy lunches and the exchange of gossip.

'I know,' she said. 'I'll call you in the morning. Thanks, Lydia, I really appreciate it.'

'Okay, then, I'll speak to you tomorrow. I'm not going to tell

Emma we spoke tonight, alright? Just call me tomorrow and accept the job, and be grateful, and come back like none of that mess ever happened. Capiche?'

Lucy cringed at Lydia's vocabulary. 'Got it, Lydia,' she replied. 'I'll speak to you in the morning.'

31

'I take it they decided to stay another night?' Lucy said to Tom as she walked into the kitchen, still in her dressing gown.

'Yeah, they're on their way back from Bristol now, but the traffic's going to be shocking. What are you up to today?'

'Not much. Warren and Charlie are arriving after lunch so I'm not really doing anything this morning.' She paused. 'Hang on, was this a trap? If I say "nothing" are you going to ask me to work?'

'Nope, if you say "nothing", I'm going to take you surfing.'

'Have you forgotten how bad I am?' Lucy asked, pouring orange juice into two glasses and passing one to Tom.

'Absolutely not. That's why you need to be taken out by someone as gifted as me.' He handed Lucy an apple, which dribbled juice down her chin as she took a bite.

'Here, let me,' Tom wiped her face with his thumb, and she didn't know where to look as he stood so close to her. She felt relief when he stepped back again.

'So what do you say?' Tom said, wiping his hand on his neon board shorts.

'Sure,' Lucy replied. 'I'd love to. I could use the exercise.'

Lucy carried Nina's board under her arm as they walked to

the beach, wetsuits unzipped to their chests. Sweat trickled down Lucy's chest.

'So what's going on with your flat?' Tom asked

'Oh, Claire's friend, well, Tim's friend –'

'Claire's husband, right?'

'Yeah, his friend Anna. She's staying there for another few days, then she's back to Manchester. It's not my flat, really. I only rent it. It's really nice'

'I thought everyone in London shared big overcrowded houses these days?'

'What, like Oliver Twist, you mean? Yeah, it's a lot like that. You have *been* to London, Tom. Don't try the Cornish bumpkin act with me,' she laughed. He was winding her up.

'No, it's cool, I'm just jealous. Sounds much more exciting than life down here. Bit of a change of pace coming back, I should think.'

'Yep,' Lucy replied. With the morning sun on her skin, her hair scraped back into a high ponytail and her feet on the sandy grass track down to the beach, she couldn't help thinking this pace was much more like it.

'If you sold the house you could buy a flat, right?' Tom said, stopping to the side to let her go ahead of him where the track narrowed.

'Yeah, I could' she agreed. 'Claire and I, we haven't spoken about it in a long, long time. She doesn't need the money and I guess it would mean sorting out the last boxes of things – all that messy stuff we never got around to.'

'It must cost you, though, to keep it there, empty, all secured and alarmed and whatever?' Lucy hadn't really thought about it. 'Claire looks after it all,' she said, feeling childish.

'I think the last person who tried to buy it wanted to convert it into a hotel,' she said as they reached the beach. 'Like this place needs more of those – it's overrun with tourists as it is.'

The beach was already filling up: garish windbreaks lined up across the sand, families marking their territory for the day.

'It's good for me, for business, I mean,' Tom said. 'My parents had some rough summers before I took over. We came pretty close to closing down.'

Lucy had wondered, when she was in London, how it was going down here for Tom's family. Nina had never been great at the details, but she'd got the gist that things were tough a few years back. In fact, she'd just never got the memo that they'd turned around so dramatically. She felt guilty that she'd not been there for Tom when it was hard – never even called him. After everything they'd been through before she left, it suddenly seemed almost perverse to her that they'd stopped talking at all.

In the water Lucy found herself even worse on her board than she'd imagined. Tom was struggling not to laugh at her attempts at standing up. She was useless.

'Oh stop it!' she shouted at Tom, catching his grin.

'It's cute!' he shouted back.

'You patronising prat!' she yelled back, taking a mouth of sea water at the same time.

'Come over here,' he called to her. She paddled over to where he was sitting on his board watching her embarrass herself. She heaved herself onto her board next to him, bobbing on the tide.

'You really are rubbish,' Tom said. 'I had forgotten after all.'

'Yep,' Lucy said, enjoying the sensation of the water lifting and pulling her around.

She wondered suddenly if Tom was going to tell her about him and Tara. It felt like he was about to say something important. But silence hung in the air, pierced by squeals of fun from children on the shore.

'I thought you couldn't surf for weeks?' she said, remembering the painkillers.

'Yeah, what do they know, hey?' Tom smiled at her mischievously. 'How can I not come in the water when the weather's like this?'

It was another seriously hot day – this summer would be remembered for its relentlessly scorching temperatures.

'I can't believe you're leaving,' Tom said, not looking at Lucy. 'It feels like you just got here.'

'It's been almost five weeks,' she said, stating the obvious.

'It feels like you belong down here,' Tom looked at her now and held her gaze.

'It's been great,' she said, not wanting to be the one to look away, not wanting to show any doubt. 'But my life's in London. I made that decision a long time ago and it'd be a bit pathetic for me to just trot back here and do what, work in your café?'

'Only you know what will make you happy, Luce,' Tom said. 'If that's London, then great, go for it. I'm not asking you to stay for me, you know, I'm asking you to stay for you. I don't think you are happy up there. But hey, I hardly know you any more, right? So I should just keep it to myself.'

Lucy had stopped listening. That confirmed it; he didn't want her down here for him – it wasn't like that. Whatever they still had between them, because surely she wasn't imagining what it still felt like when they walked close to each other, when he hugged her, it just didn't mean the same to him. He didn't want her, not like that. She felt embarrassed, but also certain; sure of what she needed to do. It had been an amazing month and she'd sorted herself out, like she'd needed to. Hell, it had been five weeks of no drugs and hardly any hangovers, she was practically in rehab. She'd put on a bit of weight and she looked better, even she could see that. *Claire will approve,* she thought.

When she got back to London she'd sort out her flat, organise everything properly, and live like a grown-up. It was exciting, the thought of taking control of her life again. She could pick up her career, at least that's what Lydia and Warren had said, she could go back to Spectrum and work her way back into Emma's good books; she was good at that job. A few years and she'd get a break on a production; she wouldn't have to be an assistant forever.

181

Nina was right, they were too old to 'be whatever they wanted to be' now; it was already decided, all plotted out ahead of them. They could fight it, try and start a new path, do something random, or they could continue on the track they'd already headed down and actually make some progress. The surge of excitement began to give way to, what, acceptance? Her life wasn't going to be extraordinary; it was just another, normal life and that was fine – she was lucky really. She had a good life in London – she just needed to manage it better.

Tom stayed in the water while Lucy headed back for the beach, to their bags and towels. She pulled the band from her ponytail, tipping her head forward to shake seawater from her hair. The water had revitalised her, she felt good – and hungry, she realised, really, really hungry.

Tara was waiting tables when Lucy arrived at the café. She smiled at Jen behind the counter and headed for the terrace, quickly, trying to limit the drips from her wetsuit. Outside she sat at the smallest table in the corner and read the menu like it was an erotic novel – salivating at the thought of all the food.

'Hey, Lucy,' Tara stood, pen and pad in hand, ready to take her order. 'What'll it be?'

'I'll have "Stef's brunch",' Lucy said, pointing at the boxed special on the menu.

'Cool,' Tara made a note. 'How was the surf?'

'Surf was good, so I'm told,' Lucy said. 'I was a disaster, utterly crap.'

Tara laughed as she walked away. Lucy texted Tom to let him know she'd ordered brunch, to see if he wanted to join her.

A few minutes later he pulled a chair up at her table, sopping wet from the sea.

'You left quickly,' he said, casually. 'I didn't mean to piss you off.'

'You didn't,' she lied. 'I was just hungry.'

'That looks good,' Tom said, picking up a piece of avocado from her plate and popping it into his mouth.

'Olly!' he shouted, his mouth full. Lucy grimaced at his table manners.

'Alright, mate?' Olly walked over and grabbed another chair.

'Can I just –' he leant over and picked up a piece of bacon from Lucy's plate as if it were totally normal. Lucy gave her best exasperated sigh and pushed her plate into the centre of the table.

Olly and Tom began analysing the morning's waves, predicting where the best surf would be tomorrow – Newquay, apparently.

'I'm just going to go and make a call,' Lucy said, standing up.

'Are you finished with this?' Olly gestured towards her plate.

'Help yourself,' she replied, as he tucked into the rest of her brunch. She wondered how she'd found him so attractive when she first saw him. *I guess personality really does matter*, she thought as she walked away. She looked back at Tom, who looked so handsome next to Olly, and a surge of love for him rushed over her before she could bat it away and lock it up again. She realised how much she was going to miss him.

She had a couple of hours until Warren and Charlie arrived but she needed to get back and get a shower. She walked up towards the house with her wetsuit peeled down to her waist, sweating in the sun. Tom had said that her friends could have the pool house, so she would check the beds were made in there. She walked to the bottom of the garden and onto the creaking wooden steps. She and Tom had spent so many nights in here after drinking on the beach, scared to wake his parents in the main house. She opened the door and the smell of cushions and sunlight escaped, hitting her with a wave of memories. She pushed them aside, making her way inside. opening the windows in the bedrooms and pulling back billowing white curtains in the open-plan living and dining area. It was so warm in there, the heat of the whole summer trapped within the wooden walls. Lucy stepped out of her wetsuit, now bone- dry from the sun, and hung it over the veranda at the back, the sea view stretching out ahead of her and a cool breeze cooling her scorching skin. She closed her eyes momentarily and took in the scent of the sea, the salty fresh air.

The beds were made – Tom must have done it already. The place looked lovely. Warren and Charlie would love it, she thought.

She remembered she needed to make a call and headed into the main house in just a bikini, her bare feet cool on the wooden floors. She ran the shower in her en suite, picked up her phone from her bedside table and stepped out onto her balcony.

Lydia answered after just one ring.

'Tell me you're taking the job,' she said, flatly.

'Yes, I'm taking the job, yes please,' Lucy said, attempting enthusiasm. 'When can I start?'

32

'Luce!' Warren exclaimed, arms outstretched, as he stepped out of Charlie's BMW estate.

'Hey hey!' Lucy called back to him, walking towards him, before being grabbed into a bear hug. Warren pulled away from her and retrieved his aviators from his hair, arranging them carefully on his nose. Lucy stepped back and took in his outfit; he had clearly gone for a 'beach chic' look. His short shorts revealed fake-tanned legs and in one hand he clutched a straw fedora.

Charlie groaned as she got out of the driver's seat. 'What a fucking journey!' She reached into the back seat and dragged out her handbag. 'Six fucking hours that took, I'm knackered.'

'Didn't you share the driving?' Lucy asked, as she helped them take their huge cases from the boot.

'Well, that was the plan,' Charlie said, glaring unimpressed at Warren. 'Someone got so drunk last night they were still over the limit this morning.'

'I'm fine now!' Warren declared, 'I'm ready for a drink, actually.'

Charlie shot him a look, then turned to Lucy. 'Isn't he a dick?'

Lucy laughed. 'Come on,' she said. 'I'll show you around and introduce you to Tom.'

'Bloody hell, nice place,' Warren said, eyes roaming around the entrance hall and out to the garden.

'Yeah, this is Tom's parents' place, but they're not here,' Lucy said. 'But you're out in the pool house. I'll show you.'

'Oh stick us in the shed, nice,' Charlie said, only half joking, Lucy thought.

'It's really not a shed,' Lucy said, feeling slightly protective. She pointed out the kitchen as they made their way out into the garden.

'Bloody hell, what a view,' Warren said, stopping at the sight of the sea while Charlie barely paused. 'Yeah, nice,' she said, disinterestedly.

'Here we are,' Lucy said, stepping into the pool house, as Warren and Charlie dropped their cases on the veranda.

'Oh this is great,' Warren said, visibly impressed. 'You didn't make it sound this nice.'

'Yeah, it's lovely, thanks Lucy,' Charlie said, as she slumped onto a chair, letting her head fall back, and closing her eyes.

'I'm not sure where Tom is, but I'll go and find him in a bit,' Lucy said. 'Do you want to get showered and settle in a bit?'

'Sounds good,' Charlie said, eyes still closed. Warren was pacing around excitedly, opening drawers and cupboards.

Lucy found Tom in the kitchen, sitting on a stool at the breakfast bar.

'Your friends here?' he asked, looking up at her. He looked like he'd stepped straight out of the shower, wet hair, bare-chested, a towel around his waist.

'Yeah, they're settling in,' she said, helping herself to a glass of water and downing it.

'What do you want to do this evening?' Tom asked. 'Do they fancy dinner at mine? My treat.'

'Ah that's lovely,' Lucy said. 'I'll ask them.'

She sat next to him and he surprised her by resting his head on her shoulder.

'I'm knackered,' he said. 'Getting old.'

Lucy laughed gently. 'You work too hard,' she said. The weight of him on her was comforting, making her feel suddenly sleepy too.

He lifted his head and looked at her, smiling. 'I'll come and say hello in a bit. Might just put some clothes on first.'

'Good idea,' Lucy said, struggling not to look at his naked chest.

'Is Tara okay?' she asked, surprising herself with the words.

'What do you mean?' Tom said.

'She just seemed a bit on edge the other day when we went out.'

'Ah, your little girls' trip to the island? She loved that.'

'Yeah, she was kind of, I don't know, jumpy?'

'What did she say?'

'She didn't really say anything. She thought she'd seen someone, but that it wasn't them or something. It was a bit odd.'

'Shit,' Tom said quietly.

'What is it? Is there something going on? Annabel said she's not really called Tara.'

'She's such a troublemaker – it's none of her business.'

'What isn't?' Lucy was beginning to get frustrated.

'Tara's ex. He's a nasty piece of work. Aggressive, controlling. She never wanted him to know she was here. But we think he's always known.'

'How would he know?' Lucy asked.

'I don't know, but I thought I saw him again the other week, and now this. Maybe he does know and maybe he's actually here.'

'Poor Tara,' Lucy wondered why she hadn't told her herself.

'She's mortified by the whole thing,' Tom said, as if reading her mind. 'She doesn't like the drama and she never wanted everyone knowing. I told most of the younger lot in the town when he first started sniffing around a few months after she moved here. Just asked that they didn't talk to strangers who asked where she was. Fucking Annabel, she's such a shit-stirrer.'

Lucy felt embarrassed again at how much she'd idolised Annabel.

'So she is actually Tamara?'

'She started using Tara when she moved down here, yeah,' Tom said, reaching for his phone. 'I'm going to give her a call. Do you mind?'

Lucy waved him away, shaking her head. He made his way up the stairs and she could hear his concerned tone drifting away.

'Poor Tara' she thought again. It sounded like a horrible situation. And if she really had seen him that evening then she must be bloody scared. She wondered what the guy was playing at. It couldn't be that difficult to track her down if he already knew she was here. It was a small place and she worked in the busiest business in town. The thought that he was biding his time was even more sinister.

'Have you got wine?' It was Charlie, peering around the kitchen door. She'd changed into a beach dress now, her hair tied up in a bun.

'Oh there's always wine,' Lucy said, her mind still on Tara. She poured a glass for each of them, and then for Warren as he appeared in a Breton-striped top and white shorts, aviators still on indoors.

They took their drinks outside and sat by the pool, chairs facing out to sea.

'Hi everyone,' Tom walked out and joined them, beer in hand, top on now. He shook hands and chatted to them about their drive, about London, about Spectrum. Lucy felt slightly on edge, watching her worlds collide like this, but it was going well. Tom made conversation easily and she could tell that Warren and Charlie both liked him.

He invited them down for dinner at the Beach Café and they arranged a table for 8pm. Tom made his excuses and left for work. He squeezed Lucy's arm as he left, causing Warren to give her a look that seemed to convey something between knowing and jealousy.

'He is fit,' he confirmed, once Tom was out of earshot.

'He's your ex?' Charlie questioned. 'Are you fucking crazy? I would be all over that.'

'That was a long time ago,' Lucy said, longing to change the subject. 'I accepted my old job back, by the way. I'll be back in a couple of weeks.'

'Oh my days! Amazing scenes!' Warren had leapt to his feet and was careering towards her to grab her.

'Great news,' Charlie said. 'I'll drink to that.'

They'd made their way through two bottles of wine in a frighteningly short amount of time and Lucy could feel her head rushing. The light was beginning to fade and she thought she ought to get changed into something nicer for dinner, but couldn't find the enthusiasm.

'Fancy a party treat?' Warren said, mischievously. Lucy's heart raced at the thought. She hadn't touched anything since she'd been down here.

'I don't know,' she hesitated.

'Oh, what?!' Warren exclaimed theatrically. 'Where's Lucy gone? Who is this imposter?'

Charlie laughed. 'Don't be a drag,' she said, following Warren back to the pool house.

Lucy was torn. The thought of the immediate rush was beyond tempting – she'd never turned it down before. But she'd felt a better person these last few weeks, and the thought of doing it in Tom's house made her feel queasy. It just wasn't right.

'Honestly, I'm alright thanks. You guys go ahead. I'll wait here.'

Warren and Charlie looked back at her in disbelief, then disappeared into the pool house, closing the door.

At the restaurant Tom had reserved them the same table she'd sat at on her first night back here. Warren and Charlie were buzzing, excited by the place, but even more so by the wine list.

'Let's get two bottles of prosecco,' Charlie announced. Lucy wondered if she actually wanted to drink any more.

She looked at the food menu, trying to decide between crab or lobster. 'Shall we get a load of things to share?' she suggested.

'Oh. I'm not really hungry,' Warren said, and Charlie murmured in agreement. Lucy knew it was the coke and she was pissed off with them. This was Tom's treat, his way of welcoming them, and they weren't even going to eat his food.

Charlie excused herself to go to the bathroom and Warren passed her a tiny parcel wrapped in clingfilm. Lucy couldn't believe how blatant it was. She cringed at the thought of how many times she'd done things like that, how discreet she'd thought she was being and how many people must have known.

'Well, I'm hungry,' she said, without looking at Warren.

'You've put on weight,' he said. 'Maybe you've had too many pasties.'

Lucy blushed self-consciously, mortified.

'You look good, don't get me wrong,' Warren backpedaled, seemingly realising what he'd said. 'It suits you.'

'Thanks,' she said, her appetite now long gone.

They talked about work, about Emma's recent hysterics over a commissioning editor's decision to rename one of their shows. It was funny hearing about some of her old friends – it didn't sound like much had changed since she'd been gone. Warren and Charlie took it in turns to disappear to the toilets and as the evening went on they became increasingly poor company, each delivering rambling, self-aggrandising monologues and not listening to anything anyone else had to say. Lucy found herself stifling yawns and checking the time on her phone. Tom kept catching her eye and smiling at her as he dashed between tables, handing over steaming bowls of mussels and bottles of wine.

'Do you fancy a big cliff path walk tomorrow to the next beach?' Lucy asked Warren and Charlie.

'Yeah, sure,' Charlie shrugged, looking away.

'Another bottle?' Warren lifted an empty prosecco bottle and raised his eyebrow.

'Yeah,' Charlie said. 'And we ought to buy some drinks to take back with us too.'

'The Spar shop's shut,' Lucy said, wondering how they were contemplating drinking even more. She felt drunk and exhausted.

'Oh God. We really are in the sticks, aren't we?' Charlie said, unimpressed. 'It's 10:30pm and everything's closed.'

Lucy chewed her final mouthful of bread and butter and finished her glass of prosecco, the bubbles burning her throat.

'I think I'm done, guys,' she said, waiting for the backlash.

'No worries,' Charlie said, looking at Warren. 'We'll finish up here and make our own way back. Hang on, do you have taxis here?'

'Yes, we have taxis,' Lucy said. 'I'll ask Tom to call you one.'

'Sure we can't tempt you with a little pick-me-up?' Warren pulled a sad face. 'You just need a second wind.'

Lucy couldn't think of anything worse. 'I'm alright, thanks. I'll see you back there, unless you just want to come with me now.'

'You're so lame!' Charlie exclaimed, pulling a cigarette packet from her bag. 'It's our first night.'

'I know,' Lucy said. 'I've got a bit of a headache, sorry,' she lied.

'Can I have an ashtray?' Charlie was leaning back over her chair, asking Jen.

'I'll see you later,' Lucy leant in and kissed them both good-night.

Tom was by the counter ringing a bill through the till. He looked tired too. 'I'm off,' Lucy said. 'Can you sort them out with a cab? They're on a bit of a mission and I'm really not in the mood.'

'No problem. You okay?' Tom held her eye as she told him she was fine, 'Just tired.'

'They're exactly what I expected,' he said, smiling at her mischievously. 'Media wankers.'

'They're not wankers,' Lucy tried to sound cross, but she secretly agreed with him. 'They're just drunk.'

'Okay, I'll give them the benefit of the doubt.' Tom made his way back into the hustle and bustle of the restaurant, brushing past Lucy and sending a shiver down her spine.

'I need to pay up, for all the wine,' she said, searching for her wallet in her handbag.

'I said it's on me,' he said, 'So consider it sorted.'

'Thanks, Tom,' she said, embarrassed all over again at the lack of food ordered, and the amount of alcohol. It seemed so rude.

'I'll see you later,' he said. He leant towards her and kissed her softly on the cheek, pausing a moment before he pulled away. Lucy froze on the spot, unsure if she was physically capable of moving like a normal person. She couldn't look at him, felt herself burn up with embarrassment and mumbled a goodbye, disappearing out the door and onto the street.

33

Nina let herself into Lucy's room, putting a cup of tea down on her bedside table and sitting on her bed.

'Morning,' she said. 'You okay?'

Nina and Kristian hadn't returned when Lucy had dragged herself to bed last night.

'I'm fine,' she groaned, stretching a yawn out and propping herself up. 'How was Bristol?'

'It was good, we stayed an extra night,' Nina said, pausing. 'In fact, it was great, we've found a place, Luce, it's perfect – the one I showed you, out by the golf club.'

'Amazing. I'm so pleased for you guys,' Lucy said, rubbing Nina's arm.

'Plenty of spare room for you to come and stay,' Nina said. 'And Tom. I don't want this to be the last time we all spend so much time together, I've had the best summer.'

'Me too,' Lucy said. 'I can't believe it's gone so quickly.'

'You do promise, don't you?' Nina said, more seriously than Lucy was used to. 'You promise you're not just going to disappear when you go back? I need you, Luce.'

Lucy felt horrible that Nina thought her capable of abandoning her now, after the last month, especially with her being pregnant.

'I absolutely promise,' she said.

'Oh God, are your friends here? Sorry, I meant to text last night,' Nina looked embarrassed to have forgotten.

'Yeah, they arrived yesterday,' Lucy said, remembering how disappointing last night had been and trying to push the thought away. 'I think we are going to go out for a big walk today if you fancy it?'

'Sounds lovely,' Nina said, 'Warren and Charlie, right? Did you guys have fun last night? What did you do?'

'We went for dinner,' Lucy said. 'It was nice to catch up.'

'I'm looking forward to meeting them. Tom and Kristian have gone surfing already – amazing waves first thing, apparently,' she rolled her eyes. 'I'll go and make us all breakfast, shall I?'

'That'd be lovely, thanks, Nin. I'll get a shower and see you downstairs.'

Lucy left her hair to dry naturally – the sun was hot already and she figured breakfast on the terrace would probably be enough to sort it out. She headed downstairs and out into the garden to the pool house. The door was closed and the curtains pulled. She thought about knocking but let herself in. The smell of alcohol hit her first, wine and spirits, and then cigarettes. They must have been smoking in here. The stench was awful. Anger rose in her chest – it just seemed so disrespectful to smoke in someone else's home. She knocked on the first bedroom door; there was no answer. She walked to the second bedroom and the door was slightly ajar – she knocked gently and pushed it open to reveal Warren on top of the bed in the same t-shirt he'd been in at dinner and nothing else.

'Warren!' she exclaimed involuntarily.

'Urh, what?' he replied with his eyes still closed. Lucy picked up a towel from the back of a chair and threw it over him.

'What time is it?' he asked. Lucy checked her phone.

'It's nearly 10am,' she said. 'Are you going to get up soon? Breakfast is ready.'

'Oh God, no,' he groaned, 'We only went to bed a few hours ago. I feel awful. I need to sleep.'

He still hadn't opened his eyes and Lucy felt a rush of disappointment in him.

'Fine,' she said, leaving his room and stepping back into the main living area. She couldn't let Tom see it like this – it was embarrassing. She set about clearing bottles and glasses. She moved a pile of magazines and found a makeshift ashtray full of cigarette butts. She threw open the windows and the front door and hoped that fresh air would be enough to revive the place.

'All okay?' Nina was standing on the terrace with a plate of bacon as Lucy walked back through the garden.

'Yeah, fine, they're having a lie-in,' she said, embarrassed by her friends.

'Oh right, okay,' Nina said, possibly sensing Lucy's suppressed anger. 'Well breakfast is ready – help yourself.'

They sat and ate. Nina was so excited by the house she and Kristian had found. It cheered Lucy up to see her light up like this. Lucy kept sneaking a look at the time on her phone, willing Warren and Charlie to sort themselves out and join them here for some food, to meet Nina, to just be bloody normal. But it was becoming clear that it wasn't going to happen. Eventually Nina began to clear the table – she looked at her watch. 'God, it's half-eleven,' she said, looking worried. 'I hate wasting a day – what are we going to do?'

'I'll go and give them a knock in a sec,' Lucy said, trying not to visibly deflate at the thought. 'If they're still out of action, let's just go the two of us.'

As she'd feared and expected, the pool house was in the same state that she'd left it in, although the stench did seem to be lifting with the flow of fresh air running through the place now. Lucy went to knock again on the bedroom doors, but couldn't face it. She remembered those hangovers, the comedowns. Warren and Charlie would be terrible company even if they could drag themselves out of bed. She'd go without them, text them to tell them where she was and hopefully they'd be in a better state later on.

Lucy's phone beeped as she and Nina were walking back towards Hideaway, the cliff path opening up as they turned the corner towards the bay, revealing the island and the beach. It was Warren.

Sorry, all sorted now. Fancy a late lunch? Thought we'd get a taxi into town.

It was 3pm and she'd already had lunch at the pub in Camel Cove with Nina.

Let me know when you're down there and I'll meet you at the café, she replied. She should've called them, explained that they could take the path from the bottom of the garden down to the town, but she couldn't be bothered. She was trying to shrug off her anger towards them, but her stubbornness was making it difficult.

She and Nina got themselves a table at the café and ordered lattes from Tara, who hugged them both before they sat down.

'Tom told me about Tara's ex,' Lucy said, remembering with surprise that she hadn't discussed it with Nina yet.

'What about her ex?' Nina said, looking at the menu, somehow hungry again despite the huge lunch they'd devoured a few hours ago.

'He sounds a bit stalkerish,' Lucy said, surprised by her reaction.

'Oh right.'

'Did you not know?'

'No, Tom's never mentioned it. Although, come to think of it, Kristian's said a few odd things about her over the years. I just figured he'd got the wrong end of the stick or something.'

Tara returned to the table with their drinks and Warren and Charlie appeared behind her, both wearing sunglasses and looking very rough.

Lucy stood, 'Nina, this is Warren and Charlie.'

They shook hands and Warren and Charlie sat down, Warren

groaned as he attempted to remove his sunglasses before promptly putting them back on.

'Nice to meet you,' Nina said. 'Big night last night?'

'Yeah,' Charlie laughed. 'I need some food.'

Tara took their orders and Nina began asking them about themselves, about where they lived in London, about their work. Warren and Charlie were polite, but short on conversation, clearly both struggling with their hangovers.

'I might have a bloody Mary,' Charlie said.

'Great idea,' Warren replied.

Lucy groaned internally.

The late lunch seemed to perk them up a bit. Lucy kissed Nina goodbye as she headed back to the house for a rest. Warren and Charlie wanted to explore the town a bit, so they walked through the cobbled streets slowly.

'Oh my God, so much shit,' Charlie said as they walked past a shop selling practical jokes, novelty t-shirts and sticks of rock.

'It's kind of cute, I think,' Warren said charitably.

'It's sweet,' Charlie agreed. 'But it's like something from three hundred years ago. I could never live somewhere like this. What do you actually *do* here?' she turned to Lucy.

'I don't know,' Lucy said. 'It's different to London, but it's just a different way of life.' She felt the clichés fall out of her mouth and cringed a little.

'Hmmm, it's giving me cabin fever,' Charlie said. Lucy was beginning to tire of her rudeness.

'Ere, Lucy, good mornin', my lover!' Louie was about to jump into his packed boat.

'Hiya, how are you doing?' she called over. 'These are my friends, Warren and Charlie.'

'Nice to meet you all.' Louie outstretched a hand towards them, which they shook in turn.

'You gang down for the Sundowner, I spose? Well I better geddon. I'll see you later, my love.'

'Bye, Louie, have a good one.' Lucy gestured to his boat, full of passengers applying sun cream and peering over the edges to look at the glistening water.

Lucy turned back to her friends, who were sniggering now. 'What?' Lucy said, pissed off now.

'That was hilarious,' Warren said. 'A proper Cornish bumpkin. Oh my God, amazing.'

He and Charlie hadn't looked so animated since last night, when they were off their faces on coke.

Lucy wanted to hit him.

'What's the Sundowner?' Charlie asked, once she'd pulled herself together.

'Nothing,' Lucy said. 'It's nothing.'

The group ate dinner together on the terrace. Tom cooked a ham and Kristian made a load of salads, while the girls and Warren chatted and watched the sunset.

'We're very glad to be having her back,' Warren said, smiling at Lucy and then Nina.

'What, in London?' Nina said, looking at Lucy. Lucy felt her heart sink. She should have told them all properly about her return to Spectrum. They shouldn't be finding out like this.

'No to work,' Charlie laughed. 'When do you actually start?'

'What's that?' Kristian was stood by Nina now, one arm draped around her neck, the other holding a plate of Greek salad.

'Lucy's going back to her old job,' Nina said, holding Lucy's gaze.

'You're what?' Kristian said. 'Seriously?'

'Yeah,' Lucy said, trying to sound breezy. 'It's great. I can't wait.' She felt sad at how little she meant this. The last couple of days with Warren and Charlie had had the complete opposite effect to what she'd expected.

'Have you told Tom?' Nina asked. Lucy couldn't look at her friend any more, afraid she'd see the truth about her feelings.

'No, not yet. Can I tell him? Actually, can we not talk about it tonight? I'll tell him myself.'

Warren and Charlie pulled confused expressions and shrugged. Nina and Kristian didn't answer.

Dinner was pleasant. Warren and Charlie went easy on the wine and were better company than the night before. They told endless stories about Spectrum, though they didn't let Lucy's return slip in front of Tom. Lucy watched her friends graciously listen to one long-winded tale after another about a bunch of people they'd never met, about a world they didn't know. Lucy wondered whether tonight had done much to counteract the media-wanker label Tom had given them yesterday and doubted it. As they cleared everything away and said goodnight she realised that Warren and Charlie hadn't asked a single question about anyone else.

34

Lucy was surprised the next morning to find Warren and Charlie dressed and ready for breakfast when she opened the door and stepped into the garden. The pool house door was open and it looked tidy inside. There were cases on the veranda, she noticed.

'We're going to head off this morning,' Warren said, looking a little sheepish.

'What? You've only been here two nights,' Lucy said, surprised but slightly delighted.

'We just thought we ought to get back, thinking about it. We should probably be at work tomorrow. They're really busy there with the new commission.'

'But you've booked it off as holiday,' Lucy said, confused.

'Yeah,' Charlie said, 'but apparently they're mad busy there, and…' She paused as if searching for something to say. 'Well, we just thought we'd get back, really.'

'It's been fab,' Warren said, hugging her. 'Seriously, can't wait to have you back.'

'Will you have breakfast?' Lucy asked.

'No I think we'll beat the rush hour and head off now,' Charlie said, flicking her car key in her fingers.

Lucy laughed inside at the notion of a rush hour here, offered to help them to their car and kissed them goodbye. It was worrying how relieved she was to see them drive off, but it felt like peace had been restored as the electronic gate closed smoothly behind them. She thought she could see them laughing as they sped off, but she could only see their silhouettes – maybe she was imagining it.

When she told the others at breakfast they seemed a bit surprised, but not too put out. It had been an odd couple of days and Lucy felt a residual embarrassment from the whole thing. Kristian pulled her to one side after breakfast and asked if she could help him now that she had an unexpected free day, and Lucy agreed, happy for the distraction.

Nina found her sitting on the edge of the pool, with her feet in the water.

'I'm going in to Truro in a bit – need some bloody maternity jeans. Fancy joining me?'

'I can't,' Lucy said, reaching for her tea and searching for an excuse. 'Tom's roped me in for a shift at the café.'

'It's going to be fucking hideous in town, isn't it, in this heat? Oh well, I literally can't get into my clothes any more, so I'll just grin and bear it.'

'`Don't get angry with people,' Lucy could picture the scene.

'I'll try my best,' Nina said. 'I wish you could come. I need to talk to you about Kristian – he is being so bloody weird at the moment. I think he's stressed about the move, but he won't talk to me like a normal person,' Nina got up with a groan.

Lucy sipped her tea and looked down over the beach as the realisation that she needed to tell Tom that she was going back to her old job began to weigh on her mind. She tried to tell herself he'd be supportive of her decision, but couldn't make herself really believe it. He was due to be in the café this morning. She remembered, suddenly, that she hadn't told Claire yet either; she'd call her on the way down to town.

'Morning,' Molly raised a coffee as a greeting in Lucy's direction. She looked harassed – the café was busy.

'Morning, Molly,' Lucy said, looking around for Tom.

Claire had sounded happy enough about Lucy's plan when she'd phoned her on the walk down to the café, although somewhat nonplussed, maybe. Lucy had heard Tim sounding miserable in the background, trying to get Claire off the phone. She'd asked her what Tom thought, which seemed strange to Lucy, since when was Tom her keeper?

There was no sign of Tom in the café. Lucy checked the terrace, weaving through tables full of people eating and ordering. She reached the stairs at the edge of the decking that ran down to the beach and heard a noise below. Walking down she caught sight of two figures, entwined, against the white wall. She could see Tara's hair knotted at the top of her head. She was pressed hard into a large, male figure in neon board shorts, whose hands were running all over her body, his face obscured by the angle of the wall. But she didn't need to see his face to know it was Tom – she recognised the neon-pink shorts, his surfer's physique. Her heart raced at the sight and she froze momentarily on the spot, praying they hadn't heard her coming down the steps. She turned, as soon as she had composed herself – how long had it taken? Minutes? Seconds? She walked back up the stairs, her heart pounding, legs jelly. It shouldn't have been such a shock. She'd known, really, all along, but seeing it with her own eyes – it felt like her heart was breaking.

She walked quickly back through the café, smiling at Jen, trying to look breezy. *Please don't mention I was here*, she thought, mortified at the prospect of Tom and Tara bonding over how awkward it all was, how pathetic she was. Back out on the street she realised she was red with embarrassment and wiped the sweat away from her hairline. She tried to push the image of the two of them away. Pulling her phone from her pocket she called Kristian.

'Luce, sorry, just out the water – are you still free?' He sounded so happy.

'Yep, free as a bird,' she said.

'Shall I meet you at the café?'

'No,' she said, slightly too quickly. 'I'll walk up to the house. I'll be half an hour,' she said, trusting that Kristian wouldn't have read much into her tone; she could count on him for that.

She walked so quickly back up to the house that she was out of breath halfway up the hill. She stopped to catch her breath, finding herself needing to bend over, as if she'd run it. Kristian appeared behind her, wetsuit on and a huge grin plastered on his face.

'Wow, need to work on your fitness,' he said, waiting by her side. 'You okay?'

'Fine,' Lucy said, her breath returning. 'Just took the hill too fast.'

'I just need to jump in the shower,' he said. 'I'm really sorry. I was going to come straight back after I spoke to you, but then –'

'You went back in? Don't worry.' Lucy smiled at Kristian's sincere face, still so boyish.

'Give me a knock when you're ready,' she said. 'Are we going to Truro? We need to be careful. You know that's where Nina's gone shopping don't you?' she asked him.

'How did you know I want to go to Truro?' he said, looking genuinely perplexed.

'Because I'm guessing you want me to help you pick a ring and despite this being the 'Champagne Coast' we aren't exactly spoilt with jewellery-shopping opportunities around here.' Lucy looked at him, so sure she was right.

'You haven't mentioned it to her, have you?' She looked a bit disappointed, 'I really don't think she's expecting it.'

'She's not,' Lucy said. 'She's pissed off with you acting all strange – she thinks you're nervous about the move. She doesn't have a clue.' She loved seeing Kristian's face light up with the affirmation.

Still such a nice boy, a gentle giant – he was huge, she noticed all over again, six-foot something; a big beast of a man.

In the car Kristian quizzed Lucy about just how sure she was that Nina didn't suspect his proposal was on the cards. Lucy was glad of the distraction from what she'd seen at the café and genuinely thrilled by the prospect of Kristian asking Nina to marry him. She knew from their late-night conversations that Nina had all but given up on the idea – she'd always been uncharacteristically un-pushy about the whole thing. Lucy had noticed it before. It turned out it was one of a very small number of things Nina cared so deeply about that she didn't want to meddle with it. She really wanted the magic of a genuine proposal, not one of those 'oh go on then' marriages, where the guy finally relents – she wanted the fairytale. Lucy loved that about Nina. She knew people could find her abrasive, hard even, but she wasn't, not at all really. She had a wicked sense of humour and a bit of a mouth on her when cross, but she was a good person. That's what she'd learned about her old friends, being back in Cornwall, maybe about the town itself. There was a sense of wholeness and goodness that she'd missed in London. Maybe she was simplifying things, buying into the Corny-ishness of the place, but she didn't think so. There was something special down here.

'That one,' Kristian said firmly to Lucy, pointing at a single sapphire on a gold band. 'That's it.'

Lucy leant in to look closer. It was beautiful, although not your typical engagement ring, she pointed out to Kristian. But certainly undeniably beautiful.

'Nina's not your typical girl, I guess' Kristian said, pride in his voice. 'She'll love this.'

He was right. It was totally Nina's style; almost vintage-looking, but new – and expensive. Bloody expensive.

'Three thousand pounds? Kristian, are you serious? How minted are you guys?'

'That's okay,' he said, quietly. 'She's worth far more than that to me and I've planned this for a long time.'

Lucy carried on inspecting the ring; its ornate settings glittered in the jeweller's bright display lights.

'Will you try it on?' he asked her, taking her by surprise.

'Um, yeah, course,' she said. 'I think we have the same ring size, actually.'

She slipped it on to her finger and suddenly thought she might cry. Kristian looked at her with something between confusion and sympathy on his face. This was probably up there with his worst nightmares, a girl about to cry in front of him and no one else to help.

'You're right,' she said. 'She'll love this – you should get it.' She slid the gold ring off her finger and placed it carefully back on the velvet stand, which the assistant whisked away silently.

'Are you okay?' Kristian said. 'I mean, I can see you're not. What's wrong? It's Tom, right? London? What is it?' He looked like he might cry himself, the earnest expression enough to make Lucy almost want to laugh.

'It's Tom,' she admitted. 'It's not a big deal. I just, I saw him with Tara earlier, I knew already, really, but, you know, seeing it, knowing for sure, it was just weird. I am being ridiculous.'

'Are you sure?' Kristian said, looking confused. 'I really don't think there's anything there. I mean, I've asked him and he said there isn't.'

'Maybe it's not a big thing, just a fling, whatever,' Lucy said. 'But I saw them – it's something.'

'I just thought it was you,' Kristian said, looking straight at Lucy. 'It was always you. He never got over it. I do know that. He never got over you.'

Lucy didn't know what to say. It was sweet of Kristian to try and make her feel better, but it wasn't going to work.

'I am seriously not going to let this become about me and Tom,' she said, pulling herself together as the shop assistant

205

returned to speak to Kristian. 'I'm so sorry. Do what you need to do – buy it, it's perfect. I'm so, so happy for you. I'll just be outside.' She walked out of the store, refusing to let tears fall, mortified that, yet again, she'd made a bloody scene.

What a fucking train wreck.

35

'Last day, huh?' Stefan was loading pallets of fish from the market in through the back door of the kitchen.

'Yep, that's right,' Lucy said, picking up a bag of mussels and lifting it onto the work surface.

'Who's covering your shifts, do you know?' he asked.

'Jen, I think,' Lucy said. 'I was just helping out. Tom always knew I was going.'

'Sure, yeah, I know. We'll miss you, though' Stefan said, beginning to prep the shellfish for his increasingly famous lobster special. 'Pass me that butter, will you?'

Tara was due in, but there was no sign of her yet. Lucy walked from table to table, slotting the freshly printed daily menus between the wooden salt-and-pepper shakers. She hadn't seen Tom last night, he'd not been there when she and Kristian got back from Truro; she hadn't heard him come home at all, in fact. She thought back to the sight from the steps, the image making her stomach drop. She was glad it was her last day working here, glad to be going back to London now. Claire was collecting her keys from Anna today; she said she'd get the flat ready for Lucy's return on Wednesday. Lucy tried to tell her she didn't need to do anything, but Claire had been characteristically insistent about 'airing' it out or something; Lucy hadn't listened properly on the phone last night.

'So sorry,' Tara looked flustered, her hair loose around her shoulders. 'Overslept,' she said without looking at Lucy.

'Don't worry,' Lucy said. 'I think we're all set, I just need to go and pick up the scones.' She walked through the café towards the large glassy entrance, and out onto the street. Walking through town she smiled at the guys at the fruit-and-veg shop, and exchanged 'good mornings' with the ice-cream girl, whose name she really should've asked by now. It was strange, being surrounded by so many vaguely familiar faces. So many people from school had stayed, you couldn't take more than five steps without bumping into them, or their parents, or someone you half-recognised from childhood. She wasn't sure whether she felt more like an outsider here or in London. It was strange how neither was really home. She'd not let Claire book her train ticket back to London, despite her protests. Tom had paid her for all the hours she'd worked in the café, and it had ended up being a fair sum of money, not London money, but enough to pay for a standard-class train ticket and enough left over to get through the first week or so back in the flat. Lucy felt newly determined to not depend on Claire when she was back, not in the way she had before, at least. Lydia hadn't discussed salary with her. She assumed she'd be on the same wage as before, and maybe she'd be able to get an increase in six months or so.

The smell of freshly risen bread cloyed in the air of the bakery, unpleasant in the heat of the day. Martin recognised Lucy and dipped behind a counter to retrieve a tray of fruit and plain scones. Lucy could feel the heat coming from them as she thanked him and carried them out of the shop. Late August always saw an influx of university-age students descend on the town, staying at their parents' holiday homes, partying on the beach late into the night. Lucy passed a group of hung-over-looking girls in tiny shorts and bikini tops, drinking from coconut-juice cartons, all big shades and long limbs. At the entrance to the campsite, cars were pulling up to sign in at reception. More people than looked feasible, given the size of the car, piled out of an Audi TT. The driver, a young, good-looking brown-haired guy smiled at Lucy. She remembered how much promise this place had offered when she was young, how full of hope their summer evenings had been. So carefree. There was something about the beach that brought that out of everyone, made everyone young. She pictured her family home, sitting above them at the top of the valley, its stark white walls and dark-brown floorboards aching with years of emptiness. She wondered whether she should walk up there tonight, take one last look before she went home.

Tara was at the counter when Lucy got back to the café, folding napkins and enjoying a rare quiet moment.

'Tom's on his way down,' she said. 'He's just at the cash and carry.'

'Oh right,' Lucy replied, she hadn't realised she was going to see them both today. She wasn't sure how she felt about it.

'There's something I want to talk to you about, actually,' Tara said, continuing to pile navy napkins into a wicker basket.

Lucy felt her pulse rate rise slightly. *You don't need to do this*, she thought. She felt sorry for Tara – it wasn't her mess, she hadn't actually don't anything wrong. The thought was inter-rupted by a hand on Lucy's waist. She turned to see Annabel.

'Hey,' Lucy said. 'How are you doing?'

'I'm good,' Annabel said. 'I just wanted to pop by. Tom said it's your last day today.'

'Yep,' Lucy said. She'd forgotten what it was like to live some-where where everyone knew your news – and where they seemed to care.

'You make sure you come back and see us again soon, okay?' Annabel said, pulling her into a hug. 'And bring that sister of yours next time.'

'Let me get you a coffee,' Tara said. 'On the house.'

Annabel shot her an unmistakably filthy glance and looked back to Lucy. 'I need to open up the shop. You take care Lucy, look after yourself.'

'What was that about?' Lucy turned to Tara. 'Do you know Annabel?

'Yeah,' Tara said. 'She doesn't like me. She's been the worst of everyone – ever since I moved here.'

Given her previous conversations with Annabel and Tom, Lucy was contemplating asking Tara what had been going on when Tom arrived with boxes piled under his arms. He looked exhausted.

'Are you okay?' Tara asked him. 'Do you want some help bringing stuff in?'

'No, no, it's fine, cheers. Hey, Luce,' he turned to her and smiled.

'Hey,' she said. 'We missed you last night.' It was true. They'd waited around for him and hadn't cooked dinner until 9pm in the end. 'No one could get hold of you.'

She felt Tara shift her weight awkwardly next to her.

'Anyway, I need to sort these out' she said, nodding towards the scones on the side. 'And there's loads to get ready for tonight.'

Tom was hosting the late-summer Sundowner party at the café for the first time this year. It had always been at the campsite until now. It had been Stefan's idea, the chef himself told Lucy proudly. He was going to run a huge barbecue stand on the terrace, people could take food down to the beach from there and he was making toasting sticks of strawberries, marshmallows and chocolate for kids to toast on the enormous bonfire that they lit for the event on the beach.

Tom dumped pile after pile of outdoor fairy lighting at the back door of the kitchen, ready to be strung around the decking and down to the sand. A van was unloading DJ equipment around the front, whilst Tara moved tables and chairs to try and make space for the sound desk. Lucy was glad she was here for the Sundowner; it had always been her favourite night of the summer.

The town heaved with a younger crowd than usual in the days before the event – there was more of a buzz about the place, a sense of excitement. Tom looked nervous about it all, she couldn't help but notice. He could have done with his parents around to help him sometimes, she thought. It was a bit much carrying all of this on his own. She looked to her left to see Tara joining Tom at the strings of lights, helping him to untangle them, laughing together now. *Or not on his own*, she thought.

Her last day in the café went quickly, with the preparations underway for the evening's festivities. Stefan closed the kitchen at 2pm, so the rest of the afternoon was just a scone-fest; easy-peasy compared to the past few weeks. An astonishing amount of alcohol continued to arrive throughout the afternoon: mini champagne bottles, crates of beer, pitchers of gin cocktails. Lucy served her last customers and joined Nina and Kristian outside as they hooked multi-coloured paper lanterns from the wooden banisters.

'I think he's mental,' Kristian carried on talking to Nina as Lucy sat down on a chair beside them.

'It's a great idea,' Nina said. 'It's going to look great out here when the sun goes down.'

'Do all the shops still put stalls outside?' Lucy asked, remembering how the streets used to fill with trestle tables, bunting zig-zagging from the shop roofs.

'I think so,' Nina said. 'We've not been here for the last few years, though.'

When she was a child, Lucy's dad had always brought them out to the Sundowner and bought them a bag of fudge each to eat as they watched the bonfire spit embers into the sky. The same lady who had always served them still ran the sweetshop. Lucy had been so pleased when she spotted her in the shop, behind the same counter, the old rickety model of a farm girl still churning an urn of butter in the window. It was funny how, despite the massive leaps certain parts of the town had taken, the café being a prime example, so much of it was exactly as it always had been.

'Have you told Tom about Spectrum yet?' Nina asked, passing Lucy a pile of plastic cups to go on the table.

'No, haven't had a chance yet,' Lucy said. 'Have you told him you're sticking around for a few more weeks? He'll be made up.'

Nina and Kristian's new house wouldn't be signed and sealed until September, which meant they were effectively homeless, Nina had informed her last night. Another few weeks at Tom's wasn't a particularly hard life, as Kristian had pointed out, but Lucy could see that Nina was enjoying the drama of being pregnant and homeless. This development had put more pressure on Lucy to stay around for longer too, but everything was set for her return to Spectrum and she was starting to actually look forward to it – especially since seeing Tom and Tara with her own eyes. It had been helpful, in some ways, at least.

Lucy looked around at the café, the decking was covered in a canopy of tiny bulbs now. Nina was right, it was going to look spectacular tonight. The sound of the DJ checking his equipment boomed from inside and more and more young girls and guys in dark-blue polo shirts with white-stitched 'Beach Café' logos assembled at the tables inside, ready to take their instructions for the evening from Tom.

Lucy finished helping Nina and Kristian with the lanterns – hundreds of tiny coloured paper balls now hung around the decking. She needed to go back and get ready for the evening. Her hair felt limp, the back of her neck slightly damp with sweat. She wanted to enjoy her last few nights in Cornwall, to relax before going back to work. She'd tell Tom this evening about her job – he'd understand. In the storeroom she collected the few bits of clothing she'd accumulated over the past weeks: a cardigan she'd brought down in case it got cold in the evenings, never needed; a dress she'd thought she'd change into if Tom had asked her out for a drink after work, unworn. As she walked out into the warm evening air, towards Tom's house, she realised they'd not had the chat Tara wanted. She hoped the pair of them weren't going to make some formal announcement tonight in front of everyone, confirming their golden-couple status to the whole of the Champagne Coast.

36

The air was thick with the smell of barbecued food, hot bodies and after-sun lotion. Music played from the café; Lucy could feel it through the boards of the terrace under her feet. Stefan was in his element; she watched him dashing from the kitchen back to his barbecue, loading more and more meat and fish onto the huge grill. The place was heaving. Waiting staff delivered individual bottles of champagne to tables of locals; groups of tourists drank beers on the sand beneath the restaurant. The effect of the lights, so artfully installed by Tom, was stunning. Looking up, it appeared as if the entire sky was stitched together with fairy lights.

Lucy was wearing her coral dress, pulling at its hem from time to time, concerned that it was too short. Nina was eating a lobster roll, leaning on the banister next to her, giving a running commentary on the fashion choices of the people making their way from the beach to the café.

'Here comes Big Bird,' she pointed at a girl in an unflattering yellow dress.

'You're so mean,' Lucy poked Nina's arm. 'I don't know why I'm friends with you.'

'Because I'm fabulous,' Nina replied, a piece of lobster falling out of her mouth as she spoke.

'You're certainly something,' Lucy replied.

'Hello girls,' Tom put an arm around each of their shoulders. He was wearing a crisp white shirt, rolled up at the sleeves, his top two buttons undone, showing bronzed skin. He smelt divine, Lucy noticed, recognising the Hugo Boss cologne.

He had a mini Pommeroy champagne bottle in each hand and passed one to Lucy. She took a sip from the foil spout, bubbles fizzing in her mouth.

'It looks good, right?' Tom said, admiring his own handiwork.

'It looks brilliant,' Nina confirmed, 'And the food's great.'

'Are you off duty, then?' Lucy asked. He seemed so relaxed – he must be. There were certainly enough staff around to take care of things.

'I sure am,' he said. 'I'm going to enjoy myself tonight.'

Cheers came from the beach and Lucy leant over the banister to see the bonfire erupting into flames. Children were running around the sand with sparklers, looking like the 'what not to do' section of a firework safety advert.

'I'm going to find Kristian,' Nina said, balling up the napkin in her hand and tossing it into the bin. 'Have you seen him?'

'He was at the bar a minute ago,' Tom said.

Nina rolled her eyes in reply and left.

'Sure you want to leave this place?' Tom said loudly to Lucy, competing with the music booming from the speakers. Transfixed by the bonfire, she mumbled a response, before turning to meet his eye.

'It is beautiful here,' she said. 'I've had the best time down here, seeing everyone again, working here, it's been great.'

'You could stay,' he said. 'You don't have to go back. I know it's not much, but you could work here, you could be a manager, whatever. I can pay you properly. More, I mean. We don't close until October, we might not close at all this winter, actually. I told you Tara reckons we could stay open right through. I think she might be right – if we just change the menu a bit.'

'I've taken my old job back,' Lucy said, still watching the growing fire.

'You have to be joking!' Tom said, loudly. 'Spectrum? You can't go back there.'

'I don't really have a choice,' Lucy said, disappointed by his reaction. She wasn't in the mood to justify herself to him, and she didn't want tonight ruined by an argument.

'I don't think you should,' Tom said, he sounded deflated. 'But you know what we all think. Even Claire agrees.'

'You've spoken to Claire?' Lucy asked, blood rushing to her cheeks.

'Yes,' Tom admitted. 'A few times. She just wanted to know you were okay.'

Lucy didn't have anything to say, it was mortifying that Claire had been speaking to Tom like he was some kind of social worker.

'She says Anna would have stayed on in your flat if you wanted to stay down here a bit longer. You don't need to go back next week. Have you told her your plan? Your latest, brilliant, plan.' His tone was mocking now – she could have hit him.

'I don't want to stay down here,' Lucy snapped. 'Did you ever consider that? That I don't want to be around you, feeling the way I feel about you, while you and Tara run around having your secret little relationship. Playing the perfect couple. God, it's so embarrassing, Tom, can't you see that? I feel like a total fucking idiot for having come down here. For thinking that…' She stopped herself, furious that the words had fallen out before she could stop them. Furious that he'd pushed her to it.

She walked away, moving as quickly as she could into the bodies gathered by the outside bar, willing it to swallow her up. She moved fast through the crowd, towards the beach.

'Lucy, stop, please.' It was Tom; he had his hand around her wrist, trying to slow her down.

Lucy pulled away from him, determined to walk towards the

beach. She wanted to go home. She certainly didn't want a show-down here in front of the whole town.

'Tom, drop it,' she said firmly, stopping but not turning around to look at him.

'What did you mean about me and Tara?' he said, standing next to her now, trying to make her look at him.

'Nothing,' Lucy said, 'I just want to go back to the house, okay?'

'We're not a couple,' he said, insistently. 'Is that what you thought? Did you think I'd invite you down here to meet my new girlfriend?' He was almost laughing, which infuriated Lucy.

'It's up to you who you date,' she said insincerely, glancing at him briefly, seeing him smile at her.

'Oh, for goodness' sake, Luce,' he said, as he put his hands on her waist now. He stepped forward towards her body and she could feel the heat of his skin on hers.

'I saw you, together, at the café,' she said, close to tears. What was he doing this to her for?

'I don't know what you saw,' he said, stepping closer to her, 'but it wasn't me. I asked you to come back because I've never stopped thinking about you.' He leant in, his hands rising to hold her face and kissed her, hard on the mouth. Lucy's hands met his on her face and she kissed him back. They stood, lips touching, noses side by side, like that for what felt like minutes.

'I've wanted to do that since the moment I saw you again,' Tom whispered.

Lucy didn't know what to say, she kissed him again, his lips soft on hers. She ran her hand through his hair. He put his mouth to her ear. 'I love you, Lucy,' he whispered, 'I've always loved you.'

A solitary firework squealed and banged, chased by streams of smaller glittering trails into the sky. Tom and Lucy stood next to each other looking up at the sky, their bodies pressed into one another, their hands entwined. Lucy pulled hers away at the sight of Nina and Kristian approaching. Tom gave her a puzzled look as she let his fingers slip from hers.

'Top work, mate,' Kristian said, thrusting his hand into Tom's in a congratulatory handshake.

'I love fireworks,' Nina said loudly, competing with the bangs. The crowd at the café had shifted towards the edge of the terrace, hundreds of faces staring up at the fizzing neon sky. Down on the beach the group was surrounded by families, children on parents' shoulders pleading to be bought the fibre-optic wands for sale at the stall by the surf school.

Lucy's mind raced with thoughts of the kiss. She could feel the heat of Tom's body next to her now. *He loves me*, she ran the words over and over in her mind. She loved him – she'd realised that not long after she first saw him again. She'd never stopped loving him. As the fireworks climaxed and finished, the crowd seemed to loosen around her. She thought, too, of her return to London, looming in just a few days' time and tried to push away fresh question marks over just what the hell she should do. She stood, half-listening to her friends discussing the music, the beer, the crowds. Kristian had his big arms wrapped firmly around Nina's waist, holding her against him as she talked animatedly. Tom's arm grazed Lucy's side, making her skin tingle. She wanted to kiss him again.

They moved, in search of beer, towards the bonfire. Stefan's toasting sticks were being held towards the flames by happy-faced children. Lucy smiled at a girl with long blonde hair and a big gap-toothed grin of sheer, innocent joy. The cracking and banging of the bonfire was surprisingly loud. Lucy struggled to hear Nina's story about the man she'd met on the cliff path walk that morning, but grasped something about 'him looking like a paedo', so risked a laugh in acknowledgement, which seemed to satisfy her friend. Tom handed Lucy another champagne, brushing her hand and meeting her eye. Could Nina and Kristian see this, she wondered? She felt exposed and unsure why it would matter if they did notice what was going on, anyway. It had been so long since anyone had kissed Lucy, had held her, put their hands on her, desire swept through her at the thought of Tom, of going home with him tonight. She remembered the last time they'd spent the night together, the night before she'd left for London; how silent and intense it had been that night; how much they didn't say. She thought of Tom's body, his surfer's physique, the way his hands had felt on her waist, the anticipation of them on her bare skin. *He loves me*, the words ran over and over.

With the families beginning to drift back to their hotels and villas, the crowd on the beach was now mainly made up of groups of young people who'd had a few drinks and showed no signs of slowing down. From the café the music continued to get louder and in the dark of the night the DJ's lights now swept across the beach through the glass wall of the café. The four of them had found a quiet patch of beach where Kristian had put a blanket down for Nina to sit on; she insisted Lucy joined her so she didn't 'look like an invalid'.

'So?' Nina widened her eyes at Lucy.

'So, what?' Lucy replied, looking away.

'Oh come on, we saw you two on the beach. Took you long enough!'

'I don't know, Nin,' Lucy said, looking down at the sand. 'He said he still loves me.'

'Well, yeah, obviously, we all know that!' Nina said rolling her eyes. 'And you still love him, right?'

'Yeah, I do, it's ridiculous isn't it? After all this time. But I do.' Lucy could feel herself smiling at the thought of it all.

'It's not ridiculous, it's brilliant,' Nina said. 'Does this mean you're going to stay around down here?'

'Oh God, no. I mean, I don't know. I've just accepted my old job back. And I don't know what Tom's thinking about the future. It'd be pretty weird for me to just stay down here and be his girlfriend and basically regress to my sixteen-year-old self, wouldn't it?'

'I don't think it'd be weird,' Nina said, 'I think you were always

219

meant to be together and it's just taken you both a ridiculously long time to figure that out.'

Lucy saw Nina's face change, forming a grimace. She clutched her stomach and bent over slightly.

'Are you okay?' Lucy asked, worried.

Nina seemed to be catching her breath, breathing slowly in through her nose and out through her mouth. 'I'm fine,' she answered eventually, forcing a smile. 'I've been getting these weird pains. Apparently they're normal, but my God, they hurt.'

Kristian returned with two beers before Lucy could ask anything more. Nina gave her a look that she knew meant she shouldn't mention anything to Kristian. He passed a beer to Lucy.

'Can I borrow you a sec?' he asked Nina. She stood up and walked away with him towards the fire.

Tom sat down next to Lucy, his arm pressed against hers. He reached for her hand, and slipped his into hers on the sand.

'Guess tonight's a success, then,' Lucy said, looking around at the crowds of people drinking and dancing on the beach and on the café terrace.

'Yep, I guess it is,' Tom said, raising his beer to hers and clinking the glass bottle.

'We need to talk about what we're going to do,' he said, looking at her. 'You can't just go back to London.'

'I can't just stay,' Lucy said, with a sigh. She thought about her job, about walking back into the production office, and it felt a million miles away.

'We can talk about it tomorrow,' Tom said, looking out to sea now. 'I just want to enjoy tonight.'

Lucy didn't reply. She followed his gaze out to the ocean as a slight breeze swept over her face. The night sky was packed with stars, glittering in the darkness. The bonfire cracked and spluttered, its orange glow seeping into the sky around it. The DJ had moved onto the house section of his set and groups of people were dancing with their drinks in the air.

'Oh, my God,' Tom said, taking Lucy by surprise.

'What?' she said, panicked.

'Look, over there,' Tom pointed to the left of the fire.

'What?' Lucy repeated, no idea what she was supposed to be looking at.

'That's Kristian, isn't it?' Tom said, still pointing.

'Where? Where am I looking?' Suddenly Lucy realised where Tom was looking. A figure was at half height next to all the others, and it was Kristian. Tom was right. He was down on one knee, hand outstretched towards Nina.

Tom squeezed Lucy's hand in his. 'I can't believe it,' he said, leaning in to her ear.

'No,' Lucy said. 'When did we get so grown up?' She turned and kissed Tom lightly on the cheek.

'She said YES!' Kristian said, almost running back towards Lucy and Tom, with Nina following him, grinning.

'Congratulations, bud,' Tom stood and pulled him in for a big hug.

'Let's see,' Lucy held her hand towards Nina's to inspect the ring. 'Beautiful,' she smiled at her friend.

'Finally making an honest woman of her,' Kristian said, his arm around Nina's waist. He kissed her on the forehead and she smiled at him.

'I'm so happy for you guys,' Tom said.

'And we're happy for you two,' Kristian said, his eyes moving from Tom, to Lucy, and back. 'It's meant to be; this is what life's meant to be like.' He gestured to the scene around him.

Lucy paused for a moment. *He's right*, she thought, *this is what life is meant to be like.*

37

The next morning Lucy woke late, feeling a little delicate. She reached across her crisp white sheets for Tom, but there was no one beside her. She remembered their night together and smiled, pulling the sheets tightly over herself and stretching awake. Light poured through the curtains and music was playing downstairs. She must be the last one up, again, she thought. She showered and dressed, catching herself grinning in the bathroom mirror as she did her make-up. Being with Tom again felt new and exciting, totally right and somehow normal. She remembered, with a jolt, that she was booked on a train back to London in a couple of days, and pushed the thought away, unwilling to give up the feeling of total happiness that kept washing over her this morning.

Downstairs Lucy found Kristian outside reading the paper.

'Some absolutely classic letters in here this week,' he said to Lucy, as she sat down. The *Cornish Times* letters' page had provided them with endless entertainment as youngsters, the angry locals enraged by the pettiest issues.

'Where is everyone?' Lucy asked. She'd hoped they could all do something together today.

'Oh, Tom and Nina have gone on one of their walks,' Kristian said. 'I feel like death, couldn't face it. Tom wanted to let you sleep in.'

Lucy tried to hide her disappointment. 'Oh right,' she said. 'What are you doing then? Fancy breakfast somewhere?'

'If, by somewhere, you mean the Beach Café, then yes,' Kristian replied.

'Okay, let me grab my bag,' Lucy said, suddenly ravenous at the thought of a bacon sandwich.

The café was still partly decorated from the night before and hung-over teenagers were slowly taking down fairy lights and lanterns on the terrace. Inside had been deep-cleaned in the early hours and smelled like buttered toast after the morning breakfast rush. A few families were finishing cooked breakfasts, kids colouring in the pirate pictures on the backs of their menus with the little pots of crayons handed out to families. Lucy and Kristian chose a table by the window and Lucy collapsed into a cushioned chair with a groan.

'You feeling as bad as me?' Kristian asked.

'I'm not sure,' Lucy replied. 'Do you feel like you drank cotton wool all night, and maybe finished off with a few swigs of sandpaper? I need a coffee.'

'I need food,' Kristian said, thanking Molly for the menu she handed him.

'So,' he said, seriously all of a sudden. 'You and Tom, huh?'

'I'm more interested in you and Nina,' Lucy said. 'You know, the small matter of you guys getting engaged last night. What did you say?'

'I can't really remember, not exactly,' Kristian said. Lucy thought she might advise him not to tell their engagement story quite this way in front of Nina.

'I think I said, 'you are my whole world and I want you to be my wife'. It was something like that, anyway, but she said yes, and that's all that really matters.'

'It's very exciting,' Lucy said, scanning the menu, even though she knew she'd end up ordering a bacon sandwich. 'Do you think you might get married here or in Bristol?'

'I've got no idea. I imagine I'll have very little say. Have you met Nina?' He smirked and Lucy laughed.

Molly returned to take their order. 'Have you seen Tara?' she asked, after she'd finished writing on her pad.

'No, why?' Lucy asked, feeling guilty, though she had no idea why.

'She was meant to be here to open up,' Molly said. 'It's fine, I've got a set of keys, but it's just pretty busy. I'm not sure how lunch service is going to go without her.' She looked very concerned, her little brown bob framing a furrowed brow.

'That's not like Tara,' Kristian said. 'Have you called Tom?'

'No,' Molly said. 'I don't like to bother him. Tara always says not to bother him.'

'You can't do lunch on your own here,' Lucy said, 'I'll help you, but I think we ought to track Tara down. It's weird that she's just disappeared.'

'Yeah, she's not answering her phone,' Molly said. 'Anyway, let me get these over to Stef.' She raised her pad and walked away towards the kitchen.

'Stef must be absolutely hanging,' Kristian said. 'Did you see him dancing at the end of the night? I mean the guy doesn't normally like speaking to people, but he was out there throwing shapes and downing jaeger bombs. I prefer drunk Stefan, for sure.'

Lucy nodded in agreement, her mind elsewhere now with the mystery of Tara's no-show at work. She's probably just hung over, she tried to tell herself, but something in her gut told her there needed to be a better reason for her to let Molly down, to let Tom and the café down. It just wasn't her style, and she remembered Tom telling her about Tara's troubles with her ex. She wondered suddenly, irrationally, whether she'd seen Tom and Lucy's kiss, if she'd run away upset at the sight of them back together. She felt guilty, as if she'd done something wrong, but she hadn't. Tom and Tara weren't a couple, that's what he'd said. And anyway, there was almost no chance Tara had seen anything anyway. Something just felt wrong. Lucy couldn't put her finger on it.

The bacon sandwich really helped Lucy's hangover and Kristian seemed to be coming back to life too after his huge cooked breakfast. Lucy had never seen one person eat so much food. Molly cleared their table, still looking fraught; there was no sign of Tara and she still hadn't answered her phone. Lucy, with her renewed enthusiasm for the day, offered to help Molly out in the café, which was heaving now.

'I called Jen,' Molly said. 'She's coming in, so you don't need to work, but thanks, Lucy.'

'Oh, okay,' Lucy said. 'I think I'm going to walk up to Tara's, then, just to check she's okay.'

'Yeah, I'll come with you,' Kristian said. Lucy was surprised by how concerned he seemed. She hadn't realised he was close to Tara. Perhaps he knew her story; Tom may well have told him everything.

As they walked through the town Kristian told Lucy about his job in Bristol, about their new house, about their favourite Thai restaurant. Lucy felt the fondness for Kristian that she'd had since they first met in a maths class at school, when he'd sat down next to her, all floppy hair and big eyes, flustered because he hadn't done his homework. Lucy had let him copy hers over the course of the lesson; by the end of class he had homework to hand in and she had a new friend. It was Kristian who had introduced Lucy to Tom, they'd been friends since primary school. Lucy remembered the first times they'd all hung out together, so young, all the funny things they'd done together. They'd loved going on long bike rides out into the country; she remembered one that had ended with them finding a fun fair, its neon lights glowing in the distance – they'd been drawn to it like moths. She thought about them eating candyfloss, riding the dodgems, every memory seemed to have a soundtrack of laughter.

'How about you?' Kristian asked,

'What about me?'

'London, here, Tom, what's the plan?'

Lucy smiled at Kristian's straightforwardness – it was something she'd always liked about him.

'I really don't know,' she said.

'But you can't just go back now, not with Tom down here.'

'It's not that simple, though. I've got a job to think about, a flat. I can't just leave it all behind. I've worked for five years to make something of myself up there. When everyone told me to go to uni and I decided to work in telly instead, so many people thought I was making such a big mistake. But I've done alright. I've got a decent job at a good company. If I stick it out I could really make something of myself.' Lucy found herself speaking too fast.

'I know, I get it, Luce,' Kristian said. 'But is that really what you want? Is that how you're going to measure success? Because, to be honest, when you turned up down here a month ago, you looked totally destroyed. If that's what success looks like then I think you need your head checked.'

Lucy felt like she might cry. She knew he was right. But it wasn't that simple. Nothing ever was, was it? What could she do down here? She didn't want to be a full-time waitress. And what was to say things were going to work out with Tom anyway. It felt right now, but that might change. What if it was just the emotion of being back here, of it all being temporary? What if Tom didn't actually love her, just loved the idea of her, loved his memory of eighteen-year-old Lucy? She pictured their old house, sitting at the top of the hill, empty, all those memories she'd locked away for so long. Could she really come back here and walk among them all again? She thought about what Claire would say. She'd probably encourage her to stay, she thought.

But Claire hadn't been back here either, so what did she know? She'd run away too, built herself a life in London, so why couldn't Lucy do the same? Why did everyone have to act like she'd fucked everything up and needed to return to Cornwall to recover? Things weren't all bad in London; she'd done alright for herself.

'There's no answer,' Kristian said, ringing Tara's buzzer for the third time.

'Do you think we should walk around the back? See if we can look through the window?' Lucy didn't know what she expected to see through Tara's window, but it seemed worth a shot.

They walked around the large white building and Kristian pointed out Tara's living-room window. The blinds were open and a light was on.

'It's open,' Kristian said. 'I think she's there. Hang on.' He walked over to the gravel boundary to the garden and picked up a handful of stones. He began throwing them at the window and shouting Tara's name. Lucy still couldn't quite believe Kristian's concern for Tara. 'Is there a reason you're so worried?' she asked. 'Do you think it's something to do with her ex?'

'I hope not. She's just had a rough time of it, before she came here, some not very nice people around her, you know. TARA!' Before she could ask him any more, a voice called back.

'Kristian? Okay, okay, I'm here. Stop throwing things, will you?'

'Can you buzz us in, please, Tara. I'm worried,' he called back to her.

'Us?'

'Yes, I'm here with Lucy.'

'Oh, for God's sake! Alright, I'll buzz you in.'

They walked back around to the main door. 'What the hell's going on?' Lucy wondered out loud. 'How did you know she was in there?'

'She never leaves the window open, not unless she's in there,' he replied, seriously. Lucy realised they must all have been more worried for Tara than she'd appreciated. Even Kristian seemed to be taking this ex situation seriously.

The door buzzed open and Lucy and Kristian climbed the stairs to Tara's front door. It opened and Tara stood in her hallway. Her face was covered in scratches, her left eye socket purple and swollen.

'Oh my God,' Kristian rushed in ahead of Lucy and held Tara by the shoulders. 'What happened? Are you okay?'

'I'm fine, I'm fine,' Tara insisted, shrugging Kristian off. 'It's not as bad as it looks.'

'Who did this to you?' Lucy was shocked by the sight of Tara, her pretty face disfigured with violence like this.

'Annabel,' Tara said, sounding embarrassed.

'What the hell?' Kristian replied. 'Annabel Carmichael?'

'Yep, pathetic isn't it? A proper girly fight. She pulled my hair and everything,' Tara said, trying to smile, running her hands through her hair. Lucy recognised that she was in pain, she looked so sad.

'Why?' she said, stepping towards Tara, putting an arm out to hers, rubbing her shoulder gently. 'What happened?'

'She caught me and Olly,' Tara said, quietly. 'We didn't realise anyone else was around. We were in the storeroom.'

'Olly?' Kristian said, puzzled. 'You and Olly are a thing?' He was smiling now.

'Yes, we didn't want anyone to know,' Tara said, looking at Lucy. 'Annabel's his ex and she's a fucking psycho. And anyway, this whole bloody town is so gossipy, we didn't want everyone talking about us, judging us, waiting for us to break up.'

Lucy couldn't believe what she was hearing; all that time she'd thought Tara had feelings for Tom she'd been wrong.

'I couldn't face coming in to work looking like this,' she said. 'I should've called. I did text Molly, but her signal's terrible down there, did she not get it?'

'No,' Lucy replied. 'No one knew where you were. We were worried.'

'I'm really sorry,' Tara looked mortified. 'I didn't really know what to do.'

'It doesn't matter,' Kristian said. 'As long as you're okay. I'd started to worry, you know.'

Lucy looked at Kristian, then over to Tara, who looked embarrassed. 'I know, I should've thought it through. I didn't think what it would look like to you. I'm so sorry. Please tell me you haven't mentioned it to Tom. You know what he's like about it all. And anyway, I actually heard from a friend back in Exeter, my ex is repping in some holiday resort in Spain. He's long gone.'

'Thank God for that,' Kristian said. 'And no, we haven't told Tom. You're alright, that's all that matters.'

'How badly did Annabel come off, by the way? Does she look as terrible as you?'

'Oh God,' Tara groaned. 'It was a pathetic scene. She waited until Olly had gone, 'til I was on my own. She bloody pounced on me. I didn't see her coming. She's mental!'

Lucy struggled to picture Annabel behaving like that, but girls could be crazy when boys came into it.

'Shall I stick the kettle on?' Tara asked. Lucy and Kristian agreed to stay for tea.

'Make me a cup too, mate, will you?' Olly appeared from the bedroom, grinning as usual, seemingly untouched by either his hangover or the situation with Annabel. Lucy noticed his shorts; bright, neon surf shorts. The same as Tom's, the ones she'd seen Tara tangled up in a passionate embrace with behind the café that day.

Of course she's with Olly, she thought, and it all started clicking into place. Kristian's phone rang and he stood to retrieve it from his back pocket.

'Hello?' He answered, as if he hadn't recognised the number calling him.

'Yes, that's me.'

'From where?' He walked closer to the window, as if trying to get better reception.

'Oh my God.' His face dropped, startled by the tone of Kristian's voice.

Tara came back in with a plate of mugs and biscuits, but she froze at the sight of Kristian on the phone, holding the tray in mid-air.

'Yes, okay, I'll come now. I'll be half an hour.' He sounded efficient now, business-like. He hung up the phone.

'Who was that?' Lucy asked

'It was the hospital,' Kristian said. All the colour had drained from his face and his phone was still outstretched in front of him.

'Oh my God – Nina,' Lucy said, her heart racing as she remembered, guiltily, the pain she'd seen her in last night. She'd known that something wasn't right. She was standing now, walking to Kristian.

'Collapsed,' Kristian said, to the window. 'Just collapsed on the cliff path. They had to send the air ambulance.'

'Is she okay?' Lucy asked, frantically. It felt as though her heart might stop. 'Is she going to be okay?'

Kristian didn't answer. 'What?' he replied, after what felt like minutes of silence. 'It's not Nina,' he said, looking confused.

'It's Tom.'

38

Tara sprung into action as Lucy fell apart. The news that Tom had collapsed was too much to take in. She couldn't understand it. Tara offered to drive them to the hospital. She picked up Lucy's handbag from the floor on the way out and put it in the car next to her.

'What happened?' Lucy asked Kristian.

'I don't know, they didn't say. They just said he'd collapsed on the cliff path and had been airlifted to hospital. He's in intensive care.'

'Intensive care?' Tara asked, as she accelerated away from the apartment building. 'Are you sure that's what they said?'

'I'm pretty sure,' Kristian said quietly.

'Oh my God,' Lucy repeated herself over and over. 'Oh my God.'

They drove in silence the rest of the way to the hospital. Tara dropped them at the main entrance and went to park the car. 'I'll find you,' she said before she drove away.

Lucy asked at reception and was directed to the third floor. She and Kristian walked quickly, close together. In the lift, Lucy was overcome with emotion and the tears fell. Kristian grabbed her quickly, to hold her against his chest.

'He'll be okay, he'll be okay,' he said, as if convincing himself.

Lucy tried to pull herself together; the last thing anyone needed was her tears. The lift doors opened and she could see Nina sitting on a plastic chair halfway down the grey and beige corridor. That hospital smell hit the back of her throat. Bleach and fear.

'Are you alright?' Kristian said, almost running to Nina, grabbing her and kissing her head, holding her tightly. Lucy felt suddenly, painfully lonely.

Nina took her hand and pulled her towards the two of them and they stood for a moment, a strange trio of confused, panicked faces.

'What happened?' Lucy asked.

'We were walking,' Nina said, her voice shaking. 'We'd walked miles. We were nearly at the Packhorse in Saltheart. We were going to get some lunch. Tom wanted a ploughman's. He just stopped walking. I didn't realise right away. I carried on walking, and then I saw that he wasn't there. I looked back and he was just frozen on the spot. He looked so pale. I called to him, asked if he was okay and he just dropped to the ground. I ran. I ran to him and tried to wake him up and there was just nothing.' Nina was crying now, big heavy tears rolling down her pale face. Kristian stroked her hair lovingly.

'He wouldn't respond. I didn't know what to do. I didn't have my phone. There was an old couple on a bench behind us, they must have seen what happened, and the man came over, offered to call an ambulance. I just sat on the floor and tried to talk to him, tried to get him back. There was just nothing, nothing. I didn't even know if he was breathing.'

'It's okay, it's okay,' Kristian said, trying to slow her down. Nina was becoming increasingly upset as she spoke. Kristian looked fraught too, the seriousness of the situation sinking in.

Tara appeared from the lift and walked towards the group. 'Where is he?' she asked. She looked like she had been crying.

'He's in there,' Nina said, pointing to a closed door, 'I haven't seen him since they took him in there.'

'Excuse me,' Tara stopped a nurse walking past. 'We're here with Thomas Barton, he's in there, and we need someone to tell us what's going on.'

'Of course,' the nurse looked sympathetically at the group. 'I'll see what I can do. In the meantime, why don't you take a seat in the family room? There's a tea and coffee machine in there.'

She directed them down the corridor, to a room fitted out with tasteful sofas and inoffensive neutral prints on the wall. Lucy knew it was a room designed to calm, a bad-news room. It sent a chill through her.

After what felt like hours, a middle-aged nurse with dark hair and a kind face opened the door and stood in front of the group, who were gathered on the sofas drinking tea from plastic cups.

'He's awake,' she said. 'You can see him now.'

'What happened?' Kristian asked.

'I'll let Thomas explain,' the nurse said.

'Tom,' Lucy corrected her, without thinking.

'Sorry, Tom,' the nurse said. 'He's still weak, so please be gentle with him.'

'Of course,' Tara said. 'Is Dr Jenkins here?'

'He's on his way. He'll be here this evening at the latest,' the nurse said.

'Who's Dr Jenkins?' Nina asked, turning to Tara.

'He's Tom's consultant,' she replied.

Lucy's mind spun and she felt sick, as if something dark was settling among them.

'Why does Tom have a consultant?' It sounded to Lucy as if the words were coming from someone else, as if she was floating up into the corner of the room and observing the scene from outside herself.

'I can't – I need Tom to tell you,' Tara said, visibly upset now.

In his hospital bed, Tom was propped up slightly on pillows.

A drip was hooked up to his arm, its plastic bag emptying slowly into his bloodstream. An assortment of monitors bleeped softly. Lucy walked in first. He smiled at her.

'Tom,' she said, choking on tears at the sight of him like this, he looked so frail.

'Luce,' he reached out to her, and she took his hand in both of hers, kissing it softly.

'I'm fine,' he said, ridiculously.

'You collapsed,' Nina said, sadly, 'You're not fine.'

'What's going on, mate?' Kristian said, joining them at his bedside. 'You've given us one hell of a fright.' Lucy could hear that he was trying to sound light-hearted. 'Tara,' Tom said, noticing her at the back of the group. 'What's happened to your face? Are you okay?'

'I'm okay,' she said. 'It's nothing. You need to tell them, Tom. You should've told them before now.'

'Tell them what?' Lucy said, her heart sinking into her stomach. 'Tell us what, Tom?'

The silence in the room made Lucy feel sick as she stood waiting for his reply, her hands clammy, her throat drying up.

'I'm ill,' Tom said, simply.

'What do you mean, 'ill'?' Lucy asked. 'What's wrong?'

'I've been ill for a long time,' he said. 'I didn't want to tell you.'

'What?' Lucy couldn't take in what he was saying. 'What's wrong, Tom, what is it?'

'It's a primary brain tumour,' he said, without emotion.

Lucy felt her legs weaken. 'A brain tumour?' she repeated. She heard Tara begin to cry quietly behind her.

'What are you talking about?' Nina asked, sounding almost angry. 'You don't have a brain tumour. What the hell are you on about, Tom?'

'I'm sorry, I should have told you all before now,' he said, without looking at any of them. 'I didn't want to ruin everything. I just wanted it to be like old times. I didn't want to be the ill one.'

'What do you mean?' Lucy said. 'What are they doing about it? Is that why you collapsed? What treatment are you having?'

As Tom looked the other way. It felt like Lucy's heart was breaking into pieces. She stifled her tears; she felt like she could scream. This just didn't make any sense.

'There is no treatment,' Tara said, breaking the silence. 'He's stopped treatment.'

Lucy looked at Tom. He couldn't be that ill. He didn't look that ill. He just looked tired.

'It had stopped working,' Tom said, looking at Lucy briefly. 'It was making me so sick, Mum and Dad were having to care for me like a baby, it was unbearable. And it wasn't even achieving anything. It was ruining my life. What I've got left of it.'

'What you've got left of it?' Kristian said. 'What the hell, mate?'

'I'm not getting better,' Tom said, firmly. 'I'm not going to get better.'

Lucy felt like she might collapse onto the floor. 'Of course you'll get better,' she said, reaching for his hand again. He pulled it away.

'No, Luce, I won't. There's nothing left that they can do. It's game over.' He tried to smile, but Lucy could see the pain in his eyes. The urge to hold him was overwhelming. She sat next to him, put her head on his chest and spoke into his body. 'I don't understand. I don't understand. This can't be happening.'

'I think we should give them a minute,' Tara said.

Lucy stayed on Tom, her head pressed against him, heaving sobs pulsing through her now. He stroked her hair gently and let her cry.

'Why didn't you tell us you were ill?' Lucy asked eventually. 'How long?'

'I was diagnosed a year ago,' he said, 'had a few awful headaches, then the seizures started. Mum made me go to the doctors, it all happened pretty quickly.'

'There has to be more they can do,' she said, 'there's always some trial going on, or research programmes, my friend's mum had–'

' Don't, please, Luce' Tom said, stopping her, putting his hand on her face. 'I know my options, and I made my choice when the radiotherapy stopped working. I don't want to go like that. I wanted this – one last proper summer with my best friends, with the girl I love.'

Lucy still couldn't believe what he was saying, and her mind raced through possibilities.

'Why aren't your parents here, if you're so ill?' It was as if she might catch him out on a technicality, like he couldn't actually be this ill if she could just trip him up on a detail.

'I begged them to go,' he said. 'They spent six months taking me back and forth to hospital, carrying me back up to bed, cleaning up my sick. It was absolutely terrible, Luce, it was no life, not for any of us.'

'And you didn't tell anyone? How does no one know?'

'Tara knew,' Tom said. 'I had to tell her, she found me once, my second seizure, I think it was. Plus I needed her to run the café for me while I was in treatment. She's been amazing.'

'I don't understand,' Lucy said, it was all too much. 'Why is this happening?'

'I don't know,' Tom said. 'It's unfair, it's awful, and there's nothing at all I can do. Realising that actually set me free, really. Fighting it didn't work, Luce. I gave it my best shot. I was so convinced that I'd be okay. You hear about those brave people "battling" against cancer and things – that's what I was going to do, I was all set. Turns out it's not actually just about positive thinking; it has more to do with how aggressive the cancer is, how quickly it grows. Mine's a fucking bitch.'

Lucy sat in silence. The machines were still bleeping quietly, a clock ticking on the wall.

'Do you want me to call your parents?' she asked eventually, a sudden desire to be helpful.

'It's okay, I'll call them,' he said, 'I'll call them tomorrow. It's late now and I know they'll rush back.'

'Of course they'll rush back, they'll want to be here, with you,' Lucy said, annoyed by his casualness. 'You can't not tell them. You should have told *us* a long time before now.'

'So you could what, Luce? Rush back from London to see the invalid? You think I wanted you to see me like that? Like this? I spent a month trying not to fall back in love with you because I didn't want to hurt you like this. But then I realised it was too bloody late because I'd never stopped loving you at all. I knew that the moment I saw you again.'

'I knew too,' Lucy said. 'It's always been you, Tom. Always.'

'I'm so sorry,' he said. Lucy thought she could see tears in his eyes. 'This isn't what I had planned. This isn't what I wanted. I thought you'd come down for a month, and then go, and you wouldn't get caught up in this messy stuff. I thought you'd be long gone.'

'How long?' Lucy asked.

'What do you mean?' Tom replied

'How long have you got?'

'I don't know,' Tom said. 'Weeks, I guess, at most. My consultant's speaking to me later, but I don't think it'll be longer than weeks. The seizures are back. That means I'm deteriorating. I always knew this would be the first sign.'

Blood pounded in Lucy's ears. This couldn't be right. There must be some mistake. She imagined Dr Jenkins arriving and explaining that it had all been a terrible error. Then she looked at Tom, saw the expression on his face and realised with terror that this was actually happening. To Tom. To the love of her life.

'I only just got you back,' she whimpered. 'You can't leave me, Tom. You can't leave me too.'

'I know,' he said, stroking her face, crying now. 'I'm so sorry, I should never have brought you back here.'

'Are you joking?' Lucy said, looking him in the eyes. 'You saved me, Tom, this summer, it saved me from myself. I was going to self-destruct in London. I had all these ridiculous ideas about things, and then you asked me to come back, and you brought me home.'

Tom smiled at her and she kissed him. He still smelled of aftershave. She buried her head into his neck and breathed him in, running her hand through his hair.

'You're my home,' she said quietly. 'You're everything.'

She must have fallen asleep on the bed with Tom, because the next thing she knew there was a serious-looking man in a suit arriving. He introduced himself as Dr Jenkins, shook her hand and greeted Tom like an old friend. He was a calming influence in the room and Lucy's fantasy of him sorting everything out and sending Tom away with a telling off for causing such an unnecessary fuss returned briefly. Then he started discussing symptoms with Tom, asking how his pain relief had been working. Lucy remembered the pills in the storeroom, the surfing injury he'd claimed to have had. She had missed the signs.

Lucy excused herself, kissed Tom on the cheek, awkwardly in front of Dr Jenkins, and made her way out of Tom's room. Kristian and Tara were in the hallway, they both looked exhausted.

'Nina's gone home to rest,' Kristian said, rubbing the back of his head.

'How is he?' Tara asked.

'I don't really know,' Lucy said, feeling weak.

'I think we need to take you home too,' Kristian said, looking at Lucy.

'I want to stay,' she said, 'I want to be with Tom.'

'You'd be better off letting him rest, and you won't be any good to him without a proper night's sleep yourself,' Kristian said, kindly.

Lucy knew she wouldn't sleep, but also knew he was right. The clock on the wall showed it was gone 11pm now.

'Come on,' Tara offered her hand to Lucy in an unexpectedly

intimate gesture. Lucy took it and they walked together down the hallway, into the lift, and out of the hospital into the cool night air.

'Can you drop me here?' Lucy felt Tara's car slow to a standstill.

'Here? Are you sure?' Tara looked confused.

'Yeah,' Lucy replied, opening the car door, before leaning back in to kiss Tara on the cheek. 'I'll walk the rest of the way. I need the fresh air.'

She closed the door before Tara could reply and watched her pull away slowly, her car lights disappearing over the crest of the dark hill.

Lucy's heart thudded in her chest, hard but slow. Her body was tired, but her mind raced as she walked towards her old house. Thoughts of Tom flashed into her mind with each step: disconnected, random images of him, of their life together, of the future. She walked quickly, hoping to chase them away.

She felt numb as the big white house appeared when she turned the corner towards her driveway. The fencing standing between her and her childhood home making it seem like a fortress, but she remembered the spot to the side where Tom had helped her into the garden. She found the dipped section and used a reserve of strength she'd not known she had to pull herself over the wood and metal, landing heavily on the other side.

It was so quiet here. Tucked away behind the supposedly secure fence, she felt as though she was in a different world. She walked to the French windows of the living room and forced them open. A red light blinked quietly in the corner of the ceiling, some kind of alarm or camera, she wasn't sure which. She began pulling white dustsheets off old and familiar furniture. Dust puffed into the air, lit with moonlight that flooded through the huge windows. Standing back to observe the scene was surreal, her childhood home stood as she'd left it the day she'd left for London. It looked as if it had waited all this time for her. She made her way through the house, floorboards creaking underfoot, opening curtains, removing dustsheets and revealing her old home. Each room was filled with its own distinct memories; Richie's bedroom with its glow-in-the-dark stars stuck all over the ceiling, still lighting up after all these years; her mother's dressing table, half-empty perfume bottles still waiting to be finished; her dad's study, meticulously neat, folders and papers at right angles on his mahogany desk. *It should be creepy*, Lucy thought. But somehow it all felt comforting.

She thought of her family, of how they'd disappeared from her life in a flash of terror. How she'd spent so many years running away from the memories of them. She'd never really faced up to it, not really said goodbye. She'd just kept on running. She wished her mum was here to talk to about Tom. Making her way back downstairs to the pearly light of the living room, she sat on the soft leather sofa, her body rigid. How long did she have with Tom? She felt as though she'd forgotten everything he'd said. Was it months? Weeks? Or did he not know? It felt separate from her, the pain of it all now. Sitting here, surrounded by ghosts of her childhood, she felt safe and alone all at once. The evidence all around her of how badly she'd handled what had happened to her family spoke to her loudly. She had a chance this time, at least, to say goodbye to Tom, to make the most of him for now. Tears fell down her cheeks as she thought of him in this way, of the ending to their story. How could something like this happen to someone so young, so happy and so alive? It wasn't fair; but she knew all too painfully that fair didn't matter, it didn't count for anything.

Lucy wrapped her arms around herself, suddenly aware of the cold. She took the cashmere throw from the back of the chair behind her and pulled it over her body, lying down on the worn, weathered fabric beneath her. Her eyes stung with tears as she closed them and drifted into an anxious sleep.

39

'So, you knew,' Lucy said to Tara, as she lifted a tray of glasses into the dishwasher. She'd offered to help out at the café, welcoming anything that might take her mind off everything.

'Yeah,' Tara said. 'He swore me to secrecy. It was the only way I could get him to ask you to come back here.' She was standing still, apron on, looking at Lucy sadly.

'What do you mean 'get me to come back here'?'

'He wasn't going to ask you, Lucy. You know what he's like. He's proud. We spoke about it all when he decided to stop his treatment, what he was going to do with this summer. He wanted you all back together; I don't think he ever really moved on from those summers you all spent together, before you left. I thought it was all pretty straightforward; he'd call you, tell you what was happening and you'd all come down and rally around. But he wouldn't do it that way.'

Lucy began polishing cutlery, happier to have her hands occupied. Tara carried on speaking.

'He's proud, isn't he? Didn't want you all knowing he was ill, didn't want anyone's pity. He wasn't going to ask you to come at all. He said it had been too long, that you'd moved on. But, Lucy, the way he talked about you, I knew, really, that he didn't just miss you as a friend, he was still in love with you. Even after all this time. It was kind of romantic, but sad, really, too. I couldn't believe he was caught up on some girl he hadn't seen in however many years.' She paused.

'You have no idea how hard it was to convince him to ask you to come down here.'

'I thought you two were an item,' Lucy said, shifting awkwardly on the spot. 'I thought you liked Tom.'

'Yeah, well, I guess I did once upon a time,' Tara said, looking away, half-smiling. 'When I first came down here, I suppose I thought something might happen between us, eventually. But then we became friends and I realised no one had a chance against you – and you weren't even bloody here. It was mad. And then I met Olly, so that was that.'

Lucy felt a wave of relief that they'd finally got it all out in the open – it shouldn't have taken this. But her mind spun with what Tara was saying. All that time she'd missed Tom in London, thinking he'd forgotten her, hated her, even, and he'd been down here thinking about her. They'd wasted so much time. She felt tears in her eyes and tried to keep them in by pressing a napkin to her eyes.

'I'm sorry I didn't tell you,' Tara said, misunderstanding Lucy's emotion. 'It's been so hard. When Tom was off in Plymouth at hospital, having to lie to you, I hated it. But I had to respect what he wanted and he kept telling me he would tell you all when the time was right. I know this wasn't what he was planning.'

Lucy looked at Tara, her black eye masked with concealer, the tiny scratches healing on her cheeks. She felt so sorry for her, carrying around Tom's secret. It must have been horrible for her, she realised.

'Thank you,' she said. 'You've been a real friend to Tom, and you've been a friend to me too. I was a bitch when I arrived here. I was so jealous of you – this gorgeous blonde girl, so close to Tom. I totally misjudged it all. And I'm sorry, I must've seemed awful.'

'Not awful,' Tara smiled. 'You were just a bit scary. I wanted you to like me.'

'I do like you,' Lucy said. 'A lot.'

'Have you heard from Tom yet this morning?' Tara asked, changing the subject.

'No, Kristian did, though,' Lucy said. 'He's coming home in a couple of days, now he's stable.'

'That's good,' Tara said, although it sounded like she thought the opposite. 'Did they say how long they think he has?'

'No' Lucy said, 'Kristian didn't say, but Tom said weeks, I think. I just can't believe it, Tara. How is this happening?'

'I don't know,' Tara said. 'The whole thing's been fucking crazy, just the absolute worst. He was fine, surfing every day, working here, then the next thing he's having a seizure and then he's in hospital. His mum sat me down and told me he had a tumour. I couldn't even believe it, not until I saw him.' Tara was talking quickly, the words pouring out now the terrible secret had been revealed.

'The radiotherapy was just awful for him. It nearly destroyed him, I think, being that dependent on his parents, being so weak –' Tara stopped to wipe her eyes on her apron. 'I'm sorry,' she said, 'I just still can't really believe it. It was like he was better, when he stopped going to the hospital each week, he became Tom again, and now this, it's all happening. We always knew it would come, but I think I'd kind of pushed it away, started to forget. He's been so bloody happy with you all back here, it's just so fucking unfair.'

The involvement of the air ambulance had made Tom's collapse on the cliff path big news in the town. After keeping it all a secret for over a year, suddenly everyone knew he was in hospital, even if they didn't know why or how serious it was. A stream of people came into the café to ask how he was and to send their love. Lucy thanked them, told them he'd be home in a couple of days, tried not to get upset in front of them. The tourists, of course, had no idea that anything, everything, had changed; they were still on holiday, still enjoying themselves. Lucy served them with a smile. It helped to take her mind off things for a few seconds at a time.

Olly came in at lunchtime and kissed Tara on the lips in the middle of the restaurant. Lucy watched him walk through the door, spot his girlfriend and march purposefully over to her and kiss her like he had a point to prove. She understood. It was the kind of news that made you want to grab hold of the people you love and hold them tight so you'd never lose them. She thought about her kiss with Tom on the beach, how electricity had jolted into her, how it felt like coming back to life. *He loves me*, she remembered, *and he's going to die*.

She had called Claire when she got back to the house last night. It had been too late for phone calls, really, but she'd needed to hear Claire's voice. Claire had been in shock when she told her. There had been a long silence, then she'd let out a terrible sob and they'd cried together. Eventually she asked Lucy what she was going to do, and Lucy had realised right there and then that she couldn't go back to London, couldn't go back to her job. It all seemed so obvious; of course she'd stay here. Tom needed her. Helping at the café gave her a practical way of helping out for now. And she wanted to be with Tom, after all the time they'd been apart they suddenly had this countdown clock over their heads and she wasn't going to miss any more. She thought of him in his hospital bed: pale, weak, but still her Tom. Still those big arms, that hair, his smile. She was going to go and see him this evening. She was going to take him some surf magazines and she was going to climb onto that bed and lie down next to him and hold him and never let go.

'What time do his parents arrive?' Tara asked as they cleaned the café after closing early for the evening.

'I'm not sure, late, I think,' Lucy said. She couldn't wait to see them again. She just wished it wasn't because Tom was in hospital.

'I'm going to see him in a bit,' Lucy said. 'Do you want to come?'

'No, thanks,' Tara said, sweeping behind the counter, 'I'll leave you two to it. Can you give him my love, though? Tell him I'll see him back at home.'

'Sure,' Lucy said. 'Of course.'

The door of the café opened with a slight creak and Lucy went to call out that they had closed early tonight. She looked up and saw Annabel standing in the doorway; she looked incredibly glamorous in a snakeskin-print black dress and gold high heels.

'Hi,' Annabel said, meekly, to Lucy. She looked at Tara. 'Hi, Tara.'

'Hi,' Tara said, looking unmoved by the sight of the girl who had given her facial wounds a few nights earlier.

'I came to apologise,' Annabel said, walking a little closer.

'Sure,' Tara said. She sounded like a little girl. Lucy felt protective of her.

'No, I really mean it,' Annabel carried on, a pleading tone to her voice. Lucy suddenly wanted her to go away. It wasn't the time for this.

'I didn't mean to punch you,' Annabel said, looking away, almost smiling. 'I'm sorry.'

'It's fine,' Tara said. She carried on sweeping, as if to signal to Annabel that the conversation was over.

'It's just complicated,' Annabel said. 'I don't suppose Olly told you how serious we were, but it wasn't just a casual fling, if that's what he said. We were together for nearly three months.'

Annabel sounded so pathetic it made Lucy cringe a little for her. She didn't know where to look and wished she wasn't standing here witnessing this exchange. Tara didn't say anything, but this only seemed to rile Annabel, who took another step towards her.

'And then when we slept together again last month, well, I just thought maybe things were going to go somewhere again. And then I saw you two, and – oh, sorry, did he not tell you about last month?'

Tara had stopped sweeping and it was written all over her face that Annabel's revelation was news to her, news that hurt.

'Anyway, I'm sorry. I hope you two are happy together. Just watch him, because he's a total dickhead.' With this, she turned to leave. She turned back after a couple of steps and looked at Lucy now, confused. 'Lucy, you're still here? I thought you were leaving. Tom proving too hard to resist after all, huh? Well, it's cool. Come and see me in the shop. I've got a top I think you'll like. See ya!' Annabel walked out of the café and pulled the door shut with a bang.

'She's just being a spiteful bitch,' Lucy said to Tara, who had tears running down her cheeks.

'Do you think that's true? About last month?' Tara said, quietly.

'No, I don't think it is, but I think you should speak to Olly,' Lucy said. 'Trust me, don't waste time wondering whether, and what if, and whatever. Just speak to him, find out the truth and go from there. I saw him kiss you earlier, Tara. I don't think he's got eyes for anyone else. I think he adores you.' Lucy meant it. She'd looked into Annabel's eyes as she'd let her little secret slip and she'd had the look of a snake about her. It was strange seeing her in this new, unpleasant light. It was strange feeling such fierce loyalty to Tara.

'It's not important, anyway,' Tara said, clearly trying to pull herself together. 'I'm sorry you had to see that. How embarrassing. And you need to get to the hospital. I'll finish up here. You go.'

'Are you sure? Thanks, that's really kind.' Lucy gave Tara a quick hug, then untied her apron and dropped it into the laundry bag by the kitchen door.

Out on the street she saw Annabel standing outside the pub, smoking and laughing with another glamorous girl who Lucy didn't recognise. She spotted Lucy and called her over. Lucy walked over calmly and asked, 'What was that about in there?'

'What?' Annabel said, smiling but obviously slightly cross.

'What you said to Tara. Is it true?' Lucy felt the early buzz of anger in her chest.

'Ha, well, sort of,' Annabel laughed, clinking her glass of wine against her friend's. 'She deserved a bit of a shock, the little slag.'

Without thinking, Lucy took the glass of white wine from Annabel's hand and tipped it straight over her freshly blow-dried hair.

'Whoops' she said, as Annabel stood, dripping with Sauvignon blanc, in such shock at what happened that she couldn't say a word.

Lucy walked away quickly, the realisation of what she had done settling with each step, her heart pounding. At the entrance to the path leading towards the house, she felt a car's headlights sweep over her, flashing on and off. Someone was calling her name. She turned around towards the lights, which blinded her. The car dipped its headlights towards the sand and the passenger door opened. The silhouette walked towards her and she suddenly recognised the voice calling her name in the darkness. It was Tom's mum.

40

Sarah held Lucy in a tight squeeze, smelling her hair and kissing her head. Lucy felt twelve years old again.

'Oh Lucy,' she said, eventually letting go. 'It's so good to see you. How are you?'

Lucy felt overcome by the emotion of seeing Sarah again like this, because of this. It was horrifically surreal.

'I'm okay,' Lucy said. It was second time in her life that it had become the hardest question to answer – how are you?

'Can we drive you to the hospital?' Sarah gestured towards the car. Neil lifted a hand in greeting.

'That'd be great, thanks,' Lucy replied, walking towards the car, Sarah's hand on her back.

Lucy sat in the back of the Freelander, the bumpy Hideaway Bay roads giving way to larger, smoother, dual carriageways and lights speeding overhead. Sarah asked Lucy about London, about her job, about Claire. It was comforting speaking to her. She had a way of never sounding judgmental and she was so calm. She had always been calm.

'And Tom's told you what's going on with him?' Sarah asked.

'Yes,' Lucy said, the realisation dawning all over again. She lowered her window slightly to let some fresh air in.

'And you met Dr Jenkins? He's a good man.' Sarah's voice caught.

'He's really not going to get better, is he?' Lucy asked, not wanting to hear the answer.

'No, love' Neil said. 'He's not.' There was something like frustration in his voice.

'We are so glad you all came together like this,' Sarah said, clearly trying to lift the tone. 'When Tom insisted we went back to France, it felt awful, but then he said you were all going to come to the house, and, well, I suppose I sort of understood.'

'He didn't tell us he was ill,' Lucy said. 'We only found out when he got taken to the hospital.'

'Yes, I gathered that, stubborn boy,' Sarah said, fondly. She was so proud of Tom, always had been – he was her only son.

'He missed you,' Sarah said. 'He always missed you. We all did. I'm so glad to have you back here, even if it is only for a few more days.'

Lucy didn't reply. The prospect of returning to London felt so alien, almost ridiculous, now. She wouldn't go, at least not right away. She would cancel her train.

Tom's room was overflowing with flowers and baskets of cakes and biscuits. Lucy picked up a couple of cards, read names she didn't recognise, as his parents hugged him on his bed.

'I've never been so popular,' Tom said, watching Lucy. 'Come here'.

Lucy went to his side and he raised his arm for her to lean against his chest. She kissed him instinctively on the lips, then remembered with minor embarrassment that his parents were there. Tom didn't seem fazed, taking hold of Lucy's hand as they discussed France, his parents' journey over here, and, eventually, his current condition.

'They're letting me go home,' Tom said, attempting a smile. Lucy examined his face as he spoke, the little lines around his mouth, his sparkling eyes.

'We've spoken to Karen,' Sarah said. 'She's available straight away. She can come to the hospital tomorrow to meet with your medical team.'

'Karen is Tom's nurse,' Neil explained to Lucy. 'She's cared for him at home for the last year, as and when we've needed her.'

Tom looked embarrassed, Lucy thought.

'Don't worry, she's not hot,' Tom's eyes lit up a little with this. 'She's an old lady nurse.'

'She's MY age!' Sarah exclaimed, mock hurt in her voice. It was so strange, Lucy thought, the way they were bantering, as if this were normal to all be sitting around his hospital bed.

'How is the café?' Tom asked Lucy, raising her hand to his mouth and kissing it lightly.

'It's good,' Lucy said. 'Tara sends her love. Actually, everyone sends their love.'

'Lovely Tara,' Neil said. 'Is she okay?'

'She's, you know, doing alright,' Lucy said. No one was really okay any more.

'I bet you two get on like a house on fire. What a pair!' Sarah smiled at Lucy, who cringed again at the memory of how much she'd mistrusted Tara to begin with.

Lucy went to the reception area to buy coffee for everyone, the Costa stand still busy with late-night visitors. She wanted to give Tom and his parents some time alone, so seeing the queue, she headed outside to get some fresh air. The nights were getting cooler, she noticed, pulling her grey knitted cardigan around her front, shivering slightly. Her phone beeped and she retrieved it to read a message from Nina asking how Tom was. Poor Nina had been in a total state since the incident on the cliff. It had shaken her more than Lucy would have expected; she'd hardly left the house since. Kristian was dealing with it in his own way, still surfing every morning, heading out in the early hours, spending far longer than usual in the water before coming home exhausted. Looking after Nina seemed to give

250

him a way of channeling it all. Lucy recognised that need to do something; it was why she'd been so glad to work in the café. It was as if she had this whole new energy source born from a total fear and shock. If she didn't do something with it she would go crazy.

She imagined Tom coming home, a nurse looking after him. It was such an alien concept. And what was actually going to happen? Would he get sicker and sicker and fade away there at home? Or would it be dramatic? Would he end up back in hospital, machines pumping drugs into him, doctors rushing around with clipboards? She didn't know if she could ask Tom, or his parents. *What the hell is the etiquette?*, she wondered.

Back in his room, coffees distributed, Lucy sat on the chair next to Tom and listened to him speak to his parents about the café. He wouldn't be able to return to work, but he was adamant he could run the stock and finances from home. Neil said he could put some hours in in the café and Lucy reiterated that she was happy to help too.

'Are you going back to London?' Tom asked, matter-of-factly.

'No,' Lucy said, suddenly sure of her answer. 'No, I'm calling work tomorrow to tell them I'm not coming back.'

'You don't have to do that,' Tom said, genuinely.

'I know, but I want to,' she said. 'I can't just walk back into that life, not now, and not without you. If things were different, then –' she stopped herself. What was the point talking about a life that wasn't as heartbreakingly awful as this?

'Well, that's brilliant news,' Sarah said. 'You are obviously welcome to stay with us for as long as you like. It will be like old times,' Sarah said. 'Hopefully with a little less sneaking into Tom's room in the middle of the night.' She laughed at the memory.

'Thank you,' Lucy said.

'God, you look like your mum,' Neil said from the corner of the room. He'd been studying Lucy as she spoke.

'Dad –' Tom said, sounding embarrassed.

'No, it's okay,' Lucy said. 'No one's told me that for a long time. I used to love being told I had her eyes.'

'It's uncanny,' Neil said. 'Like having her in the room.'

Sarah let out a sob and Neil looked suddenly sorry for having brought up ghosts of the past.

'Sorry, love,' he said, reaching an arm around her.

'It's okay, I just need to...' Sarah stood up, dabbing her eyes with a tissue from her handbag. 'Fresh air. I just need fresh air.' She left the room and Lucy thought she heard her crying as she walked away. It was the saddest sound she'd ever heard and made tears form in her own eyes, and her throat closed up slightly.

'Look, I'm going to go and make sure your mum's okay,' Neil said, standing too. He put a hand on Tom's chest, and then, in an act that seemed utterly beautiful to Lucy, leant down and kissed his son on the head. A nurse walked in as Neil left, smiling at Lucy, and handing Tom a small paper pot of pills, which he knocked straight back, chasing them with water from the table next to his bed.

'Are you staying with us tonight?' the nurse asked Lucy, taking her by surprise.

'Oh, I, um, I don't know, can I?' she looked at Tom, then back at the nurse, unsure of who she was asking.

'Of course you can,' the nurse said. 'Let me sort something out. I think we've got another bed free. I'll be back in a minute.'

She left the room and Lucy turned to Tom. 'Do you want me to stay? Is that okay?'

'I never want you to leave,' he said. She ran her hand through his hair and kissed him again.

The nurse managed to wheel another bed into the room and line it up next to Tom's to create a makeshift double.

'Romantic,' Tom joked, as she took her dress off and climbed under the slightly hard sheets in her underwear.

Tom's parents had popped back in to say goodbye. They were coming back in the morning to pick Lucy up, hopefully Tom too,

252

if they would discharge him. Lucy snuggled into Tom's warm body, kissing his chest as he stroked her hair.

'I'm so sorry' he said. 'I never wanted to hurt you.'

'Don't say sorry to me, Tom,' she said. 'There's nothing to be sorry for. I just want you. I just wish things were different. How am I going to be okay without you?'

'You're going to do great things, Luce,' he said, running his hand down her side. 'I know you will do something extraordinary.'

'I don't want to do anything without you,' she said, crying now.

'I know,' he said, 'I know.' She felt him kiss her hair.

Tom didn't wake fully when the nurse arrived in the early morning to do her observations. Lucy pulled her dress on under the covers and slipped out of bed. She watched from the chair as the slightly stern-looking nurse took his blood pressure, writing down numbers from the display of the heart monitor above his head.

'Would you like a cup of tea?' the nurse asked as she made her way to the door, surprising her with a warm smile.

'No, thanks,' Lucy said. 'I'll pop out.'

It was 7am and the hospital held a sense of hushed anticipation, nurses and healthcare assistants bustling about the nurses' station. Other early risers were wandering in search of coffee machines, sharing smiles with Lucy as she made her way down the corridor.

Outside, the noise of the busy road the hospital was on seemed abrasively loud. Buses whooshed and squealed, impatient motorists beeped horns at slow green-light pull-aways. Lucy sat on a bench outside the main entrance. It was too early to be warm yet and she wished she'd brought her cardigan. She thought about calling Claire. She'd be up and about getting ready for work. But she couldn't muster the energy. She hadn't slept well, she felt almost jet lagged, separate from everything around her, existing in a different world. She decided to walk to find a café. Breakfast might make her feel more human. She vaguely recalled a greasy spoon somewhere down the road, towards the boys' grammar school.

The walk took longer than she'd anticipated and involved following the dual carriageway. The soundtrack of traffic blocked Lucy's thoughts and was surprisingly soothing. She walked quickly, trying to fight the cool morning air on her skin. The sun was still a pale, silvery yellow – not yet hot enough to burn off the last of the night air. Finally Lucy saw the gaudy candy-striped canopy of the café and she felt her stomach rumble in anticipation of food. She couldn't remember when she'd last eaten.

'Morning, love. What can I do for you?' The large, bleach-blonde lady at the counter hovered over the buttons of her till.

'I'll have an egg-and-bacon roll, please,' Lucy said, counting the coins from her wallet.

Sitting in a plastic chair at a table fixed to the floor, she looked at the other diners in the café: a mixture of tradesmen and students, by the look of things. She wondered what she must look like, sitting there in yesterday's beach dress, hair still in the messy bun she'd pulled it into before bed. It probably looks like a walk of shame, she thought, remembering the cruel truth. She wondered if Tom had been awake enough to register her kiss as she left this morning. He had stirred slightly and kissed her back. It seemed likely that he would be allowed home today. *Home to die.* The words forced their way into Lucy's mind. She felt her stomach twist.

'Cheer up, love, it might never happen,' Lucy looked up to see a moronic grin looking back at her. She didn't reply.

'No need to be a bitch.' The man, dressed in a garish high-vis jacket, was visibly cross now, unimpressed with her silence.

'Please leave me alone,' she heard her voice shake as she spoke. Who did this prat think he was?

'Oh, you're one of those hoity-toity, better than everyone, types, I see,' he said, still standing over her, his large physical presence intimidating now. 'Get over yourself, you stuffy cow'

Lucy was about to stand to leave when the blonde lady from the counter arrived with her sandwich.

'This one giving you bother, love?' she asked, not looking at the tanned, wrinkly-faced man.

'It's okay. Can I just get this to go?' she said, standing, handing the plate back.

'Sure.' The lady took it away and Lucy reached for her handbag from the table.

'Look, love, just a bit of banter, alright?' he was still talking to her. Lucy realized, with horror, that tears were now streaming down her face. She walked past him, brushing his arm as she left, wishing she could just tell him to fuck off, but lacking the strength.

At the door, the woman stopped her to hand her a greasy paper bag. 'Are you alright, dear? Can I call someone for you?'

Lucy told her she was fine, there was no need to call anyone, and left the café with her sandwich.

It's already fucking happened, you moron, she thought. *The world just carries on as normal, but mine is falling apart all over again.*

With the imposing hospital building in sight, Lucy took her phone from her pocket and dialed Spectrum's number. An unfamiliar receptionist answered and she asked to speak to Lydia. It was the kind of call that a week ago would have sent her heart racing, but today felt like the simplest thing in the world.

'Lucy?' Lydia answered with typical brusqueness.

'Hi,' Lucy said. 'Look, I'm sorry to let you down, but I've had a change of circumstances here. I'm not going to be coming back to London for a while, not for a few weeks at least.'

There was silence from Lydia.

'What the actual fuck,' came her eventual reply. 'Are you fucking joking?'

'No,' Lucy said, calmly. 'I wouldn't be doing this unless I had to. You know me well enough to know that. I don't have a choice.' Lydia let out a nasty laugh. 'Of course you have a choice, Lucy, you're just fucking it all up again. I can't believe this.'

Lucy could hear a commotion in the background. Was that Emma's voice? There was a stifled exchange and a rustle before Emma's voice sounded down the line.

'Lucy, if you do this you will never work in TV again. I'll see to it. I've held this position open for you for weeks. Do you know how lucky you are to have this chance after the stunt you pulled?'

'I know, I'm sorry,' Lucy hadn't expected to have to speak to Emma directly, but still she couldn't muster the usual panic this exchange would have caused.

'My friend, my boyfriend, has cancer. He is dying,' she said, factually. 'He has a few weeks to live, Emma. I'm not going to come back tomorrow. He needs me.' There was a pause.

'Well, we need you here,' came the reply, taking even Lucy, with her years of experience with Emma, by surprise.

'And unless you are some kind of cancer specialist now and are planning on curing him, it doesn't sound like you're much use down there anyway. We've all made sacrifices for our careers, Lucy.'

Lucy searched for the words to reply, but found none. Emma couldn't have done any more to convince her that her decision to stay was entirely right.

'Thank you for the opportunities you gave me,' she said, after an uncomfortable pause, and she ended the call before Emma could speak again.

41

'I suppose it should be okay,' Karen was sitting in the kitchen with a cup of tea, Kristian standing in front of her, big eyes pleading.

'We'll keep it low key,' he said. 'Won't we Lucy?'

'Yes, of course we will,' Lucy said, pouring herself a glass of water from the fridge.

'Well, okay then. I'll help him get ready.' Karen placed her empty china cup onto the marble work surface.

Tom's condition had shocked the group over the past few days. The rate of his decline unexpected, although not to his medical team, it seemed. He was on a cocktail of drugs, which kept the pain at bay and reduced the pressure in his skull, but he was weakening. Lucy could see it each day – a little more of his strength gone. He hadn't been able to leave the house, and seeing Kristian return from the beach each morning was taking its toll on his spirit – he had confided as much in Lucy. It was heartbreaking to see him like this. It had been Lucy's idea to take him to the beach. If they took the car and a wheelchair, it shouldn't be too strenuous, but his parents hadn't been too keen on the idea and insisted they run it past Karen.

'Green light,' Lucy said, walking into Tom's room. He was sitting in bed, drinking lemonade through a straw.

'Cool,' he said, not looking happy about it.

'You okay?' Lucy asked. 'Do you feel alright?'

'Yeah, fine,' he said, pinching the bridge of his nose and scrunching his face. 'It'll be good to see the sea, get some fresh air. I just wish I could get in the water. I want to surf. That's what I really want to do.'

'I know,' Lucy said. There were no comforting words to make him feel better – she'd stopped trying to find them.

'Sorry, I don't want to moan,' Tom said, trying to pull himself up further in bed. Lucy reached to help him.

'You look pretty,' he said, looking her up and down. 'You're so brown!'

'I guess I am,' Lucy said, looking at her bronzed arm next to his pale skin.

'I'm a lucky guy,' he said, pulling her in for a kiss.

Lucy needed to pop into the café to speak to Tara about the week's greengrocer order, so she left Kristian and Karen to get Tom into the car and down to the beach. Tom didn't like Lucy watching him be helped in and out of bed, so she tried to find reasons not to be there when he was moved around.

'Do you want to come with me?' Lucy asked Nina as she was heading out the door; Nina was sitting on the stairs looking lost.

'Yes, please,' she said. 'I can't stand it here at the moment.'

They walked out together, towards the beach path.

'Are you okay?' Lucy asked. 'How is baby?'

Nina instinctively placed a hand on her belly. 'Baby's fine,' she said, smiling briefly. 'This is just too much, isn't it? I can't really feel anything other than total sadness, which can't be good for this one.' She patted her stomach gently.

'I know,' Lucy said. 'What are you going to do?'

'The house is ready for us to move in,' Nina said, looking out to sea. 'I think we are going to go back to Bristol this week.'

Lucy hadn't expected the news. She'd assumed they'd all stay around to help Tom.

'I don't think we are helping,' Nina said, as if she'd read Lucy's thoughts. 'To be honest, I feel like we're getting in the way, and it'd be better for Tom's parents to have fewer bodies in the house. It must be overwhelming for them.'

'I hadn't thought of it like that,' Lucy said, suddenly wondering whether she'd misjudged the situation.

'We can still come down lots,' Nina said. 'Do you think Tom will understand?'

'I know he will,' Lucy said. 'I'll miss you, though.'

'You're hardly here, missy!' Nina said, gently poking Lucy's arm. It was true. She'd spent most days at the café with Tara and the rest of her time she was with Tom.

'I think you're doing the right thing,' Lucy said. 'I just think you need to tell Tom as soon as you can; manage his expectations, you know.'

'Kristian's telling him today,' Nina said. 'Have we got time for a coffee?'

'Yeah, I think we have,' Lucy said, as they made their way into the café, which was bustling with the early-lunchtime rush.

'We're taking Tom to the beach,' Lucy told Tara, as she pulled up a chair at their table to find out how he was doing.

'That's brilliant,' she said. 'Can I come along?'

'Definitely,' Lucy said. 'Bring Olly, if you like. We're just doing a little barbecue thing, nothing too hectic.'

'Cool, I'll see you in a few hours, in that case. I'm working till 4pm.' She left to get their coffees.

'He's not going to be there,' Nina said.

'Where?' Lucy asked, confused.

'At our wedding. Tom's not going to be at our wedding.' It seemed to be the first time Nina had thought of this, although Lucy didn't think that could be the case.

There wasn't anything Lucy could say. It was true – just one of the many moments that would happen without him there. She could think of a thousand.

She reached across the table and held Nina's hand. 'He's devastated about that,' she said, honestly, recalling the conversation they'd had on her balcony a few nights earlier. *I'd always imagined I'd be his best man*, Tom had said; he'd looked like he was fighting tears.

'Unless –' Lucy stopped herself.

'Unless…?' Nina asked.

'Unless you guys get married now, this week, here, in Hideaway.' The idea didn't seem completely ridiculous as she said it out loud.

'How the hell would we do that? *Where* the hell would we do that?' Nina asked.

'On the beach,' Lucy said, as if she had a plan in mind and this wasn't the first time she'd thought of it. 'You could just have a simple ceremony on the beach, a blessing or something, and then we could have a party here, in the café.'

Nina seemed to be considering it when Tara put two coffees down on the table.

'What do you think, Tara?' Nina said, looking back to Lucy.

'About what?' Tara asked

'Do you reckon we could host a little reception here next week, if Kristian and I had a ceremony on the beach?'

Tara clasped her hands together in excitement. 'I think that's a brilliant idea,' she said. 'We could definitely sort something out, couldn't we Lucy? Oh my God, Tom would be so happy.'

Nina smiled at Lucy. 'Well, if we can sort it out, then I'm up for it. I'll need to speak to Kristian, though. And I'll need to find a bloody dress. God, can you imagine how hideous I'll look all fat in a wedding dress? Grim.'

'You'll look stunning,' Lucy said. 'Will you speak to Kristian this afternoon?'

'Yeah, I will. Let's do this!' Nina said.

'Wheelchairs and sand don't mix,' Tom said, as Lucy and Nina approached. Tom was sat on a blanket, drinking a beer.

'Kristian carried me,' he said. 'What a fucking sight we must've been.' He clinked his bottle with Kristian's.

Lucy felt momentarily stupid for not having figured that, of course, they couldn't just wheel him onto the beach. But he was here now and he looked happy.

'Some great surf out there,' Tom said, watching surfers weave over waves. 'Man, I wish I was out there.'

'I'll carry you in for a paddle,' Kristian said, nudging Tom.

'Not quite the same, mate, but thanks,' he replied. Lucy felt like crying, but fought her tears away, determined to have a good time this afternoon.

The beach was busy, but not as crowded as it had been a few weeks before. It was coming up for the end of the season, and it felt as though the whole town was breathing a sigh of relief, loosening up, relaxing a bit. Even the sun was a little less ferocious, the air warm, the sand comfortably hot, rather than scorching.

'This was the dream,' Tom said, looking around at the group. 'Getting us all back together was all I really wanted. Does that sound a bit sad?'

'No,' Nina said. 'It's been perfect. I hadn't imagined it would be this perfect. I thought we might have drifted apart a bit after all those years, you know. Turns out we haven't grown up much at all, really, have we?'

Lucy thought about it, how true it was. All those years she'd been gone, she'd built a whole new life in London with new friends, boyfriends. She'd thought she'd become a new person, a strong, different version of herself. And if she hadn't come back here this summer, well, maybe she would never have realised that, actually, she was still the fifteen-year-old girl who liked sitting on the beach with her friends. She hadn't really grown up at all.

As the afternoon heat gave way to early evening, the beach emptied by the hour as families drifted off to get showered and sand-free for dinner. The town was buzzing with people in search of food, teenagers eating cones of chips on the wall by the campsite. Tara and Olly arrived. It was funny seeing them as a proper couple now, but Lucy could see how happy he made Tara and was pleased for them.

'I spoke to Kristian,' Nina said, quietly to Lucy as the boys talked about lighting the barbecue.

'He thinks it's a great idea, if we can get it arranged in time,' Nina said.

'I'll call the vicar,' Lucy said, 'to find out what's possible. I think he'll do it. He knows Tom's family. They're praying for him at the church every Sunday.'

'I can speak to the florist,' Tara said. 'I'll get some decorations sorted. And we have all the bits from the Sundowner, so we could pimp the café up a bit for the party.'

'Sounds good to me,' Nina said. 'Kristian said we shouldn't tell Tom, though.' She paused, looking down at the sand. 'Just in case, you know, we run out of time. We don't want to get his hopes up, or put too much pressure on him.'

The idea that Tom might not make it to next week wasn't new to Lucy. She'd spoken to Dr Jenkins, to his parents, to Karen. They all knew he was getting weaker. The medication was keeping him relatively pain-free, but it wasn't going to slow his deterioration. Tom had been totally honest with Lucy. *It could be days*, he'd said, *hopefully it's weeks*. She couldn't believe the best-case scenario was that he'd still be with them in September. It was like living in a nightmare. Except there was none of the drama she'd have imagined if someone had told her this would happen. It wasn't like in a film where everyone walked around giving meaningful looks to one another, sad music playing. A lot of things just carried on as normal. It actually hit her over and over again when she remembered what was happening; when Tom held her at night and she couldn't fight the thoughts away any more like she did when she was at work, or helping his parents; when she was stalking the miles and miles of cliff path that she now walked to keep herself busy when Tom was sleeping.

The barbecue was so heavily laden with John Dory fillets

wrapped in foil, lobster shells and burgers, that you could hardly see its glowing coals. Lucy watched Tom drink another beer, wondering whether it was interfering with his medication. He looked so happy. She walked over to him and put her arms around his shoulders, leaning in to kiss his neck.

'Oi oi!' Olly shouted. 'Enough of that, I need to borrow this gentleman,' he said, walking towards Tom.

'What?' Tom looked confused, but was smiling; he looked a little drunk, Lucy thought.

'Kristian, give me a hand,' Olly beckoned to Kristian to leave the barbecue and join them. He put down the tongs, looked seriously at his work and seemed to decide it would be alright to leave it for a moment.

'Right, one arm each,' Olly said, slipping his hand under Tom's right arm, gesturing to Kristian to take his left.

'What are you doing?' Tom said, looking slightly embarrassed.

'Taking you into the ocean, mate,' Olly said. 'If that's alright? Can't have you sat here looking longingly out to sea all night.'

'I don't think that's a good idea,' Tara said, looking around for support.

'It's a great idea,' Tom said, 'Luce, help me get this shirt off?'

Lucy hesitated, then, seeing the look on Tom's face, decided to do as he asked. She unbuttoned his shirt, and he watched her, smiling.

'Can you watch the barbecue?' Kristian said to Nina. Nothing was so important that he'd forget the food.

The girls stood in a line, in something like disbelief, and watched Kristian and Olly help Tom walk towards the sea. He didn't look like he needed much help; he looked stronger than Lucy had expected. They were laughing loudly at something as they made their way into the sea. Olly still had a bottle of beer in his free hand. *If Karen could see this*, Lucy thought.

Tara put her arm around Lucy as they watched the boys make their way into the ocean, holding on to Tom, taking him deeper and deeper into the water. Lucy thought she could still hear them laughing, even as they became miniature silhouettes in the waves.

'You've got a good one there,' she said, turning to Tara.

'So have you,' Tara said, squeezing her gently.

42

Five years earlier

Hideaway Bay, 2005

'So you're really going?' Nina asked, offering Lucy a Marlboro Light.

'Yes, tomorrow,' Lucy replied, taking a cigarette and lighting it from Nina's flame.

'And what about Tom? Have you even spoken to him properly about this? Are you sure you're not rushing it all, running away?'

Lucy bristled at Nina's questions. She'd been winding her up more and more over the past few days, her tone judgemental and annoying.

'Kind of,' she lied. Every time they'd got close to discussing it they'd ended up arguing. Tom was so adamant she should stay.

'You're going to break his heart,' Nina said, skimming a stone into the sea. 'He'd go with you if you asked him, if it's what you really want. You know that, right?'

'How are things with Kristian?' Lucy asked, changing the subject.

'Ugh, not great,' Nina sighed, lying back on the sand. 'He's just so immature sometimes. I swear he cares more about his surfboard than me.'

Lucy took a drag on her cigarette and blew the smoke into the night air above her. She was getting tired of this same conversation about Nina and Kristian, their constant break-ups and make-ups. It was pretty clear that they needed to go their separate ways once the summer was over. Nina was off to Bristol anyway, so that would be the end of it. Kristian wouldn't leave the town – he was almost as devoted to the place, and to the surf, as Tom was.

'Ladies,' Kristian sat down in between Lucy and Nina, an arm around each of them. He smelled of beer.

'The water is beaut,' he said. 'You girls should come in.'

'I might do in a bit, actually,' Lucy said. She loved an evening swim, the water still warm from the day's heat, but clear of tourists.

'We're driving over to Newquay tomorrow, if you fancy it,' Tom said, joining them now, dripping wet. He leant down and kissed Lucy, leaving salty water on her mouth.

Nina shot Lucy a look and she willed her not to say anything.

'Yeah, maybe,' Nina said, still looking at Lucy. Lucy stood up and lifted her dress over her head, revealing her neon-pink bikini with a black trim.

'I'm going in,' she said, walking towards the water. 'Coming, Nin?'

'Sure,' Nina said, wiggling her shorts down and pulling her vest top off.

'You haven't even told him you're leaving tomorrow?' She sounded exasperated. Lucy carried on walking.

'It's better this way,' she said, unsure of whether she really believed this herself.

'It's cruel,' Nina said. 'Don't make me cover for you, please.'

'You just have to not say anything tonight, that's all,' Lucy said, annoyed again. It was typical of Nina to make everything about her.

'Look, Lucy, I know you've been through hell the last couple of years, but Tom's done everything for you, to support you. You just leaving like this, it's a massive betrayal. I can't believe you'd do it to him, to all of us, really.'

'I can't stay,' Lucy said, stepping into the water. It was surprisingly cold. 'He'll understand one day. It's not good for either of us in the long run. If I stay here, it'll drive me crazy.'

'Where are you going to stay? Claire's?' Nina asked.

'Yeah, 'til I get myself sorted,' Lucy said.

'I don't think you should do this,' Nina said, sadly.

'Well it's not your call.' Lucy dived under the water – better to get the shock of the cold over in one go. She knew she was being hard, selfish, unfair, but what were her options? This town would drive her slowly mad. There were too many memories; the house, even Tom – everything reminded her of her family, of what she'd lost.

Nina didn't say anything. Despite her protests she kept Lucy's secret. As evening turned to night Lucy had her moments of doubt. She had it all written down, what she wanted to say to Tom, how much she wanted him to come and join her in London. She nearly gave the letter to him a few times. But then she saw his face as he talked about the beach, his parents' café. She couldn't ask him to leave all of that – it meant too much to him. She had to do the harder thing and let him live his life here; she would build her own life somewhere else.

She hugged Kristian and Nina goodbye and walked hand in hand with Tom across the beach towards his house. He stopped, abruptly, to go back and pick up the board wax he thought he'd left where they'd been sitting. Lucy carried on walking, slowly, pulling her toes through the sand, leaving spidery patterns. A solitary campfire dwindled on the sand ahead of her, its creators probably back at the campsite drinking in the bar, its embers still glowing, but flames fading. She carefully slipped the letter from her pocket and dropped it onto the orange lumps, watched it catch and shrivel into itself, and then into nothing.

43

'Thank you so much for this,' Lucy said, walking with the vicar towards the beach.

'It's my pleasure,' he said, spotting the arch of flowers erected by the cliff side, the row of lanterns leading towards it. 'You've done a great job, especially given the timings.'

'Thanks' Lucy said. 'Everyone's been amazing.' she looked around at the scene. Rows of chairs from the café had been carried out by the guys from the surf school and now faced the arch of flowers that Mel, the florist, and Liv's mum, had donated, refusing payment in spite of Tara's protests. Olly had strung a stream of multi-coloured ribbons down the sandy aisle, while Tara had scattered a rainbow of rose petals underneath.

'How is he feeling?' the vicar asked as he fiddled with a microphone, prompting crackles and squeals.

'He's okay,' Lucy said. 'He's not great. But he's looking forward to today. It really means a lot, the way everyone's come together like this. I don't think any of us expected quite this much.'

'Yes, this town has a real heart,' the vicar said. 'In my experience most people are genuinely kind and generous – they just need a reason to show it.'

Nina was getting ready in the Seascape Hotel, Hideaway's five-star super-resort, with her mum. Lucy was hoping to pop back there for a glass of champagne before the ceremony, but there was still a lot to sort out at the café for the reception. Nina had embraced the idea of a quick wedding on the beach with a passion Lucy hadn't expected. She had always wanted the big fairytale wedding, probably at an old house, with hundreds of guests and an amazing meal. Lucy and Tara had done their best with the offering at the café, but she knew it wasn't quite the dream Nina had always had. She'd spoken to her to check that she was truly happy with it all, and Nina had just said the same thing each and every time – *It's Tom, Lucy. All that matters is that he is there.*

Lucy had been there when Kristian asked Tom to be his best man, she had watched his confused face turn to pride and then joy as Kristian explained the plans. It had given Tom a surge of energy, that injection of anticipation. He'd pulled Lucy onto his lap, leant into her neck and whispered, 'We'll have to buy you a dress'. Lucy stroked the pink silk wrapped around her body. They'd gone to Truro, her and Nina, with Tom's credit card, to pick something. She thought he'd like this, it showed off her legs, skimming her thighs.

Nina's mum and dad had driven down from Cardiff and set themselves up in the Seascape in order to help with the preparations. Seeing Tom again after years apart had been an emotional scene. Everyone had such fond memories of him. *So many people loved him*, Lucy had thought as she watched them try not to cry at the sight of him now: weak, unable to walk unaided, fading. Nina's mum insisted on driving them to Bristol, to the bridal boutique Nina's older sister Frances had bought her wedding dress from. It was a beautiful store, cream walls lined with ornate dresses, beads and crystals sparkling in the light of the tasteful chandeliers hanging from the ceilings. Lucy couldn't believe the prices. Nina had made a real fuss about not wanting anything 'too fancy' given her growing bump, but her mum was having none of it and they'd watched her try on countless gowns encrusted with crystals, lace, appliqué roses. It had been surreal seeing Nina in a wedding dress; she looked stunning, of course, but it felt a bit like playing dress-up, like playing at being real adults. Lucy wondered if she'd ever feel like a proper grown-up; she wondered if she'd ever wear a wedding dress. She thought about those weddings you read about where people get married in hospital, when one of them was about to die. She'd never understood it until now, what the point of that was. Now she wanted to do anything to tie herself to Tom, to let him know she was his, that she would always be his, that just because he was going away it didn't mean she would forget. But they wouldn't get married; they'd watch Nina and Kristian instead. Tom would keep the rings in his pocket and she'd carry Nina's train – it was enough.

At the Seascape Hotel, Nina's parents' suite was a hive of activity.

'Oh my goodness, is this her? Thank God!' A flamboyant-looking man wearing a system of what looked like straps covered in bottles and brushes, flicked something imaginary from Lucy's arm.

'Yes, this is her,' Nina called from her chair at the dressing table, shouting to be heard above the hairdryer smoothing her long waves into place.

'Right, come with me,' the man said, taking Lucy by the hand and sitting her on the edge of the bed. He was tutting as he examined her face.

'There is not enough time,' he said, to Nina not Lucy. She laughed, loudly. 'Yes that face needs a lot of work, doesn't it?' she winked at Lucy.

'Thanks!' Lucy said to the guy, who was still looking at her, slightly too close to her face for comfort, with what was clearly disappointment.

'I just like time to work my magic,' he said, smiling suddenly, his face transforming.

'Hmmm,' Lucy said, unimpressed. She shut her eyes as he swept make-up onto her with an assortment of soft brushes.

Nina stepped into her dress with the help of her mum and her hairdresser, and turned to Lucy.

'What do you think?' she asked, looking nervous.

'I think you look absolutely incredible,' Lucy said, feeling a lump rise in her throat. Nina was draped from the neck down in beautiful, fine lace. The train ran along the floor behind her giving the impression that she never ended. Her bump sat neatly in the fabric. She looked like a model, Lucy thought.

'You look lovely too,' Nina said, as the make-up guy held a mirror up for her to take a look. He had done a good job; she had glowing, bronzed skin and subtle aqua-green eye make-up.

'Is everything okay on the beach? Thanks so much for going down there this morning.' Nina was fiddling with her train.

'It's all good,' Lucy said, hoping Nina would be pleasantly surprised by what they'd put together.

The couple of glasses of champagne had gone to Lucy's head, she realised as she stepped out of Nina's dad's Jaguar at the bottom of the hill. She helped Nina out of the car and located the end of her train, scooping it off the ground.

'I can't believe we are doing this,' Nina said, turning to her.

'I know,' Lucy said. She took Nina's hand and squeezed it.

Nina's mum kissed her and went off to take a seat. 'Be fashionably late, darling,' she said as she left, probably worried that Kristian would be.

Lucy stood with Nina and her dad, listening to the sound of the waves. The novelty of a bride at the edge of the beach was creating a stir among the tourists, and a few people stopped to take pictures. 'Who wants photos of a stranger's wedding?' Nina's dad asked, shaking his head with a proud smile.

Music sounded and Lucy took a deep breath. She felt strangely nervous.

'Ready?' Nina's dad asked his daughter.

'Ready,' Nina confirmed, and the three of them turned the corner onto the beach.

Lucy gasped silently at the scene. Every single chair was taken and people were standing to the sides and behind the rows. A sea of colourful dresses and pastel suits had assembled on the beach, and further back groups of visitors stood, smiling, watching too. Lucy looked down the aisle and saw Claire smiling back at her. The sight of her sister back here was comforting and shocking. Claire looked gorgeous, with her hair pinned up, her make-up done. Lucy was glad she'd come. She spotted Tom sitting on a chair at the front, next to the vicar. He caught her eye and smiled, his whole face lighting up. *You wouldn't even know he was ill*, Lucy thought, smiling back. He looked almost overwhelmingly handsome in his grey suit. Kristian had his back to the crowd and turned only at the last moment, when Nina was a few feet away. Lucy watched as he took in the sight of his bride, with the pride, the love, written all over his face. She felt herself well up and willed herself to hold it together.

The service was simple. The vicar's sermon was short. He talked about love, eternal love. It was poignant without being sentimental, and perfectly judged. Nina and Kristian walked down the aisle as husband and wife to the Kooks' 'Naïve', a strange choice, but it worked somehow. It was very them, Lucy thought.

Everyone made their way towards the café after the ceremony. Tara had closed it for the day to prepare and Lucy was impressed by what she'd pulled off inside. Paper decorations hung from the ceiling and jam jars full of flowers were dotted around the tables and along windowsills.

'Oh my goodness,' Nina said, as she walked in ahead of Lucy.

'This is too much, I can't believe it.' Lucy handed her a tissue from her clutch bag, pleased that Nina was so impressed, but worried about her spoiling her make-up.

'This really is something else,' Kristian agreed. 'Better than anything we'd have organised with a year's notice.'

Lucy smiled at her friends and took a glass of champagne from the tray offered to her by the waiter at the door. Kristian took hold of the other side of the glass and pulled it back to make room for Tom. He wheeled in and took a glass too, holding it in the air as he cried, 'To Mr and Mrs Hutchinson', and they all clinked in the air.

Stefan sent platter after platter of lobster rolls and steak burgers out from the kitchen, as groups mingled and talked, listening to the band playing on the terrace. Lucy stood with Tom on the boards, her arms draped over his shoulders; they stood silently, listening to the music.

'I'm so glad I could see this,' Tom said.

'And they're so glad you could be here,' Lucy said.

'I always thought we'd get married one day, when we were young, you know,' Tom said, looking out towards the sea.

'Me too,' Lucy replied.

'Who would've thought it'd be those two to beat us to it,' Tom started to laugh but it turned into a cry. Lucy dropped down to face him, held his head in her hands.

'They're a pair of gits,' she said, smiling. He kissed her softly on the lips.

'Sorry,' he said. 'This is just a bit much. Can you give me a minute?'

Lucy walked away to get more drinks, leaving Tom in his chair, facing the water, his sun-kissed hair blowing slightly in the wind. The familiar pain in her heart heaved and she felt like just falling to the floor and crying herself. Every day was a battle not to do that, to carry on, to be stronger than she felt, for Tom's sake. For his parents.

'What a beautiful service,' Tara said, offering Lucy a glass of champagne.

'It really was, wasn't it?' Lucy agreed.

'Even Olly got emotional,' Tara said. 'That's quite something, hey?'

Lucy smiled and glanced back to Tom, but he wasn't there.

'Ladies and gentlemen, if you could all take a seat, it's time for a few words,' Nina's dad spoke across the sound system. Lucy looked around for Tom and spotted him by the band, next to Nina's mum, laughing with her about something. Lucy pulled up a chair next to Tara at a table by the window, reaching for a second glass of champagne to see her through the speeches.

Nina's dad's speech was hilarious; littered with stories from their school days that Lucy had forgotten. She felt herself redden as people turned to look at her when he recounted the time he came to pick them up from The Cliff, when Lucy had had far too many vodka-and-orange juices and had promptly disappeared into the foot well of his car as he pulled away, having failed to fasten her seatbelt. In a bit of a role reversal, Tom's best man's speech was a bit more serious, the jokes about Kristian overshadowed by the collective knowledge about the situation. Tom spoke so beautifully about his friendship with Kristian that the room was littered with wet faces, the women handing out tissues and the men stifling tears. Lucy saw Tom's dad, tears in his eyes, unable to contain the emotion, his wife's hand on his leg as she smiled proudly at her son. Lucy was determined to be a support to Tom, but she could feel her heart breaking as she sat there, determinedly looking at him, smiling encouragingly.

'I suppose, ultimately, what I admire most about Kristian, is that he is a truly good, kind person. That may sound like small praise, like those are simple things to be, but it isn't and they aren't. He has been the best friend I could have ever wished for, in every situation we've found ourselves in, including this pretty shitty one,' he gestured towards the wheelchair behind him and laughed slightly.

'And Nina, I know he is going to be the best husband to you, as you deserve, of course.' She smiled at Tom and he leant over to kiss her on the cheek.

'Love is precious and I'm so happy to be here to celebrate yours,' Tom raised his glass towards Nina and Kristian.

'May love be never-ending!' He moved his glass towards the crowd, who rose to their feet to repeat his words in a toast:

'May love be never-ending!'

'And may the champagne be never ending too,' he added as everyone remained standing, breaking the atmosphere into relieved laughter.'

With the party in full swing behind them, the four of them walked slowly towards the beach, Tom holding on to Kristian and Lucy.

'This has been the best day of my life,' Nina said, as they stopped at the water's edge, the sky stretched out ahead of them above the sea.

'Bloody good job, really,' Kristian said, laughing.

'Mr and Mrs,' Lucy said, smiling at her friends. 'Who would've thought it?'

'Guys, I'm sorry,' Tom said, Lucy turned to him, concerned. 'What is it?'

'I just don't feel too good, I'm so sorry. I think I need to go home.'

'Of course, no problem,' Kristian said, looking back to the party. 'Let me just go and get your dad. Is that alright?'

'Yeah, sure, thanks. Can I just sit down a minute?'

They moved back a few metres from the water, to dry sand, and sat Tom down. Lucy sat next to him, put her arm around him and kissed his shoulder.

'Are you alright?' she asked gently. 'Have you taken your meds today?'

'Yeah, I'm just tired, Luce, that's all,' he said, looking into her eyes. 'You stay here, okay? I really don't want you missing tonight to be cooped up at the house with me.'

'No, I'm coming back,' Lucy said, feeling panicked. She didn't want to stay here without Tom.

'No. You're not. It's not up for discussion. I want to be on my own anyway. I just need some sleep. You can come and get into bed with me later, when you're drunk. Just try not to be sick on me or anything,' he smiled at her, and she realised this was a discussion she wasn't going to win.

At the back of the café, she watched Kristian and Olly help Tom into Neil's car. He hugged Nina and Kristian, and kissed Lucy goodbye, 'I'll see you later, okay?' he said, closing the door. He wound down the window. 'I love you.'

44

Eight Months Later

'Tara!' Lucy called up the stairs.

'I'm coming, one sec,' came the reply, amid thuds and wardrobe doors banging.

'Wear the red one!' Lucy shouted. She'd spent last night helping Tara decide which dress to wear today. She was sitting on the sofa with a glass of wine and waiting for Tara to appear in the living room in each of the, many, options.

'I look really pale,' Tara shouted back. This was simply untrue. Lucy was unendingly jealous of her year-round golden tan.

'Right, I'm going,' Lucy threatened.

'Okay, okay, hang on, wait,' Tara shut the bedroom door and ran down the stairs, pulling a white cardigan on.

'You look gorgeous,' Lucy said, smiling at her friend.

'Thanks,' Tara said, smoothing her dress over her thighs self-consciously. 'I hope Olly thinks so.'

Lucy found it slightly strange, but very endearing how Tara still made such an effort with her appearance for her dates with Olly. The spark hadn't faded with those two, especially not since their engagement. Tara had been excited all week about their trip today to Keeper's Island – she and Olly were going to carve their initials into the tree. Olly clearly couldn't see quite what the fuss was about, but wanted to keep Tara happy, and she'd been dropping hints for months. It had taken a quiet word to Olly from Lucy for him to get the message, but she hadn't let Tara know about that bit.

Lucy closed the door to her family home behind them, and glanced back briefly at the large white house. The outside was all that really still looked the same as when she'd grown up there. She and Tara had redecorated the interior with the unique brand of enthusiasm that grief provided, grateful for something to focus on, something to do with themselves. Claire had come to stay a few months after Tom's funeral and seemed impressed with what they'd done. The dark floorboards were now whitewashed, and there were splashes of multi-coloured pastels throughout the house. Her approval had meant a lot to Lucy.

'Sure you're okay here today? That big order's arriving at eleven remember?' Tara was waiting at the door of the café for Olly, looking hopefully up the road with the sound of each car engine.

'I've got it, you relax, please,' Lucy said, unpacking the crate of scones into the cake counter.

April was a good month for Hideaway Bay. The weather was warming up and there was the definite promise of summer in the air, but it was more relaxed than the busy summer months, a different crowd filling the hotels and holiday homes. Today was likely to be a busy one with the regatta on. Tom's parents were popping in, over from France for a few days, and Nina and Kristian were making their way down from Bristol to see them while they were in town. Lucy understood more than most why Sarah and Neil had wanted to sell up and leave town. They'd stayed for a couple of months after the funeral, but their hearts weren't here any more. When Claire had gently suggested that she could use her inheritance money to buy the café, Lucy had worried about how Sarah and Neil might feel about it, but in fact they had seemed relieved. Relieved not to be selling to a stranger, to an investor, or someone who might have changed everything. And the relief had turned to happiness, Lucy thought, as time passed. They called Lucy often, to find out how things were going with the business, to ask about what was happening in the town.

Lucy was looking forward to seeing everyone today. She hadn't seen Nina and Kristian's little one for a couple of months, and he grew so much with each week. Her phone was clogged with photos of him in their beautiful house in Bristol. It really looked like they'd nailed the whole thing. Tom would've laughed at how grown up they'd become, she thought from time to time.

She thought of Tom almost constantly and walking around the café she felt him with her all the time. She almost expected to turn around and catch him about to whip her with a tea towel as she walked into the kitchen, away from customers' eyes. Or to see him walking in from the beach, wet hair dripping on the wooden terrace boards, smiling at her. The pain didn't go away and she had begun to accept that it never would. But the terror, the horror she'd felt during those first weeks at the prospect of living without him had become less defined. She thought of the speech Kristian had read at his funeral, written by Tom weeks in advance.

I can only hope that you live incredible, happy lives and that for me, as I wait for you, time passes in the blink of an eye, and we are soon together again.

It was an idea that made things a little more bearable, the thought that Tom was standing just outside, drying off in the sun, waiting for Lucy to get ready and join him. That for him the time would pass in an instant, but that for her she needed to try and enjoy what she had here until then.

Stefan had stayed on as head chef and when they'd decided to stay open all winter he'd seemed uncharacteristically happy. He'd hugged Lucy and thanked her, then started talking at speed about the seasonal specials he could create. The café's listing in the Condé Nast Traveller guide had given them unprecedented profile and they were getting busier and busier. Tom would have been so proud to see it. The reviews were strong and people were travelling from all over Cornwall on their holidays to eat and drink at the Beach Café. Lucy had made Tara manager and she'd stepped up massively. The girl had a seriously good business brain. Now the two girls were living and working together, Tara felt like a sister to Lucy. She actually found herself dreading the day Tara and Olly bought the home they were saving for.

Olly had been an unlikely source of strength since Tom's death and Lucy had been happy to have him around all the time, doing silly, macho things around the café and the house. Just taking small things off their plates where he could, he was kinder than Lucy had realised.

'Lucy, hello, come here,' Sarah looked sophisticated and a touch Parisian in her navy outfit, removing her sunglasses as she stepped towards Lucy. They hugged and Sarah did her usual step back to look around at the café, admiring it.

'This place looks fantastic,' she said, looking at Neil.

'It really does,' he agreed. 'Are you okay with everything? All going okay?' he asked.

'It's all great,' Lucy said. 'Let me get you some coffees. Nina and Kristian won't be long. Do you want to sit outside?'

It was warm on the terrace. A few tables were occupied by stylish couples drinking coffee and reading papers.

'Look at that,' Neil said, facing the ocean.

'It never gets old, does it?' Lucy said, admiring the view. It was true; the sight of the water, its timeless power and its vast reach still took her breath away daily.

'The surf looks good,' Sarah said. 'Tom would have been happy out there today,' she smiled at the thought of him.

'How is the build going?' Lucy asked. Sarah and Neil's latest project was a conversion of a very derelict chateau in the Loire countryside. The pictures they emailed over to Lucy each week were incredible, but she wondered at times whether they'd taken on too much.

'Oh, it's going well,' Sarah said, looking in her handbag for something. Presumably more photos, Lucy thought.

'You'll have to come and stay when it's finished,' Neil said. 'There are some incredible restaurants in the neighbouring town. You will absolutely love it.'

'I can't wait,' Lucy said. She thought she probably had a few years to hold on yet, though, judging by the new batch of photos Sarah was laying on the table now of dusty-looking piles of stones that barely resembled a building.

Nina and Kristian arrived late, Nina complaining about Kristian's driving as she heaved a baby car seat into the café.

'Hello you!' Lucy said, bending down to kiss the warm little head as he woke up from his sleep. He looked up at her with big eyes and broke into a smile. She unclipped him and scooped him up into a cuddle, smelling his baby hair and kissing Nina on the cheek.

'Oh God, Nina, he is just gorgeous. I almost can't bear it!' Lucy said.

Nina laughed. 'You can change his nappy in a minute. That'll sort you out.'

'Sarah and Neil are outside. They're just about to order lunch if you guys want some too. Stef's got moules frites on today if you fancy that?'

'Perfect,' Nina said. 'How are they doing?'

'They're doing really well, I think,' Lucy said, shifting the baby to her other hip.

'And you?' Nina asked. 'How are you holding up? You look good.'

'I am alright,' Lucy said, honestly. 'I'm doing okay, keeping busy, enjoying this place and enjoying the house. Things are okay.' She smiled at Nina. 'It's so nice to see you.'

On the terrace, Sarah and Neil stood at the sight of Lucy carrying the baby. Sarah looked close to tears. She'd not met Nina and Kristian's son until now. She reached out to take him from Lucy.

'Oh Nina! Kristian!' she said, happy tears rolling down her cheek. 'Would you look at him, Neil, he is just beautiful!'

Nina lifted the baby from Lucy's arms and handed him to Sarah. 'Meet Tommy.'

Acknowledgements

I'd like to thank a few people for their encouragement whilst writing this book. Mum, Dad, Lisa and Tessa, thank you for always believing in me. Thanks to my lovely Steph for true friendship, and for being almost as weird as me. I am hugely grateful to my editor Charlotte, Dushi and the whole team at Harper Impulse for your invaluable help and guidance, and to Alex for the beautiful cover design. Most importantly, I would never have finished this book without the love and support of my husband James; thank you for making me happier than I knew I could be.